ANY FOUR WOMEN
COULD ROB THE
BANK OF ITALY

ANY FOUR WOMEN

COULD ROB THE
BANK OF ITALY

A NOVEL BY ANN CORNELISEN

A William Abrahams Book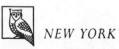
HOLT, RINEHART AND WINSTON   NEW YORK

Copyright © 1983 by Ann Cornelisen
First published in 1984 by Holt, Rinehart and Winston
383 Madison Avenue, New York, New York 10017.
Published simultaneously in Canada by Holt, Rinehart and
Winston of Canada, Limited.

Library of Congress Cataloging in Publication Data
Cornelisen, Ann, 1926–
Any four women could rob the bank of Italy.
"A William Abrahams book."
I. Title.
PS3553.0658A84   1983   813'.54   83-4342
ISBN 0-03-063254-4

First Edition

Design by Lucy Albanese
Printed in the United States of America
1 3 5 7 9 10 8 6 4 2

ISBN 0-03-063254-4

ANY FOUR WOMEN COULD ROB THE BANK OF ITALY

PRELUDE

FROM MIDNIGHT UNTIL FIVE in the morning most country railway stations in Italy are shunned by people and trains alike. San Felice Val Gufo, a junction in Tuscany, is no exception. Freight trains clatter back and forth at their own deliberate pace. Passenger trains, most of their compartments dark, whoosh by, leaving a cloud of scraps and wrappers skipping in their wake. Neither needs official attention. The station is dark, the main waiting room locked. From the police office a faint glow of light and a gentle ticking of equipment suggest a human presence. At the opposite end of the squat building another, even dimmer light in the stationmaster's office does not.

The first track is reserved for a spur line that is the only connection a neighboring regional capital has with the outside world of through trains. There, late each evening a mail car and four rusty passenger cars, so antique that each compartment has its own external door, are drawn up to await the first morning run at 5:22 A.M. Beyond, two more platforms float in a pearly mist. An occasional blur high in the roof of the sheds might be a light or only St Elmo's fire.

Quiet nights follow busy days with tidal regularity, and the night between May twenty-third and May twenty-fourth 197_ was just like any other until the express, train No. 1590, from Catania to Milan, made an unscheduled stop at 4:17. It glided to a smooth, almost surreptitious halt on the second track. The engineer had calculated his speed perfectly: his post-office car was exactly opposite the mail car on the spur line. Bars clanked, keys scratched in locks, and then two doors, one in each car, slid silently open. If the men spoke at all, it was in a murmur so quiet that no sound escaped the narrow aisle between the trains. Two uniformed guards on the express dragged a heavy canvas sack, stenciled *Poste Italiane* and bound in leather with a sturdy metal locking device, to the edge of the door—and then together, each grasping two corners, they heaved it across the gap where a guard waited to drag it deeper into his car out of the way. Six times they repeated the process and six sacks were transferred from the express to the local. A guard from the express joined the local crew, again metal bars clanked, locks scraped, and the express slipped away as smoothly as it had come.

Had anyone been watching—and a number of people should have been—he would have seen four figures, wearing the short blue cotton jackets and blue caps of station porters, push an empty freight cart around the corner of the station, along the platform past the police office and on, until it stood just below the station-side door of the mail car. They moved very quickly, very carefully, and almost soundlessly. The rumble of the express masked the dull jouncing of the cart's rubber-rimmed wheels along the brick platform. When the porters had the cart in place, they ran, Indian file, back around the corner of the station.

Again the station was deserted, waiting for dawn to bring it to life. Exactly five minutes later, the four figures, their faces now covered with black stockings and their caps pulled well down, reappeared around the corner of the station, looked carefully in both directions, then ran to the cart and climbed up onto it—the shortest had to have a hand from one of the others. When all four were safely up, one knocked on the mail-car door—three longs, two shorts. A voice inside grumbled. A bar was pulled out of its sockets, a bolt slipped, and the door rolled open on its runners. The four masked porters jumped into the car and pushed the door closed behind them.

Again the station was deserted. All was normal and quiet for twelve or thirteen minutes, until the door of the car was rolled partway open and a masked head looked out, first to his right toward the stationmaster's office, then to his left, toward the police office. No one was in sight. It took two porters to open the door all the way. Once they had, they jumped to the cart and dragged onto it enormous black plastic garbage bags as the bags were shoved through the door. The third bag thumped onto the cart and one of the porters jumped to the platform. He began working at the handle release of the truck. Another porter from the mail car took his place unloading. Three more sacks, and he too jumped to the ground. The fourth porter took his place. When the last of the plastic bags, ten in all, had been dragged onto the cart, both porters jumped to the ground and the cart lumbered slowly away, two porters pulling at the front, one on either side of the bar that served as a grip, one pushing from behind. The fourth was busy maneuvering the heavy door of the mail car closed. He strained against the weight, unhelped by any handles on the outside, until he was satisfied. For good measure he wedged a cold chisel between the door and its metal guide channel, and turning, raced after the freight cart. As he caught up with it, he grabbed the jacket of the man pushing and signaled him to leave the cart. They disappeared around the corner well ahead of the porters and their load.

A split second later the stationmaster came to the door of

his office and stood there, stretching. He looked around, saw the freight cart moving slowly along the platform, just beyond the police office, and watched it with the dull eyes of someone who is still asleep. He stretched again, turned to his left away from the cart and the porters, and went along to the public lavatories. His replacement would be coming soon.

THE PIAZZA in front of the station was deserted except for a garbage collector who pushed his dolly along with one hand, while with the other he fumbled at the buttons of his long, baggy gray coat. Two things about him were hardly characteristic of his profession: he seemed in a hurry and he wore clean gray suede gloves. At the far corner of the building another garbage collector, bent double, waged a tug of war with one end of a black plastic bag. He stopped to wait while the bag was eased around the corner by his helper, who finally came into sight, jogging along inch by inch with the bag awkwardly between his legs. He wore the white jacket, none too clean, of a barboy.

The sharp slam of a car door made the garbage collector crossing the Piazza look back over his shoulder. He jerked his cap down well over his face. As he heard footsteps coming toward him, scraping in the dirt on the road, he slouched forward, his weight all on the handle of his cart, as though the demands of his morning round had already exhausted the day's supply of energy.

At the very moment the sun eased over the horizon, casting a weak, tentative light on the station, a tall, dark, youngish man in a navy linen suit walked briskly into the Piazza. A briefcase swung in one hand. His tie, though it had been slipped under the collar of his immaculate blue shirt, was not knotted and his wiry hair needed a second combing before the curls and cowlicks were really under control. Another day his sharp features might have been austere, his blue eyes cold. Today, however, he smiled faintly at everything in the unguarded way of a man who, having performed his ritual morning ablutions, discovers he is in a good humor and does not quite know why. As he came level with the garbage collector, who shambled along with his head down, he said something. A shrug was the only answer. Still smiling, he walked on toward the station, where, at the far corner, he could see another garbage collector slumped by his cart, watching a tall, thin boy in a white jacket wrestle with a very full garbage bag.

Only that youngish man in a good humor ever actually saw any of the four, or perhaps more people, who brought off what would inevitably be called The Great Tuscan Train Robbery. *They,* along with more than a million dollars, vanished. *He* went into the station.

1

PETER TESTA, the youngish man in a good humor, did not waste attention on the station. It was too familiar. The low plaster building rejected, almost literally, all cosmetic efforts to improve it: each new coat of yellow paint crinkled into blisters, then sloughed off, and the plastic letters on the façade, which should have proclaimed the station's name, were regularly pried loose by storms and swept away. The senior stationmaster, whose title brought with it the right to the second-floor apartment, had added the only weatherproof ornament: winter and summer, from a wire just below his bedroom window, or just above the front door, depending on one's point of view, dangled a pair of his long wool underdrawers.

The interior was no more inviting. At that hour of the morning everything was closed—the newsstand, the bar, even the ticket window and the second-class waiting room. The lobby was dim and dusty, and the air sweet-sour from years of Turkish tobacco and wet wool. Unless it rained, people did not linger there. For the prosperous the bar was the normal retreat. Fresh rolls and coffee soothed. The clinking of the pinball machine and the loud discussions of the trainmen, who from habit shouted at each other, had their own lulling rhythm. But the bar was not yet open, so Peter Testa walked through the station, out past the cars of the local train, which were still dark, down the stairs into the tunnel, and up again onto the platform that served express trains. He strolled along, heading south, until he reached the third from the last lightpole, where he knew that his first-class carriage would, eventually, stop. Once there he spread his feet wide apart, clasped his hands, still holding his briefcase, behind his back, and let his mind wander in a leisurely review of the appointments he must keep at the Ministry of Justice in Rome. To him the only thing odd about the morning was that he should be twenty minutes early.

WITHIN TWENTY-FOUR HOURS people all over the country recognized his name; television viewers, even his face: he was the *only* witness to The Great Tuscan Train Robbery. Weeks would pass before he could slip back into the status of "what-was-his-name?". Journalists with reports to file and no information embroidered on their only lead. He was described as "the elusive lawyer, who has cooperated—reluctantly—with the carabinieri," then as the "lawyer implicated" in the robbery, and finally, when desperation overwhelmed judgment, the "lawyer of mixed blood, whose young wife died in mysterious circumstances."

Millions knew he was a lawyer. Few bothered to notice that he was a notary and so a public official. Antipathy toward the carabinieri was to his credit, a prejudice all true Italians share. The more intriguing insinuations about his wife's death were soon retracted (she had died in the crash of a commercial airliner) and a formal apology printed in a slot that, another day, would have been filled by a snippet of useless information. Of course, no one noticed it.

No one, that is, except Peter's mother, who was in Rome and who also considered herself a victim of these journalistic flights. English by birth, devoutly Italian by marriage, she was offended. "Mixed blood" indeed! As though her son was a half-breed, or . . . worse—whatever that might be. She was too startled at the idea that her impeccable, quite distinguished family could be the source of such genetic corruption to probe further.

Part of Peter's predicament was, perhaps, indirectly—she would admit no more than that—her fault. Her anxiety about mechanized transport was a family joke. Temperament and training blinded her to one basic truth about her adopted country: in Italy nothing *ever* happens ahead of schedule. She would not be convinced. One never knew, she claimed, and had persisted in dragging her children off so early to catch trains that they— Peter, his brother, and two sisters—thought it normal to wait an hour or more at the station. Too sophisticated to expect much of interest from the buffets or newsstands, they settled down on the luggage, where they stayed until the appropriate carriages rumbled to a stop by their platform.

As their mother, she had to admit that she was proud of their most un-Italian good behavior. She was also aware that their minds had escaped into never-never lands of their own invention. They divorced themselves from the immediate present, a pleasant enough state, which over the years settled into habit. Though her children seemed unconscious of it, she realized that they still spent rather more time in stations than other people, and probably—no reason to think they had changed— probably their minds retreated to those secret places that had always protected them from boredom. No doubt she should have discouraged it, as she had thumb-sucking and fingernail biting. Oh dear! So here was another slight flaw she must remember to put on her list for El. When the time came, she meant to warn her of Peter's failings. Gently. That seemed only fair to someone as honest as El, and of course he didn't have many. Not really. Not serious failings. When the time came . . . Or would she have to add procrastination to the list? Maybe she could prod him. He was so happy with El. She was so obviously the right . . . Just a word? No! She had never interfered, or she had tried never to interfere. There were already so many things to blame oneself for—even "mixed blood," it seemed. "Mixed blood" indeed!

Certainly Peter had been twenty minutes early. He never denied it, nor would he have denied his state of oblivion, which was hard to explain and harder yet to believe.

FOR THE NEXT FEW MINUTES Peter, bewitched to immobility by his own thoughts, was no more conspicuous than the shadow of the lightpost. The platform appeared deserted, damp, and cool, still untouched by the sun, almost inviting, but deserted. Then two slight little men with gray faces and briefcases came quietly up the stairs from the tunnel. They nodded without smiling, headed straight for the nearest bench, and sat down at opposite ends with their backs to each other. One pulled out a timetable. The other was looking for his place in a comic book when three Boy Scouts, more men than boys, tumbled up the stairs and out. The backpacks they dragged behind them by their harnesses thumped up to settle in a tangled mass on the top step. For several seconds the scouts stood, blinking in the light and tugging their shorts down, which still left most unscoutlike expanses of hairy legs and bony knees showing above their high socks. Some master's edict must have echoed in their heads, for suddenly they fell on the backpacks, trying to separate them, straighten the straps, and ease them over their shoulders.

And as suddenly they stopped, paralyzed, staring. A modern-day birth of Venus seemed to take place right before their eyes as a very tall, slender young woman emerged slowly from the stairwell with assorted layers of draperies, pink to fuchsia, floating around her, pleating across her breasts and clinging to her legs. Strands of long blonde hair rippled out behind her like pennants in a gentle breeze. She smiled at them, sweetly, vaguely, the superior being who acknowledged the presence of others without actually seeing them, and stepped daintily around them. The little gray men half rose, maybe just to admire better, maybe to offer help with the enormous suitcase she carried in one hand, or the purse of about the same capacity she carried in the other, but she dismissed them with a different little smile that said, "No, thank you. So kind . . ." and swirled on under full sail toward Peter's end of the platform.

Even at a Tuscan country station Hermione Hendricks created a stir. She enjoyed it. It confirmed something, not that she had ever defined quite what. Without the attention, the admiration, and the speculation that must follow, she would have been uneasy. She would have suspected that in some way as yet imperceptible to her she was failing and begun to worry. It is a celebrity's knack and a celebrity's need. Whether knack and need are part of the temperamental requirements of a celebrity or the state of celebrity induces these traits in them could be argued, but Hermione was a bona fide celebrity, known to the followers of every medium and to millions of the more literate (*Put That in Your Jock Strap and . . .*) as the woman who was going to liberate her sex and make men like it. Her rages were as famous as her seductions. She could turn men to stone or to jelly in any one of four languages without so much as a misplaced adverb. Five, if one counted her ripe Anglo-Saxon.

She stopped halfway along the platform, dropped her case and her purse, and glided two long steps forward, calling, "Peter!

Darling! *Ma che fortuna!*" Her voice was husky and carried without being loud. That she made such commonplace phrases sound voluptuous so early in the morning was itself proof of talent. Peter started and smiled uncertainly. Then recognizing her, he came loping toward her. She waited for him and in her waiting there was a breathless, expectant quality. As he reached her, she repeated, "Peter! Darling! But *how* lovely. Did El turf you out so early? Silly girl!" She scanned his face with wide, innocent violet eyes. She trimmed them to suit her purpose. "Oh no! I forgot 'the script'! The famous script! She has that television friend staying with her, doesn't she? Nice woman—I can never remember her name. Tracy? Lacey?" She waved a hand about her face as though shooing a fly. "So I suppose you, poor dear, hardly see El these days!" She pretended to consider, but her archness did not conceal her malice. "El's absolutely charming— of course—but frightfully *comme il faut.* You know what I mean— appearances and all that. For her, life must be a jungle of moral iss-ewes. Lucky for you she's American, not English. They can't be quite so iss-ewey—but still—truthfully, darling—don't you think she's a wee tiny bit prudish?"

"No, *mia cara,* I think you're a wee tiny bit bitchy," he said in perfect good humor. She shrugged and walked off toward the end of the platform, calling back over her shoulder,

"Be an angel and bring my things." She went unerringly to the proper lightpost and stood for a moment staring out over the tracks, her arms crossed, her hands on her shoulders, hugging herself, before she swung around to watch Peter. "Bugger," she said as he put down her bag and purse. "Why do these places have to be so beastly bare? Nothing I'd like better than a quick fuck before the train comes." She made it sound like an aspirin. "El wouldn't mind," she cooed, leaning slightly toward him. "Or would she?"

"Why not ask *her*? I'd be fascinated to hear the answer."

His voice betrayed nothing more than abstract interest, but his eyes twinkled, almost glittered.

"*Peter!* You're blushing. Surely you and El don't talk about politics *all* the time. At least—well, I assumed— Never mind, you're safe. Martha Gelder is coming along—just there." She nodded toward the station. Though she had pulled abruptly away from him, when she went on her tone was still sulky and strangely caressing. "I won't rape you. 'Never insist!' That's my motto—and I seldom have to." Peter seemed to weigh the matter very seriously.

"Umm, I did read something about a football squad—that what you mean?"

"Sod! That was a publicity stunt and you know it. Why . . ." Her voice ran down. Peter was watching, or pretended to watch, Martha Gelder's progress down the platform. She trudged along with earnest purpose and as much speed as an ample figure and tight kid pumps would allow. Every few steps she waved wildly to attract their attention, as though she were afraid of losing them in the nonexistent crowd. Hermione leaned over to hiss in Peter's ear, "You mustn't say such awful things when Martha's with us. She's a journalist and quite literal-minded. Discuss something serious, or if that's beyond you, try music. After a few drinks she's always a frustrated opera singer."

"Surely not at this hour of—" Peter was objecting.

"Oh God! Oh no!" Hermione groaned. She recovered almost immediately to point a long, bony, not very clean finger and crow in Italian, "Just *look!* See that man? He's sneaking into the ladies'!" Peter, and Martha—who was by then close enough to hear—both turned obediently to look across the tracks. A short man did go into the wrong end of the public toilets, but there was nothing furtive about his manner. Behind them the three Boy Scouts snickered.

"Good morning all," Martha greeted them with excessive

cheer. "Beautiful morning. Nice to see *you,* Dr. Testa. And you're just the person who might be able to help me. I'm about to be homeless again. Know any houses that need sitting? Or perhaps the expression confuses? The simplest explanation is . . ." But she never had a chance to make it. Hermione outchattered her in loud, clear Italian.

"That's a *porter!* Dirty old men, all of them! And government employees too! Sure sign of degeneration. National Degeneration! They're lechers, every one of them, under the skin—if you take my meaning." The Boy Scouts giggled. Hermione rewarded them with a brilliant smile.

"Do shut up, Hermione," Peter snapped.

"Oh, she couldn't do that," was Martha's prophetic comment, and Hermione rushed on into the tale of her recent encounter with her postman. Late one night she had just driven an anonymous, sexless "acquaintance" home and was halfway back up the mountain to her house when her car sank into a trough of mud and refused to move. With much eye rolling and tantalizing pantomime she made it clear that she had had nothing on except a raincoat. The Boy Scouts sucked in their breath and leaned forward not to miss a word. This was one "encampment" they would not soon forget. "You've done it this time, my girl," she had said to herself. Either a nice strong peasant—not too observant—must come along and help her or she would have to walk. Instead, who appeared but her very own mailman. She knew him, not, as she was careful to specify, in the biblical sense, but she knew him. After a lot of mucking around with a tow rope, he managed to pull her car out and to thank him, nothing else, she kissed him on the cheek. She shrieked at the recollection.

"He GRABBED me. I was *terrified!* Out there, alone in the dark. Alone—alone with a-a maniac. *I was terrified!*"

"You loved it," Martha said with devastating conviction. "Admit it. You did."

"I did *not,* and I have a good mind to report that horny little bastard over there." She waved toward the public toilets. "Women have a right to protection against . . ."

"And men don't?" Peter asked teasingly. "What if you burst into . . . ?" Bells were ringing. The train was coming. Hermione raged on.

"The stationmaster should be told. Disintegration of moral fiber—on a national level. Disgraceful!"

The rumble of the train drowned out the rest, and in the bustle of hoisting Hermione and her chattels aboard, the lusts of porters and the depravity of civil servants were forgotten. The Boy Scouts stumbled over themselves to help and then trudged sadly back toward the second-class carriages. The trip passed quickly. Hermione and Martha chirped at each other like birds after a storm. Peter, very ungallantly, slept, though he did wake up occasionally and listen to Hermione explain journalism to Martha, or Martha reorganize the feminist movement for Hermione. In Rome, as soon as he had found a porter, fortunately a tired old man who never took his eyes off the ground, he hurried away to his appointments. Hermione was in a rush, and Martha had already disappeared in a taxi.

AT THE JUNCTION STATION the departure of the 5:09 signaled the beginning of the day. The local set out on time with its meager group of passengers, mostly construction workers, at 5:22. Other trains arrived, disgorged their passengers, took on new ones, and left again. All was as it should be until, suddenly, at 5:40 nothing was. Two post-office employees in a battered little truck arrived, excited and frightened. Had the local been held for them? Their role in life was to take mail to the station, pick up any that had arrived, and transport it safely back to the post office. On special mornings, such as this, they also picked up the currency for pensions and the payroll of local government employees, along with a guard, who waited in the mail car of the 5:22. Indeed, it had been a special morning: they had had two flat tires on the road down from town. Had the train been held? The first shiver of apprehension rippled over the station staff. Each proclaimed his innocence and shortly thereafter assigned the guilt, usually on the basis of an old antipathy.

Much was said, but nothing was done until the postal clerks realized that their mail car could not, must not spend the day on a siding, its normal fate. They must have it right back. After some thought the stationmaster judged that a nonincriminating order and gave his placet. The station of the regional city was advised. Thirty minutes later an answer came back.

The mail car had been met by an armored truck and police escort. When the door was opened, the regional payroll, post, and pensions had disappeared. Two bound, groggy guards, not even three as there should have been, and some slashed mailbags were all that was left inside the car. Accusations, recriminations, and protests of angelic innocence, supported by oaths of striking originality, brought the normal business of the station to a halt. Chaos (and acrimony) reigned. It is remarkable that a serious accident was not added to the other glorious deeds of the day. That was avoided, but long before most people were fully awake, sirens screeched up and down the valley, and all intersections were blocked by the police. The manhunt was on.

2

FIVE MILES AWAY the town of San Felice Val Gufo, which lends its name, albeit grudgingly, to the station, is invisible from the highway except for the Medici fortress, a church, and a ragged string of houses all clumped together on the top of a high hill. The cathedral, the palaces and squares with their arches and loggias, are saved for a smaller, gentler valley, hidden behind the hill, away from the Val Gufo. There, Renaissance villas and large stone farmhouses sparkle in the morning light and cypress trees sway gently, nodding their allegiance to the town. Exposure, not snobbery, they say, dictates this position, southwest for the greatest amount of sun and the least buffeting from the north wind. The excuse, though always an excuse, allows the San Feliciani to be arrogant and a bit smug. As their ancestors ignored Hannibal's encampments and later those of the condottieri, so today's residents keep their backs to the clusters of concrete boxes in the valley below, the petrol stations and grain silos, the asphalt plants and building-supply yards, which the railway and through roads have attracted. A crass world, appropriate for storage, perhaps. No greater affinity need be acknowledged.

San Felice's claims to superiority are confirmed by serious guidebooks, those with small print and florid prose. They are tempted to lead the visitor from doorway to doorway on a five-hour inspection, but are too wise in the ways of tourists, who take in only what lies between the parking lot and the best restaurant in town, to put much faith in it. Instead they lavish stars and blocks of boldface on those things that must, absolutely, be seen: the Etruscan walls, the medieval battlements and portals, the Hall of the Signoria, and the museums. About two churches, one Romanesque, one Baroque, they are fulsome and at the same time resigned to the reader's inattention. Still, there can be no doubt: San Felice Val Gufo is one of those little-known gems that cognoscenti boast of as their secret discovery. It also has very good wine.

Change is not a mania in such places and too, San Felice has been fortunate. Wars and disasters have not plagued it. Already two hundred years ago there was no land left within the walls for new structures, and no real need for them. The town is much as Napoleon might have seen it. The streets are cobbled. Most are steep and uncomfortably narrow for modern cars. One just allows delivery trucks to reach the Piazza. Another shunts them straight out again. Traffic jams are not tolerated, parking spaces are few. Electrification has left braids of wires along the palace façades, and at vital corners where they must all meet and somehow join, they weave veritable pergolas. Neon has not caught on: the signs are modest and seldom lighted. No one denies the sewers are erratic. They dispose of the materials consigned to them quite efficiently, but on damp, still days they turn sulky and exhale mephitic warnings of displeasure. The Mayor and the majority of the town council, all Communists of the Tuscan, bourgeois subspecies, are, as in most nondoctrinal matters, loath to tinker with a system that works. If the weather is slow to change and the miasma too pungent to deny, they mutter darkly about political enemies, subversives all, or the nefarious activities of American nuclear submarines. Only the ingenuous try to fathom the cause-and-effect relationship implied.

The San Feliciani are happy with their inheritance and determined to take care of it. Individually they paint their shutters and repair their roofs and polish the brass mountings on their front doors. Collectively they expect the same attention for their public buildings. Italian politicians, of whatever persuasion, are pragmatic: they satisfy their constituents' more obvious whims, so that peculation may remain a private affair. All that is visible is in exquisite order. The rosy stone of the town hall, the Signoria of old, is well pointed. The clock on its tall tower still pings the quarter-hours accurately, though the adjustments required by daylight saving time stimulate attacks of tachycardia. Twice a year for several days time twirls by at a most unsettling pace. Convents, abandoned by their nuns, have been converted to other uses, to schools, even hostels, and the palaces, which now serve as museums and public offices, are maintained with a precision that would startle their former noble owners. No window pediment is allowed to crumble, no column to sag.

The services are impeccable. The sanitation workers, as they choose to be called, never strike. The garbage is *always* collected, the streets *always* swept. The town *Vigili,* in full battle dress, goggles, and helmets, strut importantly about the Piazza, looking for someone to chastise. Squads of men in blue twill trim the hedges of the public gardens, sweep the gravel of leaves, and scrub the fountains. They even sluice down the statues of long-forgotten local dignitaries often enough to keep them white and arresting in their niches. Only the pigeons who roost on the windowsills and in the crannies of the town hall have defied discipline. The slightest noise sends them up on a bombing run of the stairs, and off across to blitz the Piazza.

Not that the town is perfect. It could hardly be that. By the end of a long dry summer the water tastes distinctly peculiar, froggy. The two cinemas, one in the creaky old opera house, can rarely raise a quorum: many films are announced, few are ever shown. In the last twenty years no satisfactory site, visually satisfactory that is, has been found for the hospital the government insists it will build. Not even Michelangelo culd design a structure the size of the Ministry of Foreign Affairs that would not be obtrusive on a Tuscan hillside, so the hospital is still in a sevnteenth-century palace. The exterior is charming with its narrow arches and graceful columns, its galleries and medallions. The interior, at best, is a lazzaretto whitewashed once a year, sloshed with Formalin once a week. The equipment is mid-Victorian except for an "intensive-care unit" that was installed several years ago. As yet no technicians who understand it have been assigned to the staff. The San Feliciani admit that it is wiser to be sick in Siena. In most other ways they are satisfied with the town and themselves.

They stay there. They marry each other, gossip about each other, prosper, and die in serenity, a pattern so uncommon today that it is almost suspect. No need to be wary. The circuit is closed, and they like it: they are merely complacent. They are not attracted by life on a large scale. Industry would not have suited them. They judge the dozen or so landowners who still struggle to keep sprawling estates together as idle men with appropriate hobbies. Proper occupation is the gentle commerce of selling each other goods and services, which is much more complex than normal supply and demand. Old feuds must be honored with unflinching devotion; new ones perceived in embryo. An inordinate amount of time is spent watching neighbors through half-closed shutters on the assumption that each splinter of information has or will have its value. Skeletons are everywhere, waiting to be rattled. At least one to a family, which is a powerful incentive to tolerance and neutrality. A murmur, a shrug is warning enough. It is an armed truce and a quiet day, any day in town can be exhilarating.

The San Feliciani keep themselves armed and potentially ferocious, but are in practice quite kind to each other. They celebrate birth with smiles and delicate gold chains. To the sick they take bowls of fresh chicken broth. They mourn with grave faces. No matter what they may have said about the *caro defunto* in life, they never speak ill of the dead. They condole with the parents of a daughter who marries outside the community, a situation fraught with uncertainties. The tenor of her future life cannot be exactly analyzed, and they still hold the *tenor di vita* to be important: a question of caste. The departure of a son finds them tactfully silent. They suspect instability: ambition, for instance, is an illusional ill.

They do not doubt such judgments. They have inherited a clear code. The generalizations that follow from it assume the power of tenets. Foreign travel is dangerous and uncomfortable: the beds are poor, the food worse, and the natives thieves. All cities are corrupt and corrupting. Politicians are pirates in double-breasted suits. Civil servants are lazy and foreigners—well, foreigners have lately presented a problem for the San Feliciani.

In the summer there had always been a few tourists, German couples doggedly following Baedeker, stray Americans with hired cars and drivers, maybe a busload or two, tours in search of St. Francis or hedge gardens and herbaceous borders. They tramped down the Corso, looked around, bought postcards, and went on to the next place. At least they did until Conte Maffei married his young English wife. It was generally agreed that the change in San Felice began with Caroline's arrival, which, had she known it, would have surprised her. Like most well-bred Englishwomen she considered herself inconspicuous and far too busy keeping up with Giordano Maffei and her kennels to have any influence on town affairs.

Of course she was wrong. She might have melted into a crowd in England. She did not in San Felice where, anyway, the streets were only crowded on market day. She was too tall, too fair with her long streaked blonde hair and skin that the palest April sun could turn pink. Even the way she strode along was different, less languid than that of local matrons, less self-conscious. She was obviously pleased with the world, her world at least, which is an infectious pleasure. People who had scowled a moment before suddenly smiled broadly as she passed. Everyone knew her and spoke to her. The women said a few words and then moved quickly away from her: she made them feel dumpy. The men followed her with their eyes and enjoyed the improbable fancies that do flash across the male mind. The grocers, the pharmacists, the town clerks, the people she did business with on her daily round of errands, went out of their way to talk to her. Her pronouns were erratic and her use of the subjunctive was entirely personal, but her Italian was fluent— and they were amused by her. Her opinions were so curious, so original, and she had causes. Who but Caroline would have lectured a peasant, right in the middle of the Piazza, in front of everyone, after he had kicked a dog out of his way? "*Scusi, signora. Mi scusi,* but I didn't know the dog was yours," which enraged her further. The dog was *not* hers. She did not know whose it was, nor care. It was a matter of principle: no dog deserves cruelty. Did he understand? And, of course, he did not.

They learned soon enough that Caroline was tenacious about her causes, and were confused. What she wanted to change had long been established as man's right or man's immemorial vice. All hunting should be banned. Animals protected. Corruption in government ought to be exposed. The illegal flow of Italian capital to safe Swiss bank accounts should be curbed. So original, so very English, they decided.

The Conte had waited a long time, but it was agreed that when he finally chose, he chose the perfect wife. The twenty years' difference in their ages was unimportant. He was still a "fine figure of a man." So tall with a large head, lapping gray curls, and strong, craggy features, which, helped by a constant tan, seemed cast in bronze, he looked as a count should and was satisfactorily eccentric. He had lived in exotic places, Africa and the Far East. He toyed with the idea of sailing the Atlantic alone. Or he might do it in a balloon. Airplanes fascinated him and Chinese dialects. He had managed to learn three of them, though of the languages that might have been more useful to him he spoke only French. He was a frustrated inventor, the owner of one of the district's last large estates, therefore also the resident of its crumbling Renaissance castle, and a *soi-disant* Socialist. He saw no conflict. Certain aspects of life were as they were, inheritance being the most obvious.

Giordano Maffei admired reason and logic in all things and believed that his own decisions were arrived at through their strict application. The results, as everyone agreed, were remarkable. He had come home to manage his land, which was his main source of income. Reasonable. Logical. Now his myriad interests left him no time to do it; he had hired a factor. A liberal, he deplored the effect of prosperity on the peasants. Cars, schooling, store-bought clothes, and television had ruined them. They should have stayed in the condition natural and proper to them, that of a hundred, even two hundred years ago. With the first rumor of the oil crisis, he required Caroline to use her motorbike for all chores in and around San Felice, then bought a tractor, a medium-sized Fiat, and a Mercedes for himself. His friends listened carefully to his explanations, shook their heads, and asked him to repeat that again. Perhaps they had missed a step. Finally they gave up, dazzled by this wizardry that bent logic to prove contradictions.

Caroline, whom Giordano insisted was flighty and emotional, had surprised him by sorting out the confusion of his affairs into something close to order. He was so pleased that, when she wanted to raise Italian shepherd dogs, he encouraged her. Comfort led to benevolence, and he allowed her to invite for weekends the English and American friends he had been sure he would not enjoy. Then he found he liked them. They came back. They delighted in the countryside and their host, whose deep quiet voice seemed to confide and whose brown eyes danced with some ambiguous amusement.

They were artists, writers, journalists who could work almost anywhere, and there were at that time lots of small stone farmhouses, abandoned by the peasants who wanted modern cube houses on a paved road and "regular" jobs, even as unskilled construction workers. These Italianized foreigners bought the abandoned houses for very little and remodeled them a bit at a time or all at once, as their bank accounts allowed. Some used them for weekends. A few, like Hermione Hendricks, the inventor of "The Female Imperative," and Eleanor Kendall, who wrote highly praised, if not highly remunerative books about Italy, settled down to be permanent residents.

It was this first wave of newcomers that overcame the San Feliciani's misgivings. Foreigners were almost like real people. They would argue and explain and discuss. They *were,* of course, different—they preferred old clothes to fashionable ones, did not go to church, and drank strange fiery liquors—but they could be forgiven because they were semi-famous. They popped up on television screens or were interviewed in newspapers with gratifying regularity. Shopkeepers approved of them whole-heartedly. They were consumers of high-quality goods with high profit margins to match, and they paid their bills. When, finally, they were included in the parties of the local gentry, the matter was settled: the San Feliciani would be cordial to foreigners.

Inexplicably there did seem to be more general tourists, which gave rise to an idea that would not die: obviously all foreigners knew each other and, like migrating birds, called their friends down to share in fertile fields. Each year a few remained behind or came back out of season and more houses were bought and rebuilt and more permanent customers for high-quality goods acquired. But these did not have that other winning habit of paying their bills at once. They paid a bit this month, a bit next—maybe. The gentry did not, would not know them and, as everyone observed later, Contessa Maffei's friends were cour-teous, if they met them in the street, but they were never seen together otherwise. When this second wave sold their houses at large profit—never as outlandish as rumored—the situation was reassessed: foreigners should be treated with caution.

The San Feliciani could also speculate and did on a much more daring scale. They put light, water, and roads into several huge abandoned houses and sold them for more money than they were sure the local bank had on deposit. The third wave of foreigners knew no Italian, but that slight impediment did not make them shy. They swarmed over the town, shouting in their own languages for whatever they wanted, or grunting with simian determination. To everyone's relief the novelty of shop-ping soon wore off, and platoons of servants took over the chore of keeping their new masters and the armies of guests com-fortable. Majordomos ordered the provisions required, haggled over the prices, and at the end of each month went around, very conscious of their new importance, paying the bills. Canned and boxed goods were purchased by the case. Mops by the dozen. All most confusing, for what were these things? Corn-flakes? Tonic water? Peanut butter? Water biscuits? Mock turtle soup? Why not take a pan and one mock turtle . . . ? Bottles of whiskey and gin appeared on grocers' shelves, the toilet paper available was somewhat softer, and three new butchers sprang into existence. The San Feliciani were presiding, a bit late, over their own "Italian Miracle." Now they greeted strangers with wan, hopeful smiles and spoke only in infinitives.

Some of the more obnoxious foreigners were weeded out by circumstances beyond their control—time, two severe winters, anxiety over the Communist party's intentions, and a fix-ation about kidnapping, which, since no one had offered, sounded like another way to emphasize their eligibility. They put their houses up for sale, packed and departed for . . . ? California? The Seychelles? Who knows? Simplicity took its toll with others of more acceptable manner and greater expectations. San Felice failed them. There were no dukes and duchesses, movie stars, or heads of state they could invite for formal dinners. So they too left to follow the seasons elsewhere and talk longingly of their villas in Tuscany.

These rites of settlement puzzled the San Feliciani. For-eigners, they decided once and for all, could not be understood. They were accustomed now to the ones who had stayed. They did not panic at the sight of new arrivals or itinerant tourists. They accepted the unfathomable, but when the day was over and they met for an *aperitivo,* they exchanged funny stories about the foreigners, who were strange, very strange indeed. Society has a certain just symmetry, for when two or three foreigners sat quietly in a garden, surrounded by cypresses and the golden light of a Tuscan sunset, they exchanged funny stories too—about the Italians, who were strange people, very strange indeed, perhaps the strangest of them all.

3

THE MORNING THE TRAIN WAS ROBBED, no one in San Felice seemed to hear the sirens that wailed back and forth along the valley. They did, of course, but they ignored them. To them ignoring that vulgar lower world was a question of principle become almost a tradition. It was a difficult pose to maintain with Brigadier Cirillo, the Commander of the Second Flying Squad (there is no first!) surging back and forth through the Piazza in the mighty blue-and-white Alfa Romeo, its siren screaming indignantly. Shopkeepers shook their heads. Cirillo was a show-off, a typical southern Italian, and unfit, by local standards, for authority. Dismissing him, they went about their business of opening up for the day. There were shutters to raise, sills to sweep, windows to clean, and customers to watch.

For the last two weeks the commercial element of the town had looked forward to this particular day with anticipation that was not strictly commercial. Only the three hairdressers could expect unusual profit. Others would have to take their pleasure from information. All were satisfied to see the three signore Pomodori, which means "tomatoes" and was the local pronunciation of Pomoroy, stroll along the Corso, their hair waved, teased, and sprayed into marble sculptures. They went into the largest of the cafés, where they were soon joined by the Baroness Casale. Quite as it should be. It was odd that no one had seen signora Kendall. And Countess Maffei bought groceries, which had to be a mistake. She must have forgotten which day it was: it was inconceivable that the Maffeis were not invited. This log of movements had to do with a party, not just any party, but a rather grand one to take place that evening: the Bourton-Hamptons were announcing their daughter Joan's engagement to a Sicilian *principe,* the Prince of Ficuzza e Verdura.

Cedric Bourton-Hampton, the bride's father, had taken the time to explain the importance of this alliance to everyone who would listen. His foreign neighbors had borne it patiently. By tacit agreement they put up with his bombastic stories as long as he did not lapse into his self-appointed role of local squire. He considered himself a one-man board of governors. He insisted that anyone who showed interest in buying a house should be vetted by him. Swimming pools should not be built or land fenced off without his approval. Houseguests of friends were not included in his invitations until he had probed, subtly he thought, into their acceptability. *His* guests were always rich or titled. He would not have them offended, and he never noticed that, instead, his foreign neighbors found him offensive. His Italian neighbors agreed with Baron Casale's remark that each time he went to the Bourton-Hamptons', he felt he had been invited for ethnic balance.

The shopkeepers and clerks of San Felice were more in-clined to take Cedric Bourton-Hampton at his own evaluation, probably because he overwhelmed them in what they considered a "squirely" fashion. His voice roared with the authority of Empire, to which he had only a tenuous connection, being the grandson of small farmers somewhere in the North Country, but that made no difference: behind his back he was called "Il Milord." He had come in that last brash wave of Tuscan invaders. Unlike the others he chose to fraternize. In fact he fancied he got on well with "the natives," and it was true that on his morning progress from shop to shop and office to office, they smiled and nodded, encouraging him to expound his views on every subject from the glories of the Renaissance to the ungovernability of Italy as long as the country might be in Italian hands. He never realized that they understood little of what he said and so his analysis of the sociofinancial intricacies involved in his daughter's choice of husband had been a rich source of misinformation.

Then one morning a new dimension had been added. While Eleanor Kendall stood at the counter of the Monte dei Paschi, waiting to transact her business, the teller spent ten minutes whispering with his special friend, the clerk of the tourist office. After pooling their bits of gossip, the two men tried to estimate the value of the young prince's estates and his title. *Principe qua, Principe là* and finally El lost her patience. "Do you suppose we could get back to my deposit?" she interrupted, startling them by the curtness of her voice. They thought of her as the smiling, patient, reasonable one. "He may be rich and important. He may not, but those estates you're impressed by—Ficuzza and Verdura—are nothing more than two dry river bottoms in Sicily."

As far as could be remembered, that was the first dissenting voice. It broke the spell of obligatory admiration: negative possibilities have their own irresistible appeal. They were explored with relish. By the morning of the Bourton-Hampton party, which also happened to be the morning of the robbery, public opinion was almost evenly divided, but no one would deny that more information was needed, information that the next two days must surely provide. *It* became the business of the town.

29

Unless a customer could logically provide it, shopkeepers were inattentive, their eyes flickered away to the street. Even civil servants, in a startling reversal of character, were suddenly curious about the lives, the social lives that is, of their applicants. With such tensions arcing around the town, news of the robbery—and the ritual manhunt—created an overload. The coffee intake doubled, and suppositions, innuendos, rumors, a few facts, and hundreds of outright slanders were exchanged. In the enthusiasm of the moment all were of equal value, which made it a very busy and confusing day for the San Feliciani. The first of many and for one simple reason: the basic assumptions were wrong.

4

ROBBERY DID NOT CALL UP tortured moral evaluations.
Robbery was robbery: men had plotted against society, or worse
in this case, against The State for illegal gain; ergo the men
must be searched out and captured. The concept was obvious
and comforting to those who held truth to be self-evident. Most
men did. No contradiction was perceived. Brigades of carabinieri
were turned loose for the chase. They strangled traffic with
their checkpoints. Shoulder to shoulder they clumped through
thick woods to surround abandoned houses. They conferred
with computers, informers, and each other. The results were
meager. Fifty-six drivers were surprised *in flagrante* with expired
licenses, three soldiers were wounded by impetuous comrades,
and an unrecorded number of corps trucks collapsed ignominiously and were abandoned on the shoulders of country roads.
Hardly an impressive tally, but the best to be expected as long
as the contradiction was unperceived. *It* had been the grain of
sand to irritate and inspire. The robbery and all that happened
subsequently formed layer upon layer of nacre neatly obscuring
what would have been obvious if men had not insisted on

hunting men. Like most adventures it had started innocently, not as an adventure, but as a vacation.

The summer before, Eleanor Kendall, who was known to everyone as El, had gone south to a Calabrian beach with Lacey Wright, an old friend, a thwarted Italophile, who had renounced her happy years in the land of the Cockaigne for the solvency of being a television director in New York. They could only have gone together. Neither was fit company for a normal person.

After a season at the command of "the tube," Lacey was suffering from battle fatigue. Even her dreams were documentary. When finally she signed a twelve-week contract for ten weeks' pay and had yet another of those never-to-be-forgotten fights with Max, the photographer who was the long-term pretender to her affections, she admitted she needed a rest. And not in those chilly fjords where Max had an assignment.

El's problem, pernicious frustration, was less dramatic. A book of hers was to come out. The proofreaders had hacked unmercifully at the text: Italian phrases must conform to the Berlitz Beginner's Grammar and opinions to the *New York Times*. The corrected galleys were lost—and found, after seven trips around the world via Kansas City, at the bottom of an airplane freight bin. The man who obliged in the publicity department was too busy with "the beautiful people" to decide what could be done to/for her. Some hung-over Monday morning he might get around to considering her claims on his skill.

In short, both Lacey and El needed a rest.

Of the first week they remembered little except sleeping, sitting on the beach, and eating. The meals were memorable, if not for the food, for the service provided by the hotel's one child-waiter. The sight of two young foreign women alone seemed to mesmerize him. Gazing raptly into their eyes, he lowered their plates to approximately the spot where he had last noticed their table. With predictably sloppy results. The best beach, they decided, was a long sandy expanse about five miles from town, which they shared with one older man and his sedate, prolapsed basset hound. Each afternoon clouds appeared from nowhere and darkened ominously, or ominously enough to be an excuse for a nap at the hotel.

And just as regularly they ran into a police roadblock. After a summer of robberies and kidnappings, that was not strange. They were never delayed. As soon as El slowed down enough for the carabinieri to see into the car, they were waved on, out of the way. Lacey and El were more than uninteresting, they were a disappointment. In a bathing suit El was obviously female, but one afternoon in a canvas hat and shirt, she was not. They were stopped. Two pieces of clothing had changed her sex.

"They make me feel undesirable," Lacey complained as they were waved on with more than usual disgust. "Or at the very least persona non grata!"

The morning came when they must leave. The hotel was like an abandoned ship. Finally they found the staff(?) in the kitchen huddled over a blaring plastic box, intent on their first Radio Happening. A few minutes before eight a bank manager in a large local town had gone to open the bank and found four masked men waiting for him. The only useful information the manager could offer was that they had split up, making their escape in two cars, one heading north, the other south. El and Lacey paid their bill and left with police reports still rasping in their ears.

The first seventy miles of their trip were on a provincial two-lane road and wherever it was intersected, even by a footpath it seemed, there was a roadblock. They were waved through all of them. When El was not slowing down to be rejected, she was behind local trucks, flying blind through the noxious black smoke of their exhaust. Perhaps the fumes went to her brain.

In her irritation she muttered to Lacey that any four women could rob the Bank of Italy, take everything in the vaults, and the police would still go around looking for four men.

"Marvelous idea for a script. Think what fun we could have," had been Lacey's reaction.

That was how it started and the trip home was long.

They gave up the Bank of Italy almost immediately. They did not know enough about it. They could kidnap Gianni Agnelli or Sophia Loren's children. Both too obvious. Both impossible. They could rob a post office, very fashionable at the moment, or a bank, or a jeweler.

Lacey had objected. None of those would do. As women they had a limitation. No one must hear them speak, not just their accents, their *voices*—and it should be a big coup, not a petty crime any *delinquente* could bring off.

Crisscrossing a single railroad track, sometimes on an over-pass, sometimes at level crossings that were, inevitably, closed, reminded El of the payroll and post-office funds she had quite by accident seen delivered one gray dawn at the San Felice station. For reasons she could no longer even imagine, she had decided to take an early train to Rome, a very early train, which, according to the schedule, stopped a few minutes before 4:00 A.M. In a difference of opinion the engineer always wins, and he did, treating her to a moaned warning from his whistle and clouds of grit as he plunged past the station and on to Rome. There was no one to complain to, the 5:09 was the next train supposed to stop, and the waiting rooms were locked, so she had sat on the low wall outside the lavatories, a front seat for the show, as it turned out.

Would the post-office funds and the state payroll for an entire region strike Lacey as a coup? Roughly a million dollars by their free-style calculations. They played successfully, they thought, with the means, but ran into blind alleys trying to get

34

rid of the money. And then some fascinating subject lured them away, and the robbery was forgotten.

Ten days or so later, Hermione had wandered into El's house. The rain had depressed her. She wanted to be amused, which was not always easy. Lacey and El brought out their robbery-script idea and it jiggled her imagination. Couldn't they cast her as the "front girl"? She was too conspicuous for any other part, truth, not vanity, but she could distract attention from the others by calling attention to herself. Oh, and if they smuggled the money to Switzerland, she had a banker simply panting to do her a favor. She could arrange the numbered accounts. What fun! There must be four in the names of—she thought a while—Currer Bell, Mary Ann Evans, Aurore Lucie Dupin, and Mary Godwin. What fun! And the conversation rambled off to other more realistic projects.

That winter El's book had come out to all the usual disappointments and one or two surprises. The man in the publicity department was not one of them, so El marked time expensively in New York. Late one night she lured Lacey, who already wore sunglasses in lighted rooms and would soon be a mole, from her Movieola. El chattered along about everything and nothing to distract her and only succeeded when she remembered a clipping she had found in her files: the account of a rich Milanese's scheme, which had been successful, for driving money across the Swiss border. Clearly larceny had always been part of El's makeup.

That was it! Lacey was enthusiastic. That would work! El's ingrained pessimism, accentuated by some scotch, left her doubtful. The idea was impossible: women could never do it. Even a script had to be logical. They discussed and argued and butiffed until dawn. By nine Lacey was back in her Movieola cubicle, slightly giddy, but excited. She would come to Italy in May, they would study their plot very carefully, and over the summer write the script. Come if she liked! El had shrugged. It was as good a way to waste time as any. Irritated and exhausted enough to be sarcastic, Lacey had taunted El. There *was* a way to put down her doubts: they could organize the robbery, a real one; however, she would like to point out that the man who wrote Buck Rogers had never been in a spaceship!

THE ELUSIVE CHEMISTRY between spring and frustration softened El's resistance: the plot now seemed entirely feasible. She planned a dry run in April, a most unreliable month with religious and administrative holidays. Government offices would open and close in confusing alternation and even the most casual bureaucracy did not ship money, if there was no one to receive it. But actually, on closer study a pattern and certain rules emerged. They would be maintained at all costs: such procedures did not admit change. The traditional payday, for instance, was the twenty-seventh of the month. Someone had told her, she no longer remembered who, that three full working days must be allowed for the sorting of papers and the bookkeeping. Saturdays did not count. In a perfect month, then, the regional and provincial payrolls would be delivered on the night between the twenty-third and twenty-fourth.

She began to see that the transfer was also planned to be inconspicuous, to dovetail with existing daily routines. The stop of the Catania-Milan Express was only "unscheduled" in the sense that it was not information that the timetables offered the patient and too-often-disappointed passengers of the Italian State Railway. To the ministries concerned, the hesitation would be absolutely regular. And the local postmen could be used without disrupting their routine. The guard from the express was armed. Why did he go with the local postmen, leaving the bulk of the funds in the mail car? Probably the theorists had reasoned there could be no danger in the brief wait between the time he left and the departure of the local. The train would be met in the regional capital by squads of armed police. So, if her calculations were right, in the script they must arrange to immobilize three guards, one armed, two unarmed. Details were beginning to fall in place.

At 3:30 on the morning El had picked as likely for the April delivery, she dragged herself out of bed, dressed in a black turtleneck sweater and black slacks, and drove off to the station, feeling very, very foolish. At that hour her imagination was not awake. She sat again on the low wall by the latrines and waited.

A railway-police agent walked slowly across the tracks. With each step his large, efficient lantern flashed at a different angle, revealing a segmented world of half-objects. He stopped on the first platform, hesitated a moment, then walked over to the door of the local's mail car and tried it. Locked. He switched off his lantern and after a brief report to his brother agent in the office, went back along the platform to the first-class waiting room, where he looked carefully in both directions before he slipped inside and quietly closed the door. From his caution, El judged this was one fringe benefit not yet sanctioned by contract.

Silence except for the gentle stutter of automatic machinery. April was playing its damp tricks. It was also cold. At 4:16 a long train glided into the station from the south and the scene was played again, just as El remembered it, with the same muted sounds, the same acrid smell of oil on hot metal, and the same sense of urgency. Again she forced herself to tiptoe around the front of the local's engine and lean out far enough to see, yet be protected by shadow. Her reconstruction was exact: government mailbags were being transferred from the express mail car to the local's. She returned to her place on the wall. Seconds later, metal scraped on metal and the express slipped away as smoothly as it had come. The operation had taken less than two and a half minutes.

Again the platform was deserted. A muffled voice, the sound of cranking, another voice, more indistinct than the first—and again the soft silence of a vacuum. The stationmaster and the police agent on duty must have reported to the central office that kept traffic records, confirming the arrival of the express, the transfer, and the train's regular departure. El walked along the platform and peeked through the glass in the door of the police office. A heavy-jowled man in uniform was just nestling his head on a sweater wadded up in the middle of his desk. A goose-necked lamp, crimped sharply away from him, shone on a black telephone. Should it ring and wake him, it would be the first thing he saw.

At the other end of the building in the stationmaster's office the light from the same sort of government-issue lamp had been masked with a long pleated skirt of blue cellophane, maybe a wrapper from a candy box. The room, shimmering in dark, marine tranquillity, appeared empty. El could just make out the relaxed form of a man, tipped back in a big upholstered desk chair, his feet splayed in front of him on a straight chair. One hand was draped limply over a telephone, ready to pick up the receiver. A highly developed professional skill, El decided, this ability to function in their sleep, and a convenient one from her point of view.

She went back along the platform. No one stirred. A crack of light showed from the local's mail car. She smelled cigarette smoke. She walked on, her footsteps quiet and careful, around a freight cart. A new type with rubber wheels. She tried to pull the handle down: it was held fast by a catch. She fiddled with it, lowered the handle, worked with it until she understood that the handle was a form of brake. When it was up, the cart could neither move nor be moved. Down, she could drag the cart over the bricks easily. It was very quiet: the blessing of rubber wheels that saved it from rattle and rumble. Twice she went the length of the platform and back with it. No one stirred. She parked it carefully where it had been and resumed her walking. Still no one stirred.

At 4:44 the stationmaster came out of his office, stretched, and walked off toward the men's lavatory. He must have seen her. When he came out, buttoning his fly (was it possible the state did not yet trust zippers?), his replacement was waiting for him. They exchanged a few words. The night man left and the day man took up his post, leaning against the doorjamb of his office with his red cap, red flag, and small trumpet tucked under his arm, ready.

Just before five the mailmen from San Felice arrived, deposited their mail sack, and sauntered along the platform to the mail car. They knocked—three longs, two shorts—the door was opened, and they took possession of the payroll sack right in front of El. The armed guard jumped down and followed them, his gun in its holster. No one paid any attention to her, and there was no even minimal effort at deception. But—she realized—the local mailmen presented a problem. If they arrived too soon . . . if *they* discovered the guards trussed up and the money gone, it would be too soon. Much too soon. The robbers might still be in front of the station, loading up sacks. Or if they had gotten away, they would not be far enough away. Schemes to delay them on the road from town to the station occurred to her as she sat, waiting for the 5:09 express for Rome to stop. When it did, she walked back and forth along it, looking up into its windows, pretending to be anxious. No late passenger got off. She shook her head in disappointment, a gesture easily recognized as meaning another guest had failed to arrive when announced, left the station, and went home, convinced that she had done a good morning's work and more than ever that the script, even the robbery, was workable.

MONTHS BEFORE IN NEW YORK El and Lacey had agreed on one *sine qua non:* four somethings acceptable as identification in Europe, specifically acceptable to a Swiss bank, had to be obtained. If that was impossible, their script collapsed. The vital elements were a picture and a place and date of birth. To renew her own international driving permit El had filled out a form giving the dreary details that pursue us through life and her state license number, which looked familiar. It was, she eventually realized, her social-security number. Would they run it through a computer to discover her tax record and unpaid parking tickets? Five days later she received a new license, which, given the sluggishness of the post and caprices of most computers, must mean it had been issued without control. She had armed herself with four extra application forms.

She invented the vital statistics. George Sand burst upon life in Indiana. *Frankenstein* was written on a rainy vacation in Switzerland, so Mary Godwin became a citizen of Idaho. Currer Bell had to be content with the moors of North Dakota, and imagining the intellectual climate suitable to George Eliot, Mary Ann Evans was reborn a Bostonian. El also gave them appropriate addresses, birth dates, and then lost her nerve on their social-security numbers. They seemed to be doled out in odd nonsequences. After a demented harangue against the welfare state, El tricked three friends into showing her their social-security cards. She memorized the numbers, changed them by one digit, and reissued them to her candidates for international permits. Only the pictures were left. The idea of sending off her own did not appeal. Then one morning she met Hermione, swinging along the Corso.

"Still want to be the 'front girl'?" El asked. She was joking and her explanation was part of the joke, she thought.

"But *exactly*! You've caught on to the twist." Hermione threw her arms out in triumph, startling passersby. "Come on, we'll do them right now. If anything happens, we'll claim someone faked them. See how convenient fame is? It'll be a fake. I'll insist." No fake could have been as unflattering as what the machine churned out. "Last night *was* a bit strenuous," Hermione sighed, studying the first batch. "But I didn't realize it was *that* bad. No one would recognize me!" For once that seemed an advantage.

El stuffed the envelopes with their forms, pictures, and fees in U.S. bills and filled out the return mailing labels, two to Hermione's address, two to her own, but without their names. As far as the post office was concerned, foreign names were written in Chinese characters. A Mary Ann Evans who lived at La Volpaia was the equivalent of Hermione Hendricks. She mailed them and waited through three tense weeks, worrying over what constituted a "federal offense."

In the middle of the fourth week the international driving permits came back perfectly in order with Hermione's picture further defaced by a purple stamp. That poor George Sand was born in La Porte, but lived in Terre Haute, offended Hermione's esthetic sense.

It was just about that time, quite by accident, that Kate Pound became involved in the robbery. She was a diligent optimist, which, she claimed, was an asset for a political analyst and the essence of her skill. She was always on the bubble, and enthusiasm or rage—whatever her humor—it was contagious, just as her curiosity and interest in everything around her could stimulate the most boring to heights of animation and charm well beyond their talents. When she moved on and was no longer there to prod them, they, like Cinderella, slipped silently back into their dullness. But periodically Kate's optimism failed her, usually when her work, her business affairs, her husband, Robert, and their son, Alan, coordinated their perversities. Then, in a last lunge at perspective, she would talk to El, whose aversion to the impossible dream and penchant for the practical had a tonic effect on Kate's will.

Watching her walk toward the house, El recognized the symptoms. Kate always shriveled under the weight of her problems, seemed slighter than ever—and yes, she was muttering to herself, too. The opening of the door startled her. She smiled and apologized and explained, but with only a fraction of the psychic energy she would have wasted on a total stranger. El offered tea to soothe and revive and wondered who had decreed that every woman should marry.

Alan had turned up, prepared to spend the summer and, still more unlikely, was working on some mysterious business deal. Capital letters were implicit. So were Robert's fatherly doubts. He was a man of gentle innocence, who warded off disappointment with public statements of skepticism and then hoped to be surprised. He seldom was.

Alan, at twenty-four, was an outrageously handsome young man. He had drifted from school to school and subject to subject and girl to girl as though life were an elaborate smorgasbord of delights. Whenever he ran out of money, usually in some outpost of civilization, he called home, collect. Between interests he even "visited" Kate and Robert, doling out his considerable charm, until he was caught raising marijuana behind the municipal tennis courts, or had convinced the daughter of the local *liceo* principal to run off with him to Mexico, where he knew of a rich abandoned silver mine. Now, here he was again, unannounced, and what was more suspicious, without his beard, his beads, or apparently a problem. He had some decent clothes and money, and he talked rather grandly of going in for banking, as though it were a sport at his latest school.

Whatever his prospects in the financial world, Alan had declared himself in need of a few weeks' *total* rest, which had further antagonized his father. In fact Robert was now so recalcitrant that he vetoed every proposal, whether or not it had to do with Alan. One of them was Kate's determination to balance their budget by the sale of a beach house and parcels of land they had bought when the children were small, but had not used in the last fifteen years. True, they rented it, which brought in some income. Not nearly enough. Kate had found a syndicate that wanted to buy it, obviously for the land, which had been Robert's cue. It was morally wrong to sell to speculators. They would build more high-rise horrors, ruin the coast, overcrowd it, pollute the water. Besides, the idea of going to the sea appealed to him. He might use the house himself. Or he might simply retreat to their apartment in Rome.

Kate was exasperated, tired, and, as she recognized, on the verge of hysteria. What could she do? Her life was a perpetual greyhound race and she the mechanical rabbit who lunged along the rail with the pack snapping at her heels. No, no, she exaggerated, El teased her. The idea of having to write yet another article on the formation of yet another Italian government had unhinged her. Maybe that too, but Kate would not be comforted. She reviewed the glorious terms of the sale a dozen times. She had until the first of June to convince Robert. All he would say was No, I think I'll use the house this summer. She would *not* let this slip through her fingers. It was too perfect! Payment would be in dollars, checks deposited in her American account. When the exchange was good, she would pay off their Italian mortgages and . . . a light flashed on in El's brain.

Maybe to distract her, maybe because her own mind was

as absorbed by the train robbery as Kate's was by her problems—El did not stop to analyze—she told Kate about the script and added a new touch. If Kate changed her dollars for the stolen money, part of the loot would, in effect, be exported to the United States, could be put in government "paper" at high interest—and Kate could dump the "hot" lire on the banks that held her mortgages. A detail only, but it added a nice complexity.

Kate's enthusiasm could never be suppressed for long. What fun! A robbery! El must tell her all about the script. How were they to rob the train? The rest of the money? Where was it to go? When El reached the Italian-border section of the outline, Kate jumped up and down, saying, "Caroline would love it! Absolutely love it! And hate it too!" True, in the last year or so Caroline had become fanatic about the billions upon billions of lire Italians had calmly exported to Switzerland and the United States, illegally, to the damage of their own economy. Yes, she would love it. They had stayed up so late talking that Kate decided to spend the night and slept twelve hours. The train robbery was her antidote for insomnia. The next morning she drove off, calling, "I can't wait until Caroline hears about it all. She'll love it!"

El saw no harm in Caroline's knowing, especially if it amused Kate and took her mind off the dog pack at her heels, but she was less pleased when she discovered that Hermione had told Martha Gelder. An argument about journalism had been the immediate cause. Martha had never cared for work, regular daily employment was irksome, so she subsisted as a "free-lance" all-purpose writer, who might or might not take on any story. She preferred house-sitting and days of leisurely dreams. Young Lochinvar, by now not so young, might yet swing her up onto his saddle, which would be a burly feat, and gallop off with her. One of her seasonal laments was that there was no future for her in Italy. She had moaned to Hermione, who took seriously what she should have known was rhetorical. Look at Oriana Fallaci! Fortunately Martha's reaction to that sally was lost. Martha should be creative, imaginative—like, oh almost anything. El and Lacey—just an example—had noticed that the police paid no attention to women, as though they were incapable of crime. They'd invented a whole script around the idea. Martha could do a funny piece, a serious one, if she insisted, on the Police vs. Women. It would sell. There were a thousand other things just as simple. Try! Hermione urged her. Don't sit here and blubber into your whiskey.

It can be said for Martha that she asked El if she might use the idea; would El object? She did. She and Martha were old friends, or at times more like old enemies. Martha was so erratic herself that she found El's consistency erratic, a form of deception. Still, she was afraid to cross her. Their relations, like Martha's depressions, went in predictable cycles. Martha lectured El, accused her, sneered at her until, suddenly terrified she had gone too far and might not be forgiven, she rushed out and bought an elaborate present or performed some unwanted favor. El could not have kept her from using the idea. She did ask her to wait at least until the script was finished. Martha tugged her forelock and meekly went off in search of other, certainly more spectacular subjects. Left in peace, El continued charting the details of the robbery.

5

𝒪 SHORTLY THEREAFTER Lacey arrived from New York and El presented her with the tentative outline of the script. Experience had taught them that they worked well together. Neither thought herself a genius. Both had good minds and infinite capacity for slogging, which, contrary to popular myth, are the basic talents needed for work, creative or otherwise. Socially they were capable of acrobatic feats to avoid an argument. El rose above it into an aloofness so impenetrable that she might have soared beyond the oxygen level. Lacey pedaled backward, strewing compliments in her wake, like Hippomenes trying to distract Atalanta. But in professional questions they gave up diplomacy. They criticized each other, argued, challenged the other's ideas, and *in extremis* refused to go on "under these conditions." All without ill-feeling. Most important, they listened to each other, which explained why El was not surprised to find that as she had been convinced by Lacey's arguments, so Lacey had been convinced by hers, and they were again of diametrically opposed opinions. El now thought the robbery was plausible (always as a script), Lacey did not.

One night in a spluttering rage El gave up sweet reason. Dammit, then they would do it Lacey's way. They would rob the train and make it work, but—*remember Buck Rogers!* Lacey's own example, not El's. Remember Buck Rogers? Remember?

There was no rational explanation for how they had talked themselves into such a ridiculous position. Lacey had taken El up on it, and El found herself trying to draft Martha, Caroline, Hermione, and Kate to play in real life the parts that had so casually been assigned them in imagination. It had not really been very difficult either. Their parts were juicy. They were like eighth graders, who decided to snitch candy and then egged each other on to raid the store, kill the owner, and burn the building. Each knew that what they proposed was wrong, even when she considered it a lark, but other respectable virtues got in the way of discussion: team spirit, word of honor, courage. So they charged forward, encouraging themselves with the nobility of the probable side effects. Martha adopted Crime as the coming novelty in Italian journalism. On the spur of the moment Hermione invented "Women's Right to Equal Suspicion" and liked it. Of them all Caroline was the one with an intellectual cause. Kate, after months of angst, found it a welcome diversion: it would at least be fun. They had lapsed into total irresponsibility.

Each must have thought the scheme would fail, but they were too competitive not to use every crumb of ingenuity available. And too, at any point before they actually drove the money away from the station, they could claim it was a prank, a warning. No, there was no retreat. They rushed on, pell-mell.

Lacey and El were the tacticians. One all-important question remained to be solved: who was inconspicuous at a station and how could they assume that identity? The answer was— at dawn no one would be inconspicuous. Porters? Garbage collectors? Waiters? They were not usually so infatuated with work that they appeared an hour and a half early. Mailmen? El rejected that profession. The impersonation of a central government employee was surely a major offense. Lacey could not see why, under the circumstances, they should worry about that. No, and besides, people *knew* mailmen, recognized them. No one really recognized garbage men or porters or for that matter those dumb, sleepy boys behind the counters of cafés. They all looked alike—and at any hour they were indigenous to stations, the familiar fauna of the place. Also their "uniforms" were easily imitated. Or were they? They could not go to a shop. The purchases would seem unsuited to the customers. Where then?

Finally Lacey and El decided to try the most public place they could think of, a large town market. One morning in Arezzo and their shopping was done. They found two long gray smocks, which seemed duplicates of what older garbage collectors still wore, along with four blue twill porter-ish jackets and a waiter's white coat. Although changing from a porter's jacket to a collector's coat added a complication, it was a precaution. At the station only two porters were on duty at one time—never more. On the platform in the gloom before dawn four might pass unnoticed. If later, in better light, four appeared at the front of the station, they would not pass. Two garbage collectors, a bar waiter, and a porter would. They were all to wear blue jeans. They were so common, they were invisible and had a second convenience: once the coats and jackets were disposed of, they were more normal garments for innocent female residents than blue twill work pants.

Martha felt that the garbage collectors' coats should be old or they would be eye-catching. It was her idea. As she said, everyone knew she was crazy. Late one Saturday morning Lacey and El went with her to the main deposit of the sanitation department, a deep cavern *in* the old walls of the town with a doorway that opened onto the road. Martha counted on the market-day crowd, milling around, for cover. All three of them had peered into the cave. There was no one there: the morning rounds were over, the next would be after the market closed. Lacey and El backed off across the road and watched while Martha took the two new smocks out of her plastic shopping bag, hung them on pegs, rolled up two old smocks, and stuffed them into her bag. Lacey, who already had a deep tan, was ashen. She worried out loud about her nerve. Would it hold? El only nodded: her throat had closed. Martha, more casual than seemed possible, sashayed out of the deposit, swinging her bag.

"*Allons enfants* . . ." she trilled and not *mezza voce*.

After all that, the night before the robbery, when Lacey and El went into the *cantina* where they had hung the smocks on a nail behind the furnace, they discovered them immaculately laundered. Sweet Bianca, who cleaned for El, must have been puzzled, but ever silent, she had washed them and put them back without questions or comment.

Caps had been a problem too. In the market they had found two visored caps of blue twill, which could do for the collector-porters. The other two porters looked quite authentic with Austrian university students' caps, which Kate had bought for her children, as she said, in some other life. Years in a trunk had crumpled them efficiently and dulled the visors.

Having assembled this mixture of finery, they held an informal dress rehearsal at which Lacey was eliminated by unanimous decision from the status of garbage collector. The smock drooped and flapped around her tall, slender frame most unconvincingly. A broomstick draped in a man's suit might frighten birds, but even they would have suspected Lacey. She took her rejection as a slight and needed a lot of jollying along before she would try the waiter's jacket, which was the first time anyone had thought about a bare head. Waiters seldom wear caps and Lacey did have hair short enough to pass muster. Perfect, except her copper curls were too striking. They doused her with olive oil, slicked her hair down, and judged her perfect. She called it hazing and there may have been a pinch of revenge, for she was the drillmaster who took them over and over what they were to do, especially the four destined to climb into the mail car. Not a word must be spoken. They must be quick and sure in trussing up the guards. They practiced and they practiced binding each other up with adhesive tape until they created a shortage. In San Felice they spun yarns to the pharmacists about houseguests with sprained ankles. Anyone who left town was on her honor to return with at least two rolls. In this item no scrimping was allowed.

El had decided that the canvas post-office bags should be left in the mail car. They were heavy, hard to dispose of, and the locks incriminating. By chance a convenient substitute was provided (and something else could have beenused). On her foray into the deposit Martha had seen a pile of heavy black plastic garbage bags, stronger than any on sale commercially, and had "requisitioned" ten of them. For no particular reason they had struck her fancy.

Everyone was struck with fancies. If El considered impersonating a government employee a major offense, Lacey would not be involved in an "armed" robbery. Some nonweapon must be found. After various trial runs they settled on plastic bottles with hand sprays, the kind used for insecticides and available in any hardware store. Next they experimented with what liquid to put in them. They tried ether and almost knocked *themselves* out. Acids would not do. Eventually they settled on ammonia and counted on surprise to make up for the lethal qualities it lacked.

El was worried about the three guards. Surprise was an advantage, but if that failed and the balance depended on physical strength—well, the end was obvious. Lacey argued that luck, both good and bad, would play a large part and of course it did, but still El fretted. There had been several incidents already that spring, mentioned very much in passing by the newspapers, of passengers on *cuccette* cars being knocked out by some substance, sprayed presumably, and then robbed. If she could discover what had been used . . . from the reports it might have a chloroform base . . . She never found it. Later she was glad, considering the spectacular results of ammonia. The guards stated that they had been drugged, beaten, and tied up while unconscious, a fine bit of face-saving and camouflage for their amnesia. They remembered nothing about the four men who had burst in upon them. Not even their voices!

Toward the third week in May Lacey noticed that her helpers' attention span was very short. If they were acting like children, she reasoned, they should be treated like children. Practice might make perfect, but not if they were bored. For each run-through she devised a different schedule. The order of questions varied. Who pushed the cart? Who pulled? At what exact moment did Hermione open the trunk of Caroline's car? What went in Kate's suitcase? New exercises were jumbled in with old, mix-ups imagined and solved. Try, try! Compete! At times Lacey felt like a gym mistress.

Martha was fractious. She did not need rehearsal. She was *much* quicker than the others to grasp an idea—according to her—and she did not enjoy playing a guard who was always wrestled to the floor and wrapped in adhesive tape. That, at least, they understood. They did not trust her to be quiet in the mail car, yet it was difficult to invent enough chores for her and involve her inextricably. She had to be fully as guilty as the others, or she would be dangerous. At last they found the perfect assignment for her: a tape recording. Her voice was deep enough to confuse and her Italian almost without accent, especially when distorted with the Florentine aspirated *c*'s. It would be, she assured them, a masterpiece. It did keep her busy.

Hermione, as "front girl," had to delay the postmen. She decided on the flat tires, her own and theirs. She bought upholsterers' nails at Standa in Arezzo. The night before the robbery she punctured her own spare and loosened its bolts for quick unloading from the back of her car. Early the next morning she was out on the road with her car jacked up, the punctured spare leaning against the bumper as though it had just been changed and the nuts on her tire loosened ready to be tightened. The mail truck came down the hill, veered around her, stopped, backed up, and pulled in behind her, passing twice over the part of the road she had salted with her nails. The driver got out to help her—that was almost the end of the robbery.

They had no way of knowing the driver would be a friend of hers. The year before he had come to her for help. He had heard that she often went to Switzerland and wanted her to buy some medicines desperately needed for his little girl—that is, he wanted her to buy them as soon as he had accumulated the huge sum of money they would cost. Hermione had gone to see the child, had talked to the doctors. The medicines were vital. A collection had been taken up among the post-office employees, the father had mortgaged his life borrowing money, and still there was not enough. On her next trip Hermione bought the medicines, paid the difference herself, and became, in her own special Hermione way, a member of the family. She was outraged that *he* should be the one blamed for this crazy enterprise. For forty-eight hours El would jump every time the telephone rang for fear it would be, not the police, but Hermione from another airport or station to threaten and curse her.

When her tire was safely bolted on, Hermione had surged off down the road, and once out of sight, had circled the hill, coming back on a road above the mail truck. It was up on a jack and the driver and his mate were rolling a tire toward town. She went on to the station, put her car in the parking lot, and waved at Martha, who sat, waiting in hers. Minutes later Peter Testa arrived, shaved and neat, in his early morning fuddle, and they knew they were in trouble. El *must* have known. She should have warned them. They were to wait in the parking lot. As Caroline came across the Piazza pushing a collector's dolly loaded with the first bags of money, they were to open the trunk of her car, take out Kate's suitcase, and stand ready to pack it. She must take her forty million lire and all the jackets, coats, and caps. They *knew* they had to wait. They also *knew* someone must distract Peter. They argued in gestures, gave it up, and got out of their cars to stand together, watching the Piazza, waiting for Caroline to come into sight.

INSIDE ALL HAD GONE SMOOTHLY. El, Lacey, Caroline, and Kate had worked together with a precision that even a week before would have seemed impossible. Only their nerves defied direction. As the express pulled in, on time as always, Caroline murmured,

"My dears, I can't think what I'm doing here. Giordano . . ."

"You have the best part. The fun!" Kate hissed at her.

They waited, straining to hear the sounds they expected—doors sliding open, thumps, doors closing again, and finally the faint sigh, which announced departure. When it came, it startled them. They pushed the cart out along the platform. Any noise would be confused with the train's trucks adjusting to the rails. They left the cart in position under the station-side door of the local's mail car and ran back around the corner of the building. They waited. Tensely. At the first whiff of cigarette smoke, they took off their caps, pulled thick nylon stockings over their heads, down over their faces, resettled their caps, and almost got the giggles. Kate's had a hole that her nose stuck through in a very lewd way.

One by one they edged around the corner, ran, and jumped onto the cart. Kate came last, jumped and missed. They helped her up. El's soft knock—three longs, two shorts—was answered by grumbles. A bar rasped as it was yanked back through its iron keepers and a voice complained,

"We're short a guard and you guys. . . ." The door rolled open and El sprayed ammonia at the face behind it. Caroline stumbled in to grab him. Lacey caught the other, the armed guard, full-face with ammonia as he turned toward the door, a thermos bottle in one hand, a plastic cup in the other. Before he could think about reaching for his gun, Kate had jumped for his arms, twisted them behind his back, and was whipping, whipping tape around them. When he sank to the floor, she did too. El quietly closed the door onto the platform. This would be simpler than the plan—Lacey's bit of luck, which they would understand later. One of the local guards, who had been on a week's leave, had reported sick the night before and through some slip-up had not been replaced. First things first. The guards had arranged their own disgrace. They had their coffee and a smoke. Once the mailmen came was time enough, they thought, to press the station police into escort duty.

Under abundant squirtings of ammonia they wilted away, curling into fetal lumps on the floor. The rest was easy. Working in pairs, which they could not have done had there been three men, El and Caroline, and Lacey and Kate bound the guards' ankles and knees with untold meters of adhesive tape. They forced their arms behind their backs, crossed them, and wrapped them together from wrist to elbow. For good measure they clamped two broad strips across their mouths and two more across the eyes. El, tempted by the extra security of a stanchion at the far end of the car, away from the mail sacks, tethered

54

them to it by their feet. She was careful to shackle them face-down.

Now they were ready for the bags, which were awkward, but that had been taken into account too. Practice had shown that two must hold a garbage bag upright, while the other two slashed a post-office bag, lifted it, and funneled its contents into the garbage bag. As each bag was filled and its top securely closed with a triple-length wire fastener, it was dragged to the door. It took time. A bag a minute was the acceptable rate: El kept an eye on her watch. Eight and nine and finally the last. She glanced at the guards. They were peaceful in their mummy wrappings. Nothing else had been left behind.

El slid the door open a crack, looked out, and motioned frantically for Lacey's help in pushing the heavy door open. Then they both jumped down onto the cart and started tugging plastic sacks off the mail car. After the third, Lacey hopped quietly off onto the brick platform and went along to the front of the truck. It was important that the handle-brake be released at the right moment. Kate had taken her place, wrestled with three more bags, and joined Lacey. Caroline and El dragged the rest off onto the cart, then jumped down to the ground. Caroline began to push the cart. Lacey and Kate pulled. El was left to close the door again.

It was heavy and the angle gave her no leverage. She struggled, pushing and pulling from below until it was almost in place. She wedged it shut with a chisel she had brought for the purpose. It must not roll open! Again she looked around and started running after the cart, grabbing Caroline by the coattail as she passed. They were rounding the corner when they saw the stationmaster come to his door. They could not wait to see what he did. They had to hope that habit would draw him off in the opposite direction, toward the latrines.

Earlier they had moved their garbage dollies from the

normal parking place at the back of a freight barn to the side of the station, and had draped their coats and Lacey's waiter's jacket over the handles. Caroline and El ripped off their stocking masks and shoved them into their pockets. To save time and make herself look bulkier El pulled her collector's coat on over the porter's jacket and started out into the Piazza. Caroline was ready and helping Lacey change from one jacket to the other. Kate, with her nose still sticking through her mask and puffing from her exertions, began to drag the sacks off the cart and over to the corner of the station. El shoved the dolly in front of her with her foot while she struggled to force the buttons through the buttonholes. Damn the gloves! Mittens of chain mail could not have been clumsier and she must get the coat closed. For the next few minutes she would be the most exposed of the four.

She heard a car drive into the parking lot. A door slammed. She did an about-face, hooked one foot under the carriage of the dolly, twirling it around, and for a few precious seconds stood still, working frantically on the buttons. Footsteps came behind her. One, only one button, the bottom one, was undone. She left it and tried to lounge tiredly against the dolly. She was to ward off interference and curiosity and still time her arrival at the corner of the building just as Caroline's cart was loaded. Caroline would push hers off to her car, which was parked close by, behind a double trailer truck that chance had placed on the scene, and El and Lacey would load the next sacks.

The footsteps were very near. El pulled her cap as far down over her nose as she could and still see. Lacey was having trouble with the bags. They were monstrously heavy and wiggly besides. At the sound of footsteps Lacey glanced up. An odd expression flitted across her face before she ducked her head back down and concentrated on giving the bag another mighty heave. El almost turned to see what had thrown Lacey off her pace, decided against it, and started forward in her best slow shamble. A voice behind her said,

"Out early this morning."

She felt giddy. Peter! He had said "an early train," but *this* early? It had never entered her mind. What could she do? For one desperate second she was tempted to turn and answer teasingly,

"I knew you wouldn't recognize me, darling! I just knew it. I came down to wish you *buon viaggio!*" He would think her mad. No matter, if it saved the situation. But it would not. It would place her at the scene of the robbery in a preposterous getup. It also would leave the money out of the train, yes, but not yet in the cars—in limbo with her three helpers stuck. She took another slow step and another and shrugged. The footsteps went on toward the station and El, limp, leaned all her weight on the handles of the dolly and took a deep breath.

Once Peter disappeared into the station, Kate and Caroline could help Lacey. El speeded up, but not too abruptly, so that she reached them as the second bag was slipped into place. Caroline started off across the Piazza, pushing her treasure. Hermione and Martha ducked behind the double trailer truck ready to help her unload.

As Kate and Lacey stuffed two bags onto her cart, El wondered what would happen if the plastic ripped or the bottom gave. Maybe they should have kept the post-office sacks. No, too heavy, on top of their other hazards. They had had to divide the weight. Six bags had become ten and they were still too heavy. Luck, that was all. Pray for luck. Caroline and El met in mid-Piazza. Hermione and Martha helped El unload. She turned back. Again El met Caroline in mid-Piazza. And again. The rhythm was right. Caroline was on her last trip. El took her dolly back to the side of the freight barn and reappeared with her coat and jacket over her arm as Caroline crossed the

Piazza for the last time. El had forgotten her cap. With it hiding almost all of her face she looked a suspicious or at best drunken figure.

The last sacks were to go in El's car, which was in a more exposed spot in front of a store, but still out of sight of the parking lot. With her jacket tucked under her arm Lacey sped past El, hesitating just long enough to yank her cap off, and rushed on to open El's trunk for Caroline. They flung the sacks in as though they were full of feathers. Caroline grabbed El's coats and Lacey's jacket and started the last journey with her dolly to the side of the freight barn, dropping the bundle of clothes off with Martha and Hermione as she went. They already had the porters' jackets Caroline had brought with her first load and were packing them in Kate's suitcase. About her money they had been lucky too. The first sack they had tried produced bills counted and bound in uniform bundles. Martha had taken ten million to exchange in Rome, and Hermione her ten million to carry to London. They were in a frenzy to be on their way. Peter must be entertained.

It was contagious. Suddenly Caroline was frantic to get away from the station. She ran—she could not stop herself—from the freight barn back toward her car and right into three Boy Scouts, who had apparently walked to the station by a path through the fields. At least she was rid of the coats and jackets. She and the scouts ducked and bobbed and apologized. In a way they calmed her. They looked so funny-familiar with their kneesocks and backpacks.

Nearer the station the scouts stopped to help one boy rearrange his pack, delaying Hermione's approach. She cursed them as they could seldom have been cursed. She *had* to be out on the platform in time to divert Peter, while first Martha and later Kate visited the ladies' lavatory.

"Where's Kate's jacket?" Martha demanded, joining the others by Caroline's car. "I've got everything else. Where . . . ?"

They had forgotten it. Or was she still wearing it? They could do nothing. She was on her own. Hermione started her long-legged strut toward the station. They pushed Martha off before she could argue. She set out marching across the Piazza as though she were reporting to the militia, her briefcase in one hand, Kate's suitcase in the other. She was to keep up that gait through the station and out along the first platform into the ladies' room. Only the last twenty-five feet, when she was no longer protected by the local train and its engine, would be dangerous. Hermione was primed to create a scene, if necessary (and with Peter already waiting for the train, they knew it was). She was an artist of the impromptu. Her remark *did* startle him. His attention did not waver. Martha made it safely into the ladies' room, where she paused long enough to leave the suitcase. She slipped out again without being noticed.

Kate had been left with the heavy freight cart to maneuver at least close to its normal position on the first platform. She had to take several cuts back and then forward again before she found out quite how to steer it. It had a natural attraction to the wall. Footsteps came along the walk behind her. She stooped over to inspect a wheel. The footsteps passed, then stopped, and she heard voices. She peeked out and saw that two train crewmen had met at the corner of the building and the first platform. They were joking about a soccer bet. She waited. And she waited. Footsteps came around the corner again, at her back, stopped, and she heard a mild explosion. The footsteps came toward her. A man smoking a cigarette passed her without a glance and dropped a match. Explosion? Nerves! She eased the cart along toward the platform. She had to get away from it. There were too many people. She—she looked down and realized she still had on the jacket. She touched her head. Yes, and the cap. The man with the cigarette stood talking to the crewmen. Her way was blocked. She would have to wait. Better keep the jacket on and count on the invisibility it seemed to offer.

Later Kate could not understand why she had not taken off the jacket, turned, walked out across the Piazza to the door of the station, through it to the first platform, and along to the ladies'. It did not occur to her. She just stood, waiting, jittering. Finally the men drifted away, still talking, and Kate tore at the buttons. The gloves! She lost a second or two with them, wiggling them off, and started running for the platform. Her buttons were undone, she was about to take off the incriminating jacket and—one of the police rounded the corner from the platform, heading straight toward her. He scowled at her. She rushed on, still fumbling with the buttons, but now trying to rebutton them, as quickly as she could. She cut sharply to her left, out of sight unless he followed her. She had a feeling he had turned to watch her, and now that she was on the platform she could not take off the jacket. That would attract attention. She slowed down and tried to walk as normally as possible— at least without haste—along the entire length of the building, past the men's lavatories and on to the ladies'.

Hermione saw her and knew something was wrong. Later she damned herself for the reflex "Just look! . . ." She made the best of it at the time by playing the high-flying crank. If Kate could get into a skirt, no matter what happened, she could bluff her way. She did. The station policemen never mentioned, undoubtedly never saw, a suspicious porter.

After the 5:09 train pulled out, Kate emerged from her temporary hideaway and, carrying her bag with her forty million lire, the porters' jackets, and the garbage collectors' coats, she went along to the service door of the station bar. The owner was an old friend to early travelers. He gave her a before-hours cup of coffee and a bun. She took the next train to Rome, where a busy day awaited her. First she went home and lit a fire, an odd thing to do at the end of May, unless something needs burning, and of course the coats did. The rest of her time was taken up with the sale contracts for her house and land, her meetings with her own bankers, and the final payments of her mortgages and too, those charming politicians she had to interview. With disappearance by fire still on her mind, a visit to the Cremation Society seemed just the coda to the day.

Hermione called El twice from Rome about the postman, once from the station, once from the airport. She threatened to abandon the plan and return to San Felice—unless El promised, absolutely promised, to rescue her friend. El promised to do what she could not do, and on the second call repeated the promise even more vehemently because Hermione was about to miss her plane.

"Not to worry. That's all arranged. I've just broken the handle of my bag. On purpose. I'm going to produce an-Isterical-Fit about it, I am. The police are always *so* sweet. They'll help me. Get me signed in and since I'll insist—because there isn't time to check it and besides I can't be parted from it—that I must carry on my bag, they'll carry it on for me. You just wait and see if they don't. No security, no rummaging around, nothing. You'll see!" And she hung up.

El was furious. Pure panache to draw maximum attention. Hermione meant to enjoy her illegal smuggling. As it happened, her scene was perfectly timed. The police had been alerted to look for her. They were to ask if she had noticed any unusual activity that morning at the station of San Felice Val Gufo, which they did, while they swept her through boarding formalities and security examinations. She had a chance to elaborate on the vices of government employees, present company excluded, of course, and the degradation of porters who were dirty old men. The police were charmed with Hermione and she with them—and herself. Great fun, which was why the next day she decided to smuggle her lot of stolen money back out through British customs and on into Switzerland. Much neater. No dribs and drabs sitting around in odd banks, she later told her associates. Fortunately they had not known at the time.

Martha, who could be cavalier about anything but money, was more circumspect in her arrangements. By noon she had changed her ten million lire into dollars, had placed them in a safety-deposit box rented for the purpose, and, glad to be quit of the whole affair, had rushed to the nearest café for a drink. She was safe. No one could ever connect her with the robbery, which is just the kind of invitation Fate cannot resist.

In the meantime El, Lacey, and Caroline were busy and nervous at El's house. They had chosen the study for the exchequer. It had several advantages. Often when El corrected manuscripts or galleys, she locked the door to avoid even the most unintentional mix-up in her papers. No one who actually came in the house would be surprised to see her shut the door and pocket the key. Also the downstairs telephone was there and the front door was near. No unexpected visitor could surprise them. As soon as they had dragged in the sacks they were appalled. Obviously El had never done anything very clandestine in the room: there were windows everywhere. Rather than waste time moving, they decided to keep an eye on the drive and work as fast as they could. Time was vital. The money must start on its way to Switzerland no later than noon.

They opened the sacks one at a time, sorted out the papers, and stacked the money, once it had been counted, in piles according to denomination. Because they had no idea which surfaces kept fingerprints, they wore rubber gloves. At the

Bourton-Hamptons' party their fingertips were still delicate pink plissé. No one noticed.

In theory the sight of so much money, their money if possession established a claim, should have been exhilarating. Instead they were depressed. Each succumbed to her favorite form of guilt. Lacey, as accountant, had an excuse for her uncharacteristic silences. Off and on Caroline muttered to herself, but it was a private soliloquy, which El was too morose to piece together.

Shortly after 7:30 a white panel truck swept up the hill. The driver knew exactly what he was about. He turned, parked expertly, and tootled the horn twice. El groaned. She recognized the driver and his helper, who was taking tools out of the back of the truck. They were the two young men who had a yearly contract for the maintenance of her heating system, which was in the wine cellar they had first considered for their counting room. But for chance and a little common sense . . . She must go out and talk to them. She always did.

"Heard about the robbery?" was the driver's greeting. "Down at the station. They got the payroll and a big shipment of gold. Shot a guard and got away. The carabinieri chased them, but like I say, they got away. Typical, no signora?" El had no trouble being surprised. Far away down the valley sirens wailed.

While they worked and gossiped, she sat on a broken deck chair in the cellar doorway and listened. Roadblocks everywhere. The stationmaster had been arrested. Didn't take much imagination to see it was an inside job. Those railroad fellows always wanted double money for a half-day's work. Only ones worse were the morons at the post office. Between them . . . Rumor was someone important in town had actually planned it. . . . El felt queasy and lost the thread. Would they never finish? In less than twenty minutes they did, packed their tools up, and left. The driver had a few last words.

"Those fellows were local. Now if they had a house like this—in the country, apart, you know—well, all they'd have to do is sit here, act normal, and nobody'd know any different, and all that money'd be safe—all theirs. Too bad they didn't do something useful, like kidnap Fanfani. Be even richer. Well, call us if you need us. Otherwise, we'll see you in the fall." He shot down the drive, waving back good-naturedly at her. She waved, wondering if she would still be there in the fall.

Back inside the house no one was joking. Lacey and Caroline had stopped work to concentrate on each other. El, confused by the acrimony of their squabble, could not identify the cause. Finally Lacey suggested Caroline explain, assuming she could, her point of view to El. Her tone implied one idiot might understand another.

Caroline was adamant. They could not leave those poor people without their pensions and sickness reimbursements. Those funds had to be returned. How, for God's sake? Oh, *that* she didn't know, but she would not smuggle the money into Switzerland if the pensions had not been returned. What did she expect them to do, go from house to house paying off according to the government notations—stolen notations—and insisting on a signed receipt?

Between Hermione's calls and Caroline's defection it had dawned on El that their army had too many colonels—no generals and no soldiers—and worse, that each of them had five potential blackmailers, all willing to incriminate themselves and the others, if that was the only way to protect the innocent victims who particularly attracted their sympathy. El was no longer sure that any four women *could* rob the Bank of Italy, not if they were intelligent. Intelligence brought with it certain defects, convictions, which no matter how idiosyncratic they seemed, were not to be sacrificed. Conscience entered in too.

Label the cause as you wished, the truth was their minds had ill-equipped them to be criminals. El temporized. Whatever their decision about the pension funds, they must go back to work. They were adults. They had known exactly what they were doing and they would now have to finish it—in some way. The money and the papers could not be left on her desk.

6

⟡ JUST AFTER NINE that morning, to the delight of San Felice's shopkeepers, who, in interest, still ranked the Bourton-Hamptons' dinner party well above rumors of a robbery, Caroline and Giordano Maffei appeared on the Corso together. She walked several steps in front of her husband and looked, indeed was, very cross. He had heard her sneaking back with the Fiat, *his* Fiat, which had rekindled his rage about transportation in general and her trip to Switzerland in particular.

"I told you to get a shipping agent," Giordano announced to her back. Irritation sent his voice to sepulchral depths.

"Not *less* than a hundred times," she snapped. Several weeks of the same disagreement had exhausted any originality in their bickering. For the record they restated their positions in a kind of verbal shorthand. An exercise. Nothing would change. Caroline would drive to Swtizerland with her sister Laura's books, and Giordano, who disliked his brother-in-law, would insist the plan was ridiculous, that *his* wife was slave to no man, other than himself, naturally. Whichever way, the work involved, Caroline had insisted, was about the same. Either she packed the books in cartons and hauled them off in two batches to a shipping agent in Florence, who probably did not understand the snares of foreign export and would charge dearly for the disservice, *or* she packed the books in cartons, piled all that would fit in the car, and drove to Geneva, sending the leftovers (and incidentally the better part of a million dollars, a detail she did not share with her husband) on a normal freight train to Aosta, where, once she had unloaded the first lot, she would pick them up. From Geneva to Aosta was not far, and customs hardly glanced at what left the country in the possession of the supposed owner. Giordano still wanted her to use a shipping agent, ordered her to use one. Why should she care whether they were experts at foreign shipments? The books were Laura's.

Caroline had resorted to the simple feminine stratagem of refusing to discuss it, which, until the night before, when she realized that she was four, maybe even five cartons short, had guaranteed a modicum of peace. Giordano's groceries she might just balance on a motor bike, but not flapping cardboard cartons. She considered and rejected a taxi: too humiliating. Each morning Giordano drove the Mercedes up to San Felice, bought his newspaper, had coffee, and came home, an excursion that, even dawdling, took less than half an hour. She would swallow her pride and ask to go with him. Certainly, why? had been his answer. Reluctantly she had explained about the cartons: the books to go by train must be at the station no later than noon, the rest she wanted packed in the car before she went to the hairdresser. . . . Why, if she must go, must she leave the morning after the Bourton-Hamptons' party? She would not have enough sleep, would be tired. She might wreck the car. Was she aware that after a wreck his insurance rates would go up—considerably? That, at least, had given her an excuse to go to bed early.

In going to town with Giordano she ran a certain risk. He was very apt to forget her. When he was ready to go home, he did, sweeping back through the gates and out onto the grassy clearing in front of the castle, beating a tattoo on his horn, his signal that her presence was required. Many a time she had walked back to find him, leaning against one of the notched merlons of the battlements, glaring resentfully up at the windows from which no figure waved. This time, since his own food supply and Solomon's, his new parrot's, were at stake, he might remember. He was very worried about Solomon: he refused to eat bananas *and* he refused to talk. Suspecting that any parrot of theirs would have expensive tastes, Caroline had suggested they try pineapple. She had hoped . . . but as it turned out, Giordano was not too worried about Solomon to delight in another round of shipping agent vs. car transport.

"Not *less* than a hundred times," Caroline repeated. "If you'd let me take the Mercedes . . ." She glanced over her shoulder and discovered she was just too late. Giordano had ducked into the newspaper shop. She hurried on, determined to expect the best. Pessimism was destructive.

She left her list at the grocery. As a favor the owner would collect the items, tally and package them, leaving her free to dash from shop to shop in search of boxes. Her first four stops produced only one. Discouraged, she decided to have a cappuccino. When she saw Robert Pound standing at the counter of the café, she almost slipped out into the street again.

Even from the back the slouch of that long, lanky frame told her he was discouraged too. Little problems clustered around Robert like clouds of gnats, pestering him, until he was driven to escape, usually to town. Some mornings a sympathetic ear restored his good humor. Other mornings he was too deep in his thoughts to surface, or if he did, briefly, he might still walk off, leaving them in midsentence. As Caroline spoke to him she wondered which it would be. He looked up from his inspection of the counter with polite curiosity. The light blue eyes behind heavy glasses saw nothing familiar.

"You're in a trance again."

"Oh, uh—oh, it's you, Caroline," he finally said. "Know anything about camels? My editor in New York demands fifteen more lines of 'eyeball stuff.' That's a stunning picture, right there!"

"Humps, I suppose." Caroline was not going to be drawn along one of Robert's conversational detours. "Sorry, I'm in a bit of a rush. Giordano is . . ."

"Just one thing. I need to—ah—find Alan. You haven't—?"

Caroline broke in with a quick denial. His son Alan was always a complex subject. She must run, must find her boxes. But now that he had been pried away from camels, Robert was tenacious. Apparently he liked company. What boxes? He knew a man—he would show her where to find him. So they set out together on an expedition that would be highly satisfactory to both: Caroline knew she would be able to ship her books, and on their way down through the narrow stony lanes and on their way back up, carrying neatly folded cartons, Robert would have plenty of time to explore his son's metamorphosis from Tom Sawyer to Minotaur.

His lament was the one common to so many parents who discover they have a child too old to be spanked, too spoiled to be treated as an adult. They sense both failure and betrayal without being sure which predominates. All they can do is doubt, and at the moment Robert had grave doubts about Alan and Banking. Banking! He was simply using them to receive his mail, wash his clothes, take his telephone messages, and supply cars and "walking-around money." Now this morning, as his father was having breakfast, he had turned up, carrying a small suitcase. Been out all night. No explanation about where, with whom.

He would not discuss it, but demanded the keys to his father's car. At once. Robert refused, and Alan slammed out of the house. Kate—this was luck—had gone to Rome for the day, so he had time to find Alan and beat—

And Robert broke off, apologizing to Caroline. He had not meant to bore her—thoughtless of him—but he was worried. He did not want Kate to know *how* worried. She did understand, didn't she? Caroline nodded, knowing that he was relieved. She was relieved herself to see Giordano off in the distance, waiting by the car.

"Robert, you play chess?" was his greeting to them. He frowned at the boxes and unlocked the car, but did not offer to help with them. Robert shook his head. "Know anyone who does?"

"Sure, Peter Testa." Cardboard and the depths of the trunk muffled Robert's voice. "They say he's very clever," he added, straightening up. Giordano, who had edged over to watch him, looked puzzled.

"I don't know whether you have the same trouble with Kate, but I find Caroline's quite irresponsible. Charming, sweet, all that, but irresponsible." He had for the moment forgotten her presence. His own hurt feelings were too absorbing. "She's haring off to Switzerland on some fool errand for her sister. See what I mean? Irresponsible." Together they banged the trunk closed. "Peter Testa, you say. Maybe he'll keep me company of an evening. I'll ask him tonight at the party." Giordano went around to get into the car.

"What party?" Robert asked, alarmed.

"Oh no, you've forgotten. Kate will be cross," Caroline teased, sliding into the front seat. "The Bourton-Hamptons' and the Prince of Fruit and Veg."

"Oh no-o. She's supposed to protect me from things like

that!" He shook his head and groaned. "No! That's the last straw!"

"And you're back to camels," Caroline called as Giordano eased the car out of its parking place. She waved gaily. Robert waved too and pretended to tear his wispy blond hair.

The merchant-voyeurs, who had watched the scene from their doorways with more interest than their sleepy expressions betrayed, did not immediately dismiss this little pantomime as innocent. Well trained by the illustrated press, they considered the possibility of *un flirt*.

BY LATE MORNING Robert had exhausted the places where his son might conceivably be. Alan's friends were willing, but not helpful. They did not expect to see him until that night at the party. The grown-ups, as Robert now thought of *his* friends, had not seen his son, nor did they know anything about camels. The men grumbled about the party. The women rippled back and forth through their "I have nothing to wear" dialogue. Why did they worry, if they actually did, or had he fallen for more female abracadabra? Thank God Kate wasn't like that. She was straightforward and honest. . . . He noticed El coming along the Corso.

She would know about camels. He was sure she would. He was one of the many who counted on her to provide the disparate kinds of advice and information they needed. In spite of her protests—that having been married and divorced did not qualify her as a marriage counselor, any more than remembering the capital of South Dakota meant she was an authority on where Lewis and Clark had led their expedition—people insisted on believing her answers, however outlandish. Something about her calmness and the thoughtful, direct gaze of blue

71

eyes convinced them she was absolutely dependable, which, now that Robert thought about it, was the very reputation a clever con man hoped to win. The idea amused him. Had the feminists, such humorless ladies, had they in their linguistic purges crusaded for con *women*? Con *person*? He wondered.

Robert's idea of her would not have surprised El. Even as a little girl she had known that she *looked* serious and reliable. She had also known that it was nothing more than an illusion created by very straight, dark eyebrows, but she did not like to disappoint people and in any event, she learned, they would believe what they chose. She found it an awkward virtue, one that imposed a public persona at variance with her inner uncertainties. Still, she had accepted it and had, in time, acquired an air of detachment, which seemed natural and allowed her to think exactly as she pleased. Her exterior life was meticulously ordered. It was generally believed she had no other. She did not dither, did not forget appointments, was, indeed, too punctual for her more casual friends, and never left bills unpaid. Had she done so, it would have been considered an oversight. She was required to be not quite human and for good behavior was rewarded by the assumption that she was not.

Fortunately her old friends knew that she struggled against an above-average amount of self-doubt and a sly, unruly sense of humor, which she could disguise about as successfully as she could an attack of hiccoughs. Others saw her as a courteous, distant, chilly young woman, and it was true that her separateness was visible: she appeared to be alone, even when she was not.

Robert waited for her, pondering the question of clothes and the Bourton-Hamptons'. What, for instance, would El wear? He caught himself mentally undressing her: via the denim skirt and the navy polo shirt. The silly country clothes women liked left everything to the imagination. His functioned extremely well that morning. A nymphal vision swayed down the Corso toward him—but why was she frowning at him? Then he realized that she was unaware of him, the street, everything except the problem that absorbed her (as it happened, the margin for error in the delivery of freight shipments. What did they do if Caroline's books ended up in Palermo, not Aosta?). He imagined her rewriting a sentence, maybe a whole paragraph. Her even, unremarkable features had sharpened with tension, giving a preview of age that hardly flattered. Faint lines on her forehead deepened and a new, rather sardonic diagonal one fluttered tentatively over her left eye. Fifteen years, a bit more determination about the jaw, and she'll be formidable, he thought, touching her arm lightly to remind her of the here and now of San Felice.

"El, do you have a minute? I . . ." Almost instantly a smile blurred the harshness he had seen in her face. She had not, after all, been gone in syntax.

"Not for camels."

"Why are you women so touchy this morning? You, Caroline— Really, I can't . . ."

"But I'll make up for it." At his surprise her smile turned mischievous. "I just saw Alan, driving Kate's car. At a roadblock. The police were talking to him. He seemed to be coming from the station." She had continued walking, so Robert found himself drawn along at her side. Alan must have remembered that Kate always left the keys under the rubber matting on the floor of the car. Where he was going and when he might return remained unknown factors. They agreed that to be safe Robert should meet Kate at the station that evening. She would not relish the long walk home.

At the corner of the Piazza El stopped in front of a shop and Robert, confused, looked up at the sign.

"The hairdresser—I should have known! Women are such

sheep! And then tonight you'll all look alike—plasticized and remote. I don't know why . . ."

"You prefer the dowdy-crested pen-pusher look, I suppose." She demonstrated, ruffling her fine almost-blonde, almost-brown hair into even more haphazard curls and loops. "I have to go, but since we're back to animals—about your camels—have you considered their sex life? Assuming they have one. Almost everything does these days and the comic . . ."

The bells high in the Signoria tower began bonging their slow, dignified announcement of midday. Before the sound had quite died away, a radio inside the hairdresser's shop was turned up, and El and Robert heard an urgent male voice announce, "The Latest News." Without the customary pause he rushed, breathless, into, "Daring train robbery in Tuscany . . . Station of San Felice Val Gufo—Close to a milliard stolen . . . Band highly organized . . . Commando techniques . . . Vanished without trace . . . Two guards seriously injured . . ."

They stepped into the shop to hear better. The hairdresser stood transfixed, his brush poised, his customer's hair forgotten. Another woman had popped her head out from under the dryer. The announcer, as though he were reporting from the funeral, recited the name, marital status, and children "in tender age" of each guard. His treatment of official statements from the Minister of the Interior, the Commanding General of carabinieri, and the President of the Republic was more martial. The customer waved her hand, trying to attract the hairbrush. "At this time the police have named only one person directly connected with this startling crime, a notary of San Felice Val Gufo, a certain Dr. Peter Testa, whose whereabouts are unknown. They would make no statements as to his presumed role. The most obvious supposition is that Dr. Testa, with his intimate knowledge of local affairs, could have been involved in the perfectly timed robbery. Programs will be interrupted to report any

74

further developments. . . . Now for world news. . . ." Evidently, from his voice, a terrible anticlimax.

The hairdresser, the young girl who gave shampoos, and the two customers stared silently at El. Robert had felt her stiffen at Peter's name, but her expression had not changed. They might still be joking about camels.

"Is there anything I can do, El? I mean—not like that—but is there someone you'd like me to call? A lawyer, or . . ." He felt himself floundering. "I don't even know where Peter is. Do you?"

"In Rome—at the Ministry of Justice," she answered quickly, her voice matter-of-fact. "Ridiculous, isn't it? The one place they'd *never* look. Then he was to meet his mother for a late lunch and come back on the 4:40." She turned and looked deliberately at her audience, one by one. Embarrassed, they rushed to find appropriate reactions, waving their hands about and twittering half-phrases. "Absurd . . ." "Poor thing, don't be upset . . ." "Police bungling . . ." Police bungling, in any event, was always safe. El watched them thoughtfully, neither objecting nor agreeing. When they had gibbered themselves to silence, she made a prediction, which would be repeated that afternoon in all the town's shops and cafés. Repeated and, surprisingly, approved.

"By sunset half the San Feliciani will be saying they always knew Peter was dishonest, and the other half will be trying to think up ways to blackmail him for a share of the loot. Well—" She looked at each of them again and smiled slightly at Robert. "They'll be disappointed. Lawyers are improbable train robbers. And Peter? He's the *most* improbable I can imagine. They would do better to suspect me. Now—" She turned very pointedly to the hairdresser. "Francesco, we'd better wash my hair, or you'll miss your lunch entirely."

For the moment fashion took precedence over robbery.

75

AND SO IT WAS THAT, for very different reasons, Caroline Maffei, Robert Pound, and Eleanor Kendall were all at the station just before seven that evening. One was worried about her boxes: had they in the confusion of the robbery been put on the right train or on any train? One was worried about his wife *and* his son, particularly his son: where had he been at the time of the robbery? And one was worried about her . . . her what? Not even El could have explained quite what Peter was: she had not yet decided.

7

AS THE TRAIN TWISTED its way through Rome's concrete and garbage belt, Peter found a seat in a crowded compartment. He had to wait while the passengers reluctantly stowed
their coats and books and shopping bags elsewhere and pretend
not to notice their resentment. His mother would have said he
deserved it. In spite of, probably because of her nervous warnings, he had lingered over dessert and coffee. Almost too long
and just to tease her. He wedged his briefcase between bags on
a rack opposite his seat and sat down. Two men by the window,
who had watched him with the bland disapproval an unwelcome
intruder can inspire, dismissed him and went back to their quiet
conversation. Something about a robbery. No novelty in that.
Peter leaned his head back and closed his eyes.

His mother had been especially prickly. Her fixation about
trains seemed to worsen with age and then that business about
economizing. She must economize. All her friends were. A fine
example of female reasoning! Inflation, the new rich, the disintegration of civilized living—well, maybe she could do without
the maid. Or maybe it would be better to sell the huge apart-

ment, after all she was alone now—find a smaller one, and keep the maid. Or maybe the country—? He shouldn't have said, "Don't be silly!" *Not* to his mother, no matter how silly she was. Her insistence about El was her way of scolding him. Pick, pick, pick. How good the last book was! How talented El was! She was prodding him to say something. What was El writing now? What had she made of his shrug? It was the best he could do. There was the script, but what was it about? He realized he didn't know. He had asked. He was sure he had. El was such a private—such a . . . He dozed, trying to pin down exactly what she was.

He woke at Orte and again at Orvieto and again as the train lurched along the straight stretch before San Felice. His fellow passengers, who seemed to have become fast friends while he slept, were arguing about the robbery. It was agreed the culprits were state employees, but not which branch. Peter took his briefcase off the rack and edged out into the corridor, thinking how ambivalent Italians were: we never trust *statali* and yet 99 percent of us dream of nothing better than winning a place in the civil-service examinations. The train started its long glide into the station and Peter worked his way along to the platform. Even women. Already there were women train conductors and policewomen and judges. Next it would be army officers, he supposed. They didn't seem to recognize their own limitations. The brakes ground and he reached for the door handle. Women were—an enigma, he decided, and swung off the train.

SEVERAL CARS FURTHER FORWARD Kate, balancing an armload of packages, books, and manila envelopes, tried to pick her way down the treacherous steps of the carriage. The trouble was she could not see them. A cool dry breeze swept along the platform, lifting gentle eddies of dust. It rippled the hem of her skirt. Such a relief after the fumes of Rome and the sticky warmth of plush seats. If her nap could have been twice as long, she might even have felt like going to the Bourton-Hamptons'. She might. All things considered the day had been . . . the right word did not come. People milled around collecting themselves and their luggage. A few with connections to make pushed and dodged about, infecting the others with their haste. Kate stubbed her toe, her pile of oddments turned to jelly and began slithering out of her grasp. Just then a man crashed into her from behind.

"*Stronzo!*" she snarled with fine Roman scorn to include him, the books, the station, the world in general. She stooped, grabbing for her scattered possessions. The man, who had leaned over to help her, peered into her face. She would not look at him.

"Kate?" he asked. "And I always thought you were a lady."

"Oh de-ar! It's you, Peter. I didn't . . ." She sat back on her heels, surveyed the mess, and let out a little giggle, which exploded into a great, cheerful laugh. People, who sidestepped and shuffled to get around her, smiled and then laughed with her. She waved at them flirtatiously, her large brown eyes twinkling. Aren't I stupid and funny? they seemed to ask.

While she chattered and apologized and explained, Peter went about arranging the envelopes and books, the largest carefully at the bottom, into separate piles. He was very methodical. She envied patience and the people who had time for it, and told him so. Not that she was in any hurry now. Their fellow passengers were only a distant swarm at the top of the stairs into the tunnel. Let them hurry. The mountains were purple in the clear light, and the sun had hardened to the vitreous red-orange that warned of eventual twilight—and with the breeze, this was quite the nicest place she had been all day, a remark that, remembering the morning, shook her. She hoped Peter had not noticed her abrupt silence. She had never expected to enjoy a train platform, ever again—and here she was . . .

When Peter was satisfied, they each took a bundle and started slowly toward the station. Kate clipped through the calamities of her day: no single twenty-four-hour span should include both bankers and politicians. Lawyers and Roman taxi drivers were bad enough. And of course Robert had been so irrational with his last-minute scruples. But it was still a day of celebration. Real celebration. Peter clung to this last contradiction with patient despair. Day of celebration? Kate's voice fluted up in enthusiastic explanation.

"Oh Peter, it's marvelous! For the first time in all the years we've been married, we have *no* debts. None! The mortgages, the bills—everything paid off today. I sold the house and the land at the beach, you see. And I even deposited money, lots of it. Lots and lots!" Peter's smile was wary. He probably did not approve of debts. Neither did she in principle. Sometimes there was no choice.

"Now you'll have to buy something," he teased. "What will it be? A Rolls? A castle?"

"Hardly my style." She glanced away down the platform. "Isn't that El coming toward us?" She tried to wave and thought better of it. "Must be here to meet guests."

Peter, however, managed to wave and called out to her, "Would we do?"

"Do?" she said, rushing up to them. "I was beginning to worry. The others—never mind. Have you already heard? The radio, I mean . . . ?"

"Isn't that Robert?" Kate asked, squinting ahead into the dimmer light under the shed. "Why's—? Heard *what*, El? What's happened? Alan? Nothing . . . ?"

"No! Relax! It's not *always* Alan." El's voice was sharp, but her hand on Kate's shoulder was both gentle and cautioning. Kate understood and sighed.

"If you were his mother, you'd— What else happened? Someone rob the Bank of Italy?" El flicked an eyebrow at her for that.

"No, actually the station. Right here. You've heard the radio then?" Peter obviously had not. Even though she knew it made no difference, Kate put on her best wonder-and-attention expression and listened to El's summary. Peter's role as prime suspect surprised her as much as it did him, but he was only surprised, not worried. Nothing serious. He would call Captain Nardo when he got home. El was more upset than he. "But if you went to Nardo, voluntarily, then at least it couldn't be 'suspect captured.' That's why I came down, to warn you. Even if they were here, you could . . ." She stopped and lowered her voice. Robert had come up to them and was already announcing his decision about Alan. That little bastard was not going to ruin their summer. They could *not* live this way. Could *not* and would *not*! He scooped Kate's parcels out of Peter's grasp, and El was able to say quietly, "Peter, I mean, you'd be in a better position, wouldn't you, if you went on your own to the carabinieri? I've been worried."

"They say that's a good sign." Without warning he leaned over and kissed her lightly on the forehead. "Bless you. I'll see you in a little while," and before El could slip from astonishment to irritation he was gone. At the top of the stairs he turned and waved. Strange woman, she's embarrassed, Kate thought, and decided to come to the rescue.

"Oh Robert, I forgot!" Kate broke off in exaggerated remorse. "The camels! You must be down to the turds by now." She let out a great whoop of glee.

"That's it! Fuel! Somewhere they . . ." He stopped to turn and see who El was waving to across the tracks. Kate spun around too. In the door of the freight office Caroline towered over a young man in a light blue uniform, who was talking up to her with great animation. She nodded, keeping her eyes on him, but still waved to her friends. Her smile was triumphant. "The books must have gone. She'll . . ." Robert's voice ran down as he realized that El was not listening. Neither was Kate.

A knot of people at the top of the stairs on the opposite platform had attracted their attention. People milled around as though there had been an accident. Two carabinieri tried to move them aside without success. Darting around the fringes, looking like an illustration from a Fascist military manual was Brigadier Cirillo of the Second Flying Squad. As always, shaved, every button buttoned, his boots, belts, and holsters gleaming, he strutted in and out of sight, his hands on his waist, his chin stuck out, giving orders. A barrier might have been lifted. The crowd spurted forward. Cirillo leaned over, disappeared an instant, and rose again holding Peter Testa's arm, though not for long. Peter freed it with a gentle tug and stood talking to him, amiably it seemed. Caroline abandoned her new friend of the freight office, but was blocked by the people who had squeezed back out of the police's way. Peter and Cirillo, flanked by two carabinieri, vanished into the station, and El sighed,

"Did it *have* to be Cirillo?"

Kate and Robert nodded: though certainly the least of the problems, this was, somehow, the final insult. Only Lacey, who had spent the afternoon struggling to wash the olive oil out of her hair, would not have agreed.

8

ℐ THE BOURTON-HAMPTONS' GUESTS were stricken by a mild form of social distemper, which was highly contagious and had only one symptom: unconscious reluctance. When, toward twilight, they should have been in midtoilette, greater or lesser, they found instead chores they chose to classify as emergencies. Cesspools and well pumps suddenly demanded attention. Flats of petunias had to be planted and buttons sewn on garments that would not be worn again until winter. As a result they were all late and, having quarreled about whose fault it was, were very testy.

EL AND LACEY were not immune. The naps, which had revived them physically, had, if anything, aggravated their depression. El went off to the station to meet Peter. Lacey spluttered through her third shower-shampoo, feeling that it was only one of the absurd repetitions the day had brought. Of course it had a minor advantage: if she absolutely could *not* get the oil out of her hair, she would be excused from the dinner party. What she needed now—to join the others and create her own fair share of trouble—was a respectable *crisi di coscienza*. Hermione had her postman; Caroline, her pensioners; El, if the police arrested him, would have her Peter; and Martha would surely find someone to emote over. She and Kate were untainted. No person or principle nagged them to confess. Maybe they did not have consciences. Ridiculous! Of course they did. They were simply more experienced in the wait-and-see cure for snarls. The others ought to give time a chance! The postman would be reprimanded, the pensions would be reissued, and Peter would be released for lack of evidence. As it was, Hermione's confession was postponed by her absence. El's—they would soon know. And then there was Caroline. Nothing deflected Caroline. Lacey supposed they would have to go through with this next crazy step, invented to satisfy her.

As far as Lacey was concerned they had exceeded the most pessimistic male forecasts of women's inability to conceive, organize, and carry out a plan. In full agreement? Reasonably? Unemotionally? Elements better left unmentioned. And *if* the police were perverse and arrested Peter? She would think about that tomorrow! She smiled to herself: Scarlett O'Hara would have been a fine partner in a train robbery.

Her hair, almost dry, had finally decided to curl rather than lie in limp, discouraged strings. Lacey flipped off the dryer and heard the clatter of hangers being raked back and forth along a pole. El must be back, and if what to wear was the crisis of the moment . . . Lacey found her, holding out three different skirts by their hems and shaking her head. Damn! They needed pressing. The inconvenience did not erode her good humor, which Lacey took as a hopeful sign. She still did not ask questions: nothing could be gained by another argument. There had already been too many.

They had carped at each other through lunch. El would

not budge. She was determined to meet Peter at the station. With the excuse of warning him she would be able to talk to him about the robbery. She would know, she was sure she would, whether or not he had recognized her. What they did or did not do hinged on being sure. Although basically Lacey agreed, she had two objections: first, the money should not have been shipped; second, she favored a total change of costume and venue. Why remind Peter of what he had not noticed at the time? El at the station, no longer dressed up as a garbage collector, but in casual clothes, would jog his memory. El at her own front door or at the Bourton-Hamptons' in an evening dress would draw his attention in quite a different way.

Lacey had lost. She had known she would, just as she knew there was another reason for El's going to the station. The first radio report had planted the idea and others throughout the afternoon had nurtured it to fact. She was terrified that Peter would be arrested and charged with the robbery. For a surplus of reasons she had probably not admitted even to herself, if he was charged, she would confess. Now that calamity seemed to be postponed. Lacey listened to the first rush of explanations with some amusement and no visible enthusiasm, quite sure that the harder El had to work at persuasion, the more convinced she would be by her own arguments.

Obviously Peter had not recognized her that morning and just as obviously he was not upset by the carabinieri's desire to question him. She was still cross that Cirillo had had the pleasure of finding him, but realized, thanks primarily to Kate, that arresting Peter was neither easy nor likely: as a notary he was an officer of the law, a public official whose integrity was beyond doubt, if you believed the rule book. The carabinieri did.

Now that threats to and from Peter could be eliminated, El reverted to her recent role of cheerleader. The optimism and spurious energy set Lacey's teeth on edge. She did not deny their effectiveness. El, determined and on her way, was irresistible. Everything was easy. They must get back to the serious business of the day. It was actually quite simple. They had to live through the party and then . . . Lacey refused to think about that too. When she must, she accepted the inevitable, but she did not torture herself thinking about it. She let El prattle along, aware that it was unlike her, an index of strain and perhaps uncertainty, that state which so few people ever allowed El and which Lacey found reassuring in her. When the telephone rang, she escaped to her own room and the details of dressing. In a few minutes El called to her,

"That was Peter. No trouble with the carabinieri. Just a lot of blather about smocks and porters' jackets, I gather, but he's going to be late. I have to make his apologies to Madam Bourton-Hampton." In another few minutes she stuck her head around the door of Lacey's room and said in a high, aspirated voice, her mouth puckered up in prissy disgust, " 'How thoughtless of the police, though one hardly thinks of Italy as *having* police. Just criminals. I don't suppose there's any question about Dr. Testa's—yes, well, sweet of you to call, my dear. We won't wait for him and *you* needn't either.' " El's mouth drooped and so did her voice. "One more native stricken from the rolls of the acceptable. Poor Peter!"

"If she only knew!" was Lacey's reaction.

ENTERING THE BOURTON-HAMPTONS' GATES did nothing for their spirits. There before them, instead of the old cart track, which over the centuries had elected a gentle twisting route up the slope, was the new drive, straight as a surveyor could make it. Cedric was a great one for "improvements." Visualizing a formal alley, he had planted rows of silver spruce, but nature would neither be improved nor bullied:

the trees languished at the knee-high stage. The grandeur of the lawn, however, real English lawn, not field grass hacked into submission, could not be denied. It stretched off in all directions, dotted, at just the point where the eye might have tired, by a swimming pool, a gazebo, or a birdbath. If there should still be any doubt, the Union Jack was flown, in defiance of Italian law, from a tall flagpole.

Far above in the glow of discreetly concealed floodlights, a long, two-story stone structure masqueraded as a minor monument. From a distance, massive and aloof, closer to, it was fussy and slightly foolish. A profusion of new arches, loggias, and flying buttresses fluted out from every available plane. Turrets spouted improbably from old ovens and a cross and belfry had promoted a row of pigsties to a chapel. Cedric, who believed more was better, had had his way. No wall remained unadorned. Odd treasures had been set in at random: stone crests, columns that supported nothing more than vague Romanesque pretensions, and even by the front door the standard tile of Cerberus, warning *Cave Canem*. A dignified farmhouse had been converted, in its owner's view, to an Italian manor house; in his neighbors', to a folly, which could one day be used as a showroom for modern "antiques."

Prepared for the florid worst, the guests stepped into the hall and austerity. The floors were apricot tiles, the walls were hung with towering indistinct tapestries, and the furniture was sparse. It was also expensively monastic and uncomfortable. In the drawing room, which, to the amusement of Americans and the irritation of his wife, Cedric referred to as "the lounge," Savonarola chairs, attended by tall church candlesticks adapted to electricity, lurked in the corners for those who chose solitary contemplation. The more gregarious were at the mercy of the settees with intractable horsehair upholstery, grouped around the fireplaces at either end of the room. Two dispositions had been at work on the house: outside, Cedric's; inside, presumably a decorator's, as Mrs. Bourton-Hampton did not herself radiate spartan temperament, or any other kind, except resignation.

That evening, as usual, she received her guests just inside the drawing-room door. Small, yet bony, and blondish with fine features receding gently into dry skin, she faded against the arras of pastoral dalliance that loomed behind her. Once the conventional "how nice"s had been exchanged, she withdrew into a tense silence that could be, and often was, taken as dismissal. When pressed, she would offer a few phrases, phrases so uniquely unrelated to the apparent subject that they could only be her thoughts voiced by mistake. It was accepted in the neighborhood that she was "lapsus-prone." One evening, for example, she had told Baron Casale, who had asked if she had ever met his mother, that "the natives in Italy are much lighter than one expects"; so it was not surprising to hear her answer El's query about a rose spray with "I don't believe I've ever actually *known* anyone involved in a major crime—or a minor one." El swept on to compost beds, but Lacey was badly shaken.

Cedric had intervened: they must meet the young groom, a nice chap, not very ambitious, but awfully good family. Off he hustled them toward the library, expounding on Peter Testa's situation. Quite proper for the Italian authorities to look into the affair. Their duty, indeed. *However,* should they implicate Peter, he would deem it his duty to inform the Ambassador. One important point must not be forgotten: Peter's mother *was* English! In their steps Lacey thought she heard the firm cadences of "Rule Britannia."

The young drooped about the large, gloomy room, occa-sionally mumbling comments, which would, in time, bridge the winter months they had spent in other places. The girls were very pretty and very young in their cotton evening dresses. The boy-men were scrubbed and, to judge by their mild seizures of patting and pushing, self-conscious about their long hair. In a corner Cedric finally found the bride-to-be, a petulant blonde girl and her tall, dark young prince, who was languid and well tailored. Boredom had brought a dull, reptilian glaze to his eyes. He bowed slightly and mimed the correct almost-kiss over their hands without actually looking at either El or Lacey. After the required wedding questions, they fled.

"Thank goodness!" Lacey whispered. "They're as uninterested in us as we are in them."

"Don't you wonder what they do all day?"

"Probably sleep off what they did all the night before." Lacey was not sentimental about the young, or even very tolerant. "Once they rediscover their common tastes, they'll be livelier. You know—discos, grass, and shocking their bigoted parents, *fun* things like that." El's answer was a discouraged grunt. From the drawing room they could hear a new wave of guests bellowing apologies for their lateness. The party had mysteriously shifted gears.

STILL LATER, when Peter arrived, he found his hostess as querulous as he had feared and was embarrassed by Cedric's jolly assurances of the Queen's protection. Nor was he impressed by the Prince, who seemed positively drowsy and not very bright. At least that was the only explanation Peter could find for a florid compliment to his Italian. He eased away with a clear conscience and was stopped almost immediately by people curious about the robbery. He explained patiently that there was little to tell. The police had hoped he would describe the robbers. He could describe a waiter, and two garbage men—their uniforms, nothing more. Captain Nardo was working on the assumption that the plan was local, executed by locals. There were several leads. The missing train guard, for instance. Some young men who had hung around the station café the last few weeks. The money. It would reappear.

With several men, the same men who at parties usually wanted free advice, he sensed a vacuum behind their questions, a breathing space they had left between themselves and him just in case—one never knew—he might really be involved. El had been right to insist he put in an appearance, however late he might be. Otherwise . . . Where was she? He finally saw her at the far end of the drawing room, listening, absently he thought, to a man who looked like Disraeli grown about eighteen inches. Too many people crowded the room, he would never reach her. A drink would help. He found a bar table near the French doors and saw, not far beyond it, Lacey, a prisoner between Eddie Hughes and Webster Maddox, who took turns whispering confidentially into her ears. She waved to Peter, and fixed him with a green stare that explicitly asked for help. When he shook his head, she excused herself and slithered around a group, through another to his side.

"Coward!" she gasped with a broad smile. "You could have—"

"Not from those two clowns. I've had a long day. I saw a bench in the hall . . . ?" Lacey nodded happily and led the way, inching around knots of people. Peter followed her, secretly amused by the men who listed slightly out of their conversations for a better look as she passed. Did she notice, he wondered, this effect she had? It was more than a white halter dress and a tall, very slender, tanned body. Vitality? Light? He realized he was frowning.

"What's the matter? My nose on backward?" Lacey asked and motioned him to sit down beside her.

"No, nothing like that. You didn't see your admirers back there. I was trying to define—maybe it's the curls. Who could blame Eddie Hughes for snuggling?" She made a throaty noise of impatience. "I bet you'd look funny without those copper curls. Funny different, I mean." He reached over and would have smoothed them back from her forehead. She jerked her head away.

"You're as handy as Eddie and we know about *him*." A statement Peter could hardly deny, though he did not appreciate the comparison. Every Tuscan community has an Eddie, a man who has only identified two things in his lifetime as important: ancestry and war. Sober, he probed the social history of even the newest acquaintance; drunk, he relived the Battle of the Bulge. In between he was merely lecherous.

"But all that whispering! At your age!" Peter insisted.

"What's wrong with my age?" Lacey shot back at him and a moment later smiled apologetically. "Sorry. I've snapped at everyone tonight. Besides, this time you're wrong about Eddie. He had a secret. He suggested the garden. Who me, sir? Not I, sir," she trilled in a mincing voice. "How dare you, sir! So he did the only thing he could. He whispered it." Her expression still serious, she glanced sideways at him and winked. "Don't ask me. I swore I wouldn't tell."

Already Peter felt more cheerful. "Full of secrets, aren't you? How about the script? When can I know what it's about? You're very . . ." Peter abandoned the end of the sentence. At the mention of the script Lacey had whirled around to face him. From her icy glare he understood it was impolitic to insist.

"We needn't discuss *that* either." Her tone left no doubt, but she went on with some of the earlier bantering lilt to her voice. "You're pretty tight with secrets yourself—such as— how did you rob the train? Where did you hide the money? What's my share? No, seriously." She put her hand on his arm. "How did it go with Captain Nardo?"

He told her much more than he had told the others and had not finished when Caroline discovered them and pulled

Peter to his feet, insisting that he come to Giordano's rescue. Poor Giordano! As he stumbled after her, he admired Giordano's genius: any man who could convince his wife and neighbors he must be cared for, rescued, humored, and catered to was not, whatever they thought, helpless.

THE SECOND DRINK was having its way with the guests. They roared now in the safety of their own voices, enjoying the intermezzo between the solemn order of arrival and the solemn duties of dinner partner, knowing that no one listened. Caroline's announcement that she had found Giordano's chess partner brought a pause in the shouted conversations nearest him and left Peter feeling like a trophy, one that Giordano did not seem to want. He smiled vaguely at them both, but ignored Caroline's tug on his arm: he would not be rescued. He nodded to Peter in a distant, thoughtful way, commented that he was glad the carabinieri still had some sense, and wondered if he had met Lord Something, who had rented Somebody's villa. The name of the overgrown Disraeli and his landlord was lost forever. Caroline sighed, which gave Disraeli his opening. He must apologize to Count Maffei. Perhaps the others would interpret for him.

"I made a most frightful gaffe. Shockingly rude and I really must ask his pardon." His high, nasal voice clipped each syllable free and left it standing on its own, distinct from any other. "The Countess was good enough to bring a cable that had confused the postman. Natural, I suppose, that he'd be confused. But I was so impressed with her English—we've been having all the usual misunderstandings with the servants—and thinking she was a part-time postal employee—well, I'm afraid I tried to press her into domestic service. As cook-housekeeper. Most awfully ashamed—"

"Thaz vunderfool," Giordano interrupted, not having understood any of it. In the confusion that followed, he looked around, wide-eyed, as though he had done something very clever. Quietly he explained to Peter, "My only English phrase. Always works. Always! Tell me, does the good captain have any idea yet how these men plan to export the money? To Switzerland, I should think."

"Why Switzerland?" asked El, who had sidled in next to Peter. "From what I read, the Near East or South America would be more like it."

"Or if they had Mafia connections, they could wash it right here," Caroline suggested.

"My wife sees everything from a domestic point of view," Giordano rumbled. "*Cara,* this isn't a matter of our sheets. It's much too complex for you—"

"She meant 'launder' the money," Peter said mildly. "Recycle it, as they say. And these days a direct transfer to Switzerland is almost impossible. Remember the bulk. The sheer physical bulk. The *Finanza* has doubled its forces at the borders and with new search techniques—no, Switzerland is out of the question."

"Or foolhardy," added Giordano with conviction. "Caroline always imagines people trundling across the border with suitcases chock-full of bills, but it's not quite that simple."

Peter smiled. "I don't see *her* as a potential smuggler!"

"No, we'll leave that to you wily males," El said, catching Caroline's eye. Peter looked from one to the other, lost. What was that about? With perfect timing Disraeli's confident voice cut into the lull.

"Now, my new friends, there's one thing I must ask you. Tuscany is quite, quite lovely, but what does one *do* here in the spring? So far we've stayed inside with the shocking result that we've broken two beds and one chair."

''DARLING, maybe you should be in the furniture business,'' El crooned at Peter. He felt the sudden release of tension in her and prepared for mischief. Everyone was hyper-something tonight, he thought, or was he the one? "Although—he has a point. What do people *do* here? That's one of the ideas behind—" She stopped in midphrase and frowned. "Never mind! Quick!" She caught the fingers of his right hand. "While we can." She had seen a corner, protected by two offshore islands of people, the one dominated by Kate Pound, explaining Italian politics in her ultra-lucid way, the other rearranged itself into atolls and archipelagos around Cedric and his master plan for the salvation of Italy, based primarily on the extermination of Italians.

"Some rob trains," Peter commented, once they had slipped into the privacy of their corner. El stood very straight and still, as though he had been offensive. "Not this group, obviously, but somebody who knows San Felice well *did* rob the train. Captain Nardo thinks . . ." She listened with flattering attention to his report of the interview with the carabinieri. Once or twice he caught the sudden muscular pull of her eyebrows and the quickly subdued flash of her eyes and knew she was laughing at him. Why should *he* have thought it strange to have garbage men and porters around at that hour? The stationmaster hadn't. Hermione hadn't. Martha what's-her-name hadn't. Why should he? She seemed to think him particularly delinquent in not being able to describe the garbage man he had passed in the Piazza. He was a garbage man, that's all. Older and more tired than most. Why did she smile? It was the way he walked. Come to think of it, his walk was familiar. Must have seen him around the station. There was something else he hadn't remembered. He'd promised Captain Nardo he would try—something about the garbage man he had noticed and forgotten. He felt El waiting, motionless, and was sorry to disappoint her. "That's all there is to tell. Nardo says finding the train guard and the young men at the station bar may give them some clues, but the big thing now is where the bills show up. And they're bound to soon—very soon, he says."

"Why? As we were saying before, if our robbers are so smart, they'll smuggle the money out of the country."

"Like that?" Peter snapped his fingers at her. "Be sensible. It's not that easy."

"According to Caroline that's what thousands of Italians have done. She gave me some figures the other day—"

"Listen, El, what Caroline knows about it would go in an eyedropper. She reads a lot of magazines. It makes her mad, but *she* could no more smuggle money out of Italy than—than . . ." Peter was brought to a halt by El's cryptic half-smile. "Take my word for it, only a professional—"

"And these are amateurs, right? Which means Captain Nardo must have overlooked clues. Amateurs always leave them."

"We don't know they're amateurs."

"They can hardly be both local *and* professional. Like smuggling, logic may not be women's forte, but you're tangled in your own contradiction." She twirled the blue and green sash, which matched the speckled cotton of her dress, around her arm, switched directions, and untwirled it, smiling at Peter. In a different humor he would have recognized teasing.

"Stop twisting that thing into a string. . . ."

Robert Pound's head appeared between them. "Your conversation *looks* more interesting than the others. Besides I've heard them before. Can I join you?" He hesitated and his smile faded a bit. "Or is this a private argument?"

"Not private, not even an argument, but trying to be." El's voice had none of the bite Peter had expected. She was almost coy, which irritated him more. "If you'd referee—don't look like that, Robert. It's not personal. Would you say our train robbers were professionals or amateurs?" Robert's relief was obvious.

"Never entered my head to doubt it—professionals. They've been very thorough. Amateurs *never* are."

"Then why San Felice . . . ?" Her question was swallowed up by a roar from Kate's group. Robert leaned closer to be heard.

"After a day with lawyers and bankers, Kate's brain reels at double time." He watched his wife with only a slight smile to mask his pride of possession. "All these years later and she still surprises me." He frowned. "So does Alan. Which reminds me—did you see our embryo banker out in the library? He has the bride trapped on a sofa and is earnestly explaining the importance of frying an egg in a covered skillet. From that dumb girl's expression it might be the first reading of the Ten Commandments. She should be careful. He's not selling bonds."

"That's not fair," El scolded.

"You'd be a very permissive mother," Peter needled. He was not surprised when she ignored the remark.

"Fried eggs are a long way from seduction," she persisted.

"Not with him," said Robert. "They're the first little test. If the lady suits, there'll be field trials, which—Kate's right—wouldn't be a bad idea, if it meant a year in a two-room flat in the Bronx. But so far he's tried them in the Sahara, in the Himalayas." Robert stopped and squinted at the ceiling, deep in thought. "I wonder if that girl ever got back. Anyway—I-I think the Prince of Fruit and Veg better marry his Joan soon. Soon as he can, in fact."

They never found out whether this was speculation or prediction, for they, along with Cedric's prisoners, were drowned out by Kate's audience.

"So it's easy to understand why they can't form a government," Kate concluded and then, with her head thrown back, waited for quiet. " 'Cooperative conflictuality' is bad enough, but there are those nasty 'conservative revolutionaries,' who absolutely reject 'the workers' centrality in a pluralistic hegemony.' Really—" She swept an arm out wide for emphasis. "It proves Moro's theory was a model of clarity. In fact I'm beginning to see his 'parallel convergences' all around me." She stared dolefully at El, and dinner was announced.

TUSCANY IS AN ARCADIA of soft nights, shy nightingales, and a moon perpetually full, but the wise hostess is suspicious of the dews and damps, and Mrs. Bourton-Hampton was a wise hostess. Rather than move the party into the garden, she had moved the garden inside. Tables for eight, garlanded with every imaginable spring flower, were set in the baronial dining hall. Beyond it, on the loggia, which ran the length of the house, overlooking the garden, were more tables for the young. Candlelight flicked silver and crystal to life and cast shadows of disarming intimacy. It was rather too perfect, a warning the guests were to be on their best behavior.

They milled about good-naturedly in search of their place cards and their fates for the next couple of hours. The thorns were evenly distributed. Kate was allowed to share Eddie Hughes's secret, El steadfastly refused to understand Disraeli's orotund importunities, wondering why she expected all older Englishmen to be the Archbishop of Canterbury, and Caroline was quietly amused by the social ambitions of a bouncy Neapolitan, who had changed his first name to Barone. Lacey, between Giordano and Peter, fared better.

She had found her place so quickly that she caught Webster Maddox in the act of changing his card from one end of the table to the other. He put a finger to his lips and leered at her, giving his long, lugubrious face a look of childish conspiracy. It was already too late. The others had gathered, and besides, the new arrangement seemed as feasible as any. Baroness Casale's end of the table, now with Webster on her left, Giordano on her right, and Lacey just beyond, would suffer from non sequiturs and good humor. The other end was unpredictable. Much would depend on whom Webster had provided for Eddie Hughes's improbable Hungarian wife, Anatolia.

In looks she was very like the sorrowful stone ladies, elongated to fit into the niches of Gothic cathedrals, and her idea of social conversation was equally somber, especially with men, whom she treated exactly as she did children and puppies. Her dinner partner, she was pleased to discover, was a retired British ambassador, totally suitable in her eyes. He settled her carefully and after a quick appraisal of the large blonde on his right, turned back to Anatolia, ready for his opening gambit. Too late.

"I believe you're English," she stated, and hesitated just long enough for him to bow slightly before she delivered the coup de grâce. "I know your queen well." Lacey heard Peter choke down a swallow of water. They both knew that, had the ambassador been American, she would have offered him her father's friendship with Warren G. Harding. Now his answer would decide whether Peter must lure her with one of her pet antipathies: Communists would ensure the longest run, but Sardinian kidnappers or Democrats (U.S.) would do as well.

"How interesting." The ambassador's voice contradicted his words. He took his time, letting the seconds pass, until finally he seemed to run across a pleasant subject. "Ah yes, before dinner Cedric mentioned that you are the daughter of my old friend the former ambassador to Tasmania." Lacey shuddered. Anatolia was not up to leg-pulling. Instead she beamed.

"Tasmania is also my favorite sister. You know Father

named us for his most distinguished posts." And so began the tour of courts and chancelleries of Europe, which would last through much of dinner. Peter let out a long sigh of relief.

Webster, blithe and chatty at the other end of the table, was doing his best to entertain. Why didn't Giordano harness the power of the waterfall behind Palazzo Maffei by building a small hydroelectric plant? At least that was what intuition and semantic hopscotch suggested to Lacey. Since Webster treated Italian as a noninflected language, the project sounded an engineering miracle. Giordano was incensed. Attach a motor to himself? Why? Baroness Casale, a woman of great patience and tact, set about rearranging the verbs, and Lacey, though pretending to listen, wondered what she should do about the large blonde opposite her.

Winkie Cromwell was an Englishwoman, who ran an art gallery in New York and came each summer, ostensibly to paint. Lacey knew her only well enough to realize that she had all the problems to be expected of an outsized lady of adult years called Winkie. Her solutions tended toward an arch friendliness that assumed men were only interested in sex, that women shared all her experiences, and that both longed to compare details. If they did not cooperate, she recounted *her* latest adventures. Lacey, who had heard Winkie's confessions before and did not relish a rerun, was saved for the moment by Giordano. His voice roared in her ear.

"*You* explain it to him! Every summer the stream runs dry."

Webster, who had reeled on into technical specifications, stopped abruptly and looked at Giordano. "Runs dry? Why didn't you say so? Well," he began again dubiously. "Three car batteries would give you some light. Charge them by alternating them in your car. Have to park facing down . . ."

"Man's mad," Giordano mumbled. "I *have* electricity, lots

of it." Peter leaned across Lacey to discuss a possible evening for chess, and the Baroness asked when Webster's wife would be back from England.

Lacey missed the progression from Bee's return to the Rolls-Royce, but when she could again hear them, Webster was explaining that he had decided to buy a used Rolls. It was an absolutely sure-fire investment. He and Bee would take it to the States, tour the West, and then sell it to a rich Texas oilman. Or Turkey. It was all the same. At the end of the trip he would sell it, pay their expenses, and the rest would be Pure Profit. If Bee did not feel like traveling, it was just as sound an investment. He happened to know the company's secret policy: the sacred name must be protected. If he converted the car to, say, a chicken house or a pigpen, the company would rush in and buy it back. Truth—not fiction. Resale was guaranteed. He couldn't lose.

Baroness Casale nodded thoughtfully several times and then asked quietly, very bravely, Lacey thought, "Mr. Maddox, what did you do before you came here to live?"

She was not the first to wonder. His answers were always the same and satisfied no one. His ambition had been to retire at forty and he had. From what? Well—he would duck his head and grin—might call it International Commerce. Great way to see the world. If further pressed, he talked of Yemen, Somalia, and Libya, which, given their commercial bent, was taken as proof that he had been a CIA agent.

In contrast his present life was transparent. He had a charming wife and three children and spent his time remodeling *the* dream house. As each neared completion, he discovered another potentially more perfect gem. So far retirement had meant a great deal of work and a series of semi-elegant bivouacs. His wife was philosophical about it: unless Webster was physically exhausted, his mind was overactive. She dreaded only a rainy season.

The mention of Libya sprawled into a discussion of solar heating, which Lacey was delighted to abandon for Peter's desperate question about what she thought the meat might be or have been. Anatolia and the Ambassador had exhausted the diplomatic service and his patience. She was complaining about her son, Nicky, who at twenty-six was the doyen of the young dawdlers, and Peter wanted help. Lacey warned him not to look up. She had noticed Winkie watching him, the faintest quiver of a smile ready.

"Like a predatory porpoise, isn't she?" he whispered, then went on in a normal voice. "Where's Max?" Lacey raised an eyebrow. He always twitted her about her photographer friend, but with more curiosity than malice.

"Turkey. That's where he's supposed to be. You never know."

"He'd hardly approve of your performance tonight."

Lacey made a face at him. "Not his to approve or disapprove. Besides, by now he probably has a harem, or at least a . . ."

"Dr. Testa! Ooo-hoo, *Dottore*! Ooo-hoo," Winkie called, just below a yodel. He looked over at her, as the others did, surprised.

"A belly dancer," he commented, completing Lacey's sentence.

"I *beg* your pardon."

"Not you, signora Cromwell. I meant Lacey. That is, I meant, ah—shall we say, her fiancé. He has odd tastes." He jumped. Lacey had pinched him.

"How amusing!" Closing her eyes, she leaned toward Peter, let them fly open, and spoke very softly. They might have been alone. "I need a tiny, tiny bit of advice. Teensy, weensy really." She waited to be encouraged and was not. "I *should* come to your office, but you know how it is—on vacation and all that. Somehow . . ." Again she blinked like an animated cartoon. "You see, I'm buying a piece of land to build a garage on and—well, my 'Italian friend' says you *never* put the real price on the contract, just a fraction. *He* says . . ." She stuttered off into a slough of Italian subjunctives. *"Che dovessi fare?"*

"I'm afraid your 'Italian friend' has not studied the recent laws, signora. Perhaps, if you'd come to the office . . ."

"Com'è? Com'è?" she barked. *"Non sono capisco."*

Ah, she was one of those who slaughtered the language with irritable authority and did not understand it. Peter switched to English. "This 'Italian friend,' is he trained . . . ?"

"He's a state employee—*un impiegato statale,"* she repeated, in case his English was weak. "And we all know how shrewd *they* are." She twinkled provocatively at him. "He says—"

"Look, Winkie." Lacey knew she was about to hate herself. "Wouldn't it be fairer if you went to Peter's office? *You're* on vacation, but *he's* at a dinner party. It would save everyone . . ."

"Oh, was I taking too much of his precious attention?" Winkie snapped. "Sorry, ducks. He's all yours." She was scarlet. She clinched her fists and wheeled around to Webster, who threw his arm up over his face.

"You wouldn't hit a man with glasses," he whined. "It's really not done in polite society." He did not wear glasses, but she was beyond noticing. She swept back around and burst into the Ambassador's reconstruction of the robbery.

"My 'Italian friend' says it was very simple. Took no imagination at all, not even much planning. And he . . ."

Anatolia would not abdicate. "Greed seems to have poisoned the world. I remember once in the Sudan, it must have been the late thirties . . ."

"And *he* should know. . . ."

"The carabinieri think . . ." Peter began soothingly, and those at the other end of the table plunged into a noisy discussion of the balance of payments. Lacey chose to join them.

Naturally Webster had a scheme, a very simple one: block the entrance of foreign meat, import the cottontail rabbit, and an infinite supply of meat, at almost no cost, was assured. Giordano hailed it as Italy's salvation and Lacey thought that at last she understood why Socialists should be encouraged to talk, but never to govern. Her attention wandered to her plate and the last crumbs of dessert. Suddenly Winkie hissed across the table at her. Words spilled from her and rage. Her face was blotchy with it and her eyes popped.

Lacey boiled slowly, but she boiled. "*I* was rude?" she asked, making no effort to make her voice other than clear. "I? Oh, you're too much. Really too much!"

At that moment Giordano, still enthralled by rabbits, asked Lacey if she had ever heard of a rabbit-burger. And Baroness Casale very wisely stood up.

AS THEY WANDERED AWAY from the table Peter muttered in Lacey's ear, "Next time pick on someone your own size!"

She fixed him with narrowed eyes more ferocious than he had imagined green eyes could be. "Hardly a wrestling match." Her face set in a sneer. "That tripe!"

"Who's the friend?" he persevered, curious enough not to drop the subject as he knew he should.

She shook her head. "Who knows. Last summer I seem to remember it was an electrician." She slipped a hand through his arm. "I'm ashamed of myself, but she *was* impossible and I was a disgrace." Kate, who had come up behind them, wanted to know what had happened. Peter obliged, giving Winkie her full share of discredit, and then tried his question on Kate.

"Haven't the faintest. Does it strike you everyone's a little cuckoo tonight?" she asked instead. "What is it? Spring? Clear mountain air? The robbery?" Kate was babbling. She ignored Lacey's frown and chattered on nervously. "Even Eddie's all atwitter, as though he'd discovered the Holy Grail or the elixir of youth. We're all out of synch tonight." By the time Lacey had explained the expression to Peter, they and the others were back in the drawing room, where coffee and liqueurs awaited them.

Soon Caroline made a good-night sweep of the room, using the excuse that she must start for Geneva very early the next morning. Peter, surrounded by people, asking about the robbery, caught a glimpse of El, deep in conversation with Henry Maddox, Webster's eldest, who had always been her favorite of the young, she said because he was so shy. More than ever, bending over her, he looked a tall friendly scarecrow with his straw hair bristling out at odd angles. Their conversation was long and serious and at its end El and Lacey went home.

Peter stayed, not that he wanted to stay: he felt that he should. His clients could ask whatever they liked. There should be no doubts about his involvement in the robbery. He also listened to a lot of nonsense and more gossip and felt his resistance flagging, when somewhere behind him Winkie Cromwell announced that she simply could not *bear* to hear Italians speak French. Too excruciating! For Peter the evening had come full-cycle. It was almost one o'clock. He had lasted longer than he had imagined possible. He went in search of his hostess.

Once more she had sought the protective coloring of a tapestry and was ominously enthusiastic in her reception.

"Just the person who would know! Filippo, remember Joan's Filippo, the Prince?" Her pleasure in the title did not ease her furrows of concentration. "He just told me he's related somehow—I didn't quite catch it all, his English—to the Brontes. Obviously I was supposed to be impressed. They wrote books." She smiled vaguely to herself after this intellectual tour de force. "But, surely, they didn't make . . . that is, can it be an *important* connection? What can he have meant?"

Peter never reached the nobility and prosperity of the present-day Brontes. The information that Lord Nelson was created Duke of Bronte by Ferdinand IV of Naples sent Mrs. Bourton-Hampton fluttering off to find her husband.

"Silly, silly boy. Why didn't he tell us sooner? Why—? Oh, do come again soon. Lovely to see you. Lovely . . ." and she pattered away. Peter was not really surprised a week later when Webster, citing Cedric as his source, insisted that Filippo, Prince of Ficuzza e Verdura, was a nephew of Lord Mount-batten's.

AT THE FRONT DOOR Peter met Robert and Kate, who were sneaking out. He asked about camels.

"Eddie had a tale, some safari on camelback, but he couldn't remember—or couldn't invent—the end. Hamburgers kept coming into it." Kate choked, which changed the subject to Robert's other problem, Alan. Had Peter seen him in there, *dancing* with Joan? Kate harrumphed in a motherly way: that was not what she would call it.

"We're just tired," Peter suggested. "Let's get out of here." As they crossed the front terrace, Robert remembered that he had El's cigarette lighter. She had left it behind and the Bourton-Hamptons had asked if they would take it to her. Maybe Peter . . . ? The lighter changed hands, and they were about to get into their cars when it occurred to Peter that no one had told him Eddie's secret.

At his question Kate gave one of her great peals, now slightly subdued. "The Holy Grail? I warned you. He's—you won't believe this—he's found the only place in Florence where he can get a *good hamburger!*"

To Peter that seemed emblematic of the evening. Next summer, he promised himself, he would avoid large parties.

9

$\mathscr{D}$ "DID YOU GET the letter?" Lacey had asked as they drove away from the Bourton-Hamptons'.

"Of course." Nothing else was said on the way home. El had not intended to sound so peevish. She was tired and worried and nervous and fed up and, worst of all, she dreaded this next step. A glance at Lacey reassured her. She was not offended. She was absorbed in her own thoughts, probably dread, and if there was one thing that did not improve with sharing, it was dread. It was their own fault. Their sarcasm had angered Caroline, forced her to take a stand, which she could not gracefully abandon. Now they could pay for their sharp tongues. There was, though El hated to admit it, a certain flavor of justice about the situation. Caroline had been so stubborn about her pensioners. If the documents and checks were destroyed, they would never be reissued. The pensioners would never be reimbursed. The checks and documents must be returned. She was adamant *and* infuriating.

"Oh that's easy," Lacey had sniped. "We'll drive up to the station and leave them at the front door. If there's a policeman, so much the better. We can apologize. '*Scusi tanto,* took these by mistake'!"

"At that rate, let's dump the whole mess back at the station," El had suggested. "Why not? We've proven our point."

Caroline had stormed at them. They had made *their* point. And hers? She had agreed to be part of the adventure—and they would admit she had done her share—to show how easy it was to evade the Finance Police and export money from Italy. Italians must know! They must realize what damage a few unscrupulous people could do the country. Only something as blatant as her smuggling would shock them. (El and Lacey had stared at each other. Was Caroline going to bungle it on purpose, or did she assume that, after the fact, she could reveal her activities? Without penalty? To herself? To the others? And then too, there was Giordano.) Caroline coursed on, her reasoning crystalline, at least to herself. Now *they* were willing to do away with the one constructive element, because *their* point had been made, and . . . No! They had *not* made their point yet, not until the money left Italy. Here was the ultimatum! They could return the checks and documents and she would smuggle the money out, thus testing their theory—and hers—*or* she would confess and present the money to the authorities. They had not believed her. She would never do it. But—with Caroline one could not be sure. She might. And there was so little time.

Compromise was the only solution and El did not consider herself an adroit compromiser. Concessions were always uni-lateral. The documents and checks, even the small bills that were so bulky, could be returned on two conditions: one, that the money did not disappear into a bureaucratic sump, which meant that the return must be highly publicized; and two, that some trick be found to put distance between San Felice and the robbery. Caroline did not argue. Why should she? The conditions were El's, and El and Lacey had to solve the problems, before noon, when with their help the boxes would be packed and ready to be shipped from the station. Caroline went off to find her boxes.

"Hoist by our own tangled web," Lacey groaned. She propped her head on one hand and seemed to doze. "What now, maestro?" Without opening her eyes she raised an eyebrow in question. It stayed raised for the rest of the day. El tried thinking out loud. It had worked other times. Lacey could file her objections.

Where and how do you make announcements? Newspapers. A paid ad? No. They had to make such a splash the police could not stifle the story. Or—this is it—write a letter *to* the police, leave it with the documents and checks *and* send copies to the papers. Get as broad a political spread as possible. *Il Corriere della Sera, Il Messaggero,* and *Paese Sera.* They would do, but not through the local offices. And the letter could not be written on one of their own typewriters. Who could mail them in Rome or Milan? Wait . . . !

And so El had arrived at Kate again. Kate in Rome. *She* could write the letter and mail the carbons at the main post office. They would be delivered the next morning, so the documents and checks had to be left that night, after the Bourton-Hamptons' party. Lacey groaned even louder. At the station. Why not? Somewhere the bags would not be mistaken for garbage. By the lavatories. The stationmaster was sure to go there just before five o'clock.

Fortunately Kate was still at her apartment. Her reaction was violent. Certain processes in life were irreversible, including robbery. Surprise was the essence of deception. They could not repeat the pattern with the same results. This was madness. El and Lacey agreed. They also agreed that it was the only way out. Together they concocted a letter with a tenuous political note thrown in to confuse.

One problem remained. The typewriter. El had thought of the battered relics the post office kept chained to counters for the public's use. Never mind if the keys were missing and alignment a thing of the distant past. Kate had an alternative. Robert had given her an electric typewriter for her birthday. Her portable was part of the trade, but she had not yet given it to the dealer. She would write the letter, later take a taxi, leave the portable at the dealer's, and go on to her meetings. The typewriter would vanish, the carbons would be mailed from the main post office, and the original passed to El at the Bourton-Hamptons'. And so it was agreed.

Now all they had to do was get home, change from evening dresses to dark slacks, sweaters, and soft shoes, and load up the two garbage bags, the same bags they had so laboriously hauled away from the station less than twenty-four hours before.

It all sounded so simple, too simple. El knew she was playing tricks on herself and another glance at Lacey told her the truth: they both dreaded it.

NIJINSKY DID NOT WANT to get into the car. He was not nasty about it. He did not have to be, with 175 pounds of bone, muscle, and long white fur to support his preferences. He just sat in the garage doorway, watching El, like an apologetic polar bear. And she watched him, knowing it was useless to drag on his short, braided leather leash. She might pull his collar off over his ears, but she would not budge him. Caroline had warned her that the Maremma shepherd was stubborn, but, at the time, ten inches of white fluff had not seemed threatening, which, now that she thought about it, probably explained why her friends kept having babies. El sat down on some piled cases of dog food. Nijinsky came swaying over in his ripply three-stage walk, sat down in front of her, and offered his paw.

"*That* will get you nowhere," she warned, taking it to avoid the bruises his repeated offers would cause, if she did not. "Be sweet! Don't balk, Nijinsky. Everyone else has today. *You* be different!" Slowly he took back his paw. His tawny eyes were reproachful, so was his sigh as he sank down on the floor in his library-lion position. He could rest while they waited for Lacey to come back with her passport. At the last moment she had remembered that to be out on a dark night without identification papers was almost as serious a crime as robbing a train. The bags were already in the trunk. El had been left to lure Nijinsky onto his backseat throne, where, without effort beyond his Pavlovian talents, he could act as lookout and general distraction in case of danger. She patted his soft, colossal head. He looked very serious. "It's all your mother's fault," she said, patting his head again. There was always a mother to blame and certainly this mess could be blamed on Caroline. Nijinsky put his head down on her shoes and closed his eyes. Decidedly a watchdog, always on the qui vive!

A FAINT RUSTLE brought Nijinsky straight up into the grand jetés and pirouettes that had given him his name. One final leap took him out into the dark. Seconds later, twirling, he reappeared in a *pas de deux* with Lacey. He crouched and jumped, crouched and jumped in front of her as she pretended to duck around him. It was an old game of theirs.

"He won't get in the car," El announced. "See if you can trick him in. He's terrified of cars."

"Great watchdog!" Lacey panted, turning her back as Nijinsky danced toward her on his hind legs. "Hold the seat down. Maybe I can back into the car and get him to follow. Come on, you big lout, catch me! Catch me! That's right." She hunched over, spinning her hands in an egg-beater motion, moving them from side to side, retreating. Nijinsky bounded and lunged and pounced, trying to catch them, and she slowly folded herself into the back of the car, churning her hands right in front of his nose, until he had to make the fatal decision. He hesitated for a fraction of a second, then leapt into the backseat, burying Lacey under white fur. As she wrestled to get free, El started the car and stuck her hand up over the back of her seat, waving a bath towel.

"Take it! You'll need it. He's so scared, he hyperventilates and drools." Nijinsky began to yowl, and El shot back out of the garage. "The pitch of the motor hurts his ears, I think. When we reach the blacktop, he'll calm down." In the mirror she could see Lacey right herself and shove Nijinsky over. He drooped back on her shoulder. She struggled to get the towel around her, like a shawl worn backward, shouting the whole time. Fortunately in the general racket El could not quite hear her, but she could imagine.

EL DROVE into the Piazza very, very slowly. It was empty, so empty it was hard to imagine that people or cars had ever entered it before. In the mist the light from two tall streetlamps opposite the station were smudges, which shed a golden haze over the buildings and pavement. El swung the car around and backed carefully into a corner, along a wall at the end of the station, exactly across from where they had, that morning, shifted the bags from the freight cart to the collectors' dollies. It was so dark that only the radiator of the car would be visible. She turned the motor off. Nijinsky stuck his head between the front seats and licked her ear.

"Comparison shopping!" Lacey grumbled from the back.

"You'll have to get me out." El went around the car and opened the door.

"I've got him. Push my seat down." And Lacey was out. They closed the doors and met at the trunk.

"I'll get even with you for that," Lacey said, lifting the lid.

"If you'd been in front, it would have been worse," El whispered. "He would have joined us." She tugged a sack upright. "You can drive, going home." With her back to the trunk she bent her knees, grabbed the sack, and pulled. Lacey maneuvered the other and picked it up.

"No, no. I'll just have my fourth shower of the day—*if* we get home. Up—and away." They ducked around the corner of the station and went along its wall, always in black shadow, until a faint breeze warned they were approaching the open area of the platform. They put the bags down. Again El whispered in Lacey's ear.

"Have you got the whistle?" A nod. "Good. Take it easy. I'll count to a hundred. If I haven't heard anything, I'll haul the first bag out." A nod. "And if there's a hitch—you know about that." Another nod, and Lacey slipped back around the corner of the building, along the wall, past the car and further, until, when she turned, stepped out in the open, and started toward the station, she was on a long diagonal route across the Piazza. Anyone seeing her would assume she had come in from a side street.

She counted all the way. By forty-two she was at the station door. She twisted the handle carefully and pushed. The lower corner stuck. She used her toe for pressure and pushed again. The door gave without a squeal. In the closed room dust and fug had coagulated to an almost solid, flannelly musk. Fifty-eight now. High up on the ceiling a single neon tube fluttered and flashed, more off than on. She reached the far door in sixty-seven. Through the glass she could see a slice of the platform. The lights were on—that was odd. She could not wait. She had to go outside, casually. The door was not so important this time, not with the lights.

She opened it and stepped out, expecting to see formations of uniformed men marching up and down the platform. To her right, away from El and toward the far end of the building, two men in light blue trousers and darker jackets, Railway Police, strolled together, chatting. When they saw her, they quickened their pace. She ignored them, veering off to her left to the board of train postings. The lights on the platform made the dark beyond impenetrable, blacker than black. They would not see El, particularly if she kept them busy. She must decide. She fingered the whistle in her pocket. They would not hear it, if she blew. It was a silent dog whistle, which because of its particular pitch and Nijinsky's most particular ears, sent him into explosions of barking. He was just around the corner. He would hear and El would be warned. She would leave the bags where they were. Lacey waited, considering what she should do and appearing to study the white letters and numbers on their velvety black board. Behind her the footsteps stopped.

" 'Sera," said a male voice. She turned. Both men sketched a salute. "Can we help you?"

"That's very kind. Maybe you could." She smiled, winningly she hoped. "I wanted to find out if there's a through train to— to Vicenza—or do I have to change? It's not here." She had always wanted to go to Vicenza. At the worst she would. They were busy telling her what she already knew, that detailed schedules were posted in the lobby. "Oh fine. I'll try that— after I buy a pack of cigarettes." The machine was on the wall near the door back into the station. They followed her, watched her put the right change in, and laughed when the right brand came out. It so seldom did. By now El would be safe. How to get rid of the guards? One of them held the door open for her and smiled.

"Light's out in there. We can help you with our flashlights." He led the way and took up his position at the large framed panels of the official timetable, which hung from the wall on heavy brackets. His partner obliged with the flashlight. They were very slow. They argued about whether she should take the Venice Express and change at Padova or take the local to Florence and . . . No, no, the Venice Express. She'd stop awhile in Padova. She had— Suddenly from the dark beyond their schedule panels came loud, hysterical, baritone barks. Nijinsky was out of his mind. What had happened? His voice cracked in anxiety.

Lacey almost said, "Oh dear, I'd better go. I left my dog in the car." But on second thought, she did not. Her Railway Police would follow her. Where was El?

"Just some dog in love," said one of the guards.

"Sounds more like a lion," said the other. They both smiled at Lacey. She could feel her knees trembling.

"Isn't that the Rome-Bologna-Padova-Venice frame? Back there?" she asked, desperate to steer the conversation back to trains. God, if Nijinsky didn't stop, she—she— A motor started somewhere, very quietly, a soft purr. The men were arguing about times. She peeked around the edge of the panels. Through the door she could see a corner of the Piazza. No car lights. No movement, just her imagination. They had found her train— 1:32 P.M. any day, straight to Padova. They waited for her thanks, and she realized she could not hear Nijinsky. Now what?

She thanked them. She was lavish with her compliments. Reading a train schedule was almost impossible for the nonexpert. Without light too. She was most grateful. She shook hands with them. They followed her to the door. Bows and more thanks were exchanged and finally she was free in the Piazza.

She must not hesitate. Her friends were still watching. She walked off, calmly, toward the parking lot, beyond it, past a row of stores, and on out to the main road. El *should* be in the first lane to the right. She was, with the lights out and the motor running. Nijinsky was asleep across the backseat.

"What *happened?*" Lacey asked, flinging herself into the front seat. El swept out onto the road.

"Nothing! Really nothing!" El shook her head from side to side. "I saw you talking to the police. They opened the door—everything was perfect *until* I got back to the car. Nijinsky was so glad to see me that he put on that concert. I think he's afraid of the dark too. I didn't know what to do. I knew you were stumped. So I drove off. As quietly as I could. They didn't notice, did . . . ?" That was the end of conversation. Nijinsky had leaned over the front seat to welcome Lacey back too.

AT EL'S, Peter had been surprised to find the lights blazing, but the garage empty. No one answered the bell. An accident? He would have passed them on the road. He wandered around for a few minutes, calling, and finally, leaving the lighter on a large rock near the front door, he gave up and got back into his car. At the bottom of the drive he almost collided with El's car. She backed up, he eased alongside her and rolled down his window.

"Where the hell have you been?" He realized that he sounded more cross than anxious.

"Once and for all, Peter—where I go, what I do, is *my* business. Not yours. And I won't have you spying on me." By the dash lights he could just see her chin and a black sweater, but he hardly needed to see her face. However irrational it seemed to him, she was angry.

"You left your cigarette lighter at the party. I brought it back. Is *that* what you call spying?"

"I warned you, Peter. I can't . . ."

Lacey leaned across El, waving a package of cigarettes, and called, "That's why we went out. No genius without cigarettes, you know." Nijinsky, who had stuck his head over El's shoulder and out the window, squirmed closer and closer to Peter's face. "Come on, you two. Don't fight. We're all tired and——" El would have interrupted her, but Peter beat her to it.

"I hope you bought Nijinsky a cigar!" He let out the clutch, waved, and sped off down the hill, home and finally to bed.

It had been a very long day.

10

BEFORE DAWN the next morning, as agreed, Caroline called El. She would not leave for Switzerland unless the documents and checks had been returned. They had. She left. Shortly before seven Lacey, an ample purse hooked over one shoulder, set off on foot for San Felice. She was tired and it seemed to her that she walked very slowly. Did the human body ever run out of adrenaline? She felt as though she had a dead battery, but she actually reached town in good time and went to a very busy café and pastry shop, which also happened to have three soundproof telephone booths in a back room.

Lacey chose the one in the corner, closed the door, and for good measure turned her back to it. From her purse she brought out a tape recorder and slipped the strap over her head, so that the machine hung down in front of her like a space-age lavaliere. Then she took a deep breath and dialed a series of numbers. Clicks and clicks and a long silence before another definite clunk and a bored male voice announced,

"Finance Police. Mont Blanc Command Post."

Lacey pushed the "play" button on the recorder and Martha's voice, deep and muffled now by the soundproofing of the booth and rather too histrionically breathless, came on.

"If the *Guardia di Finanza* is interested in blocking the illegal export of approximately eight hundred million lire, a blue Fiat 128, license AR 165___, registered in the name of Caroline Thornton Maffei, should be stopped. It will pass through that border today sometime between ten A.M. and three P.M." Lacey hit the "off" button. This was the dicey part. If the soldier-operator was flustered and switched her to an officer, she had to run the tape back and play it from the beginning. If he kept his wits about him and asked her to repeat the message, which would mean that he was either recording the conversation or trying to trace the call, she was to go on with the next few feet of tape. She kept her hand on the buttons, ready to punch.

"Hold on just a second—that is—would you repeat that please?" Lacey pushed the "play" button and once more Martha's voice joined her in the booth.

"No, all you need to know is license AR 165___ on a blue Fiat 128, belonging to Caroline Thornton Maffei. Remember eight hundred million lire. A blue Fiat 128." The tape shut off and Lacey put the receiver gently back in its cradle. Martha's mispronunciation of Thornton was magnificent, perfectly Italianized to "Torn-toney." Now to get away from that telephone and out of the café.

In the main room workmen crowded along the counter, gobbling fresh buns and complaining to a woman half hidden behind the coffee machine. She was alone and could not keep up with the orders. In a minute! In a minute she would also calculate the cost of Lacey's call. The ring of the counter telephone made Lacey start so violently that she jostled the man next to her. She apologized, he bowed, and the woman behind the counter had a long conversation about four dozen éclairs needed for that afternoon. Not the *Guardia di Finanza!* Once the flavors were duly noted, Lacey was able to waylay the woman long enough to get the charges. She paid and left. Now to buy the morning papers and have a quiet coffee herself, in a café where the ringing of the telephone would not bring on surges of fear and guilt.

COUNTRY TOWNS are slow to wake up. Peasants and bakers may rise at dawn, but shopkeepers, public officials, and housewives do not venture out into the cool, damp morning air until they absolutely must. Matteo Matteucci, Peter Testa's clerk, deplored this private and commercial slackness. He considered it yet another symptom of society's disintegration, like half-day Saturday, which he still called "English Saturday." No, he was for the old way, the old morality, the old integrity. An office should open, ready for business—not for the first coffee break— at eight, so each morning shortly after seven-thirty, dressed in a gray suit and a white shirt *and* a tie, another convention he would not neglect, Matteo started along the Corso.

About his errands, as about his business activities, he was methodical. He bought a newspaper. He had a cup of coffee in one particular café, but only after he had kept his appointment with Micio, a gray tabby cat whom he had secretly adopted without, however, bothering to give him a name. Micio means "pussy." He was a thin, spiky animal, rather like Matteo himself, and was constantly terrorized by a gang of bristly, mustachioed dogs, who cruised the street, enforcing their monopoly of delicacies to be had from garbage pails. Matteo had slipped gradually into this liaison—one day a bit of leftover chicken, several days later a bit of fish—until he noticed that morning and afternoon Micio waited for him by the fountain at the head of the Corso and walked along with him, rubbing against his legs. When they reached a jog in the buildings, which offered some privacy, Micio sat down and fixed his benefactor with a dignified, greedy stare. If nothing materialized, he let out embarrassing yowls of fury. In short, he was a problem. Matteo could not take him home. His wife said pets were for children and they had none. The only solution was extensive catering, which strained his ability to deceive and left his pockets greasy. Micio repaid him with rusty purring and a sense that he was needed.

The attachment was known to one person, a greengrocer named Anna Maria, who washed the floor of her shop and culled her merchandise very early each morning. Matteo knew that she watched him. He also knew that he amused her, that she thought him a prissy old man and Micio a scruffy derelict, but he did not care. He bowed to her twice daily and occasionally, to stay in her good graces and ensure his wife's ignorance, he asked her about her liver. She replied in kind, asking about his spinal arthritis. Their discomforts, so suitable to their professions, were a bond. Especially in the morning, seeing her on the lookout for him encouraged Matteo almost as much as Micio's rapacious loyalty. The day had started properly.

But the morning after the Bourton-Hamptons' party Micio was not by the fountain. Matteo mewed softly, tried a few tentative kissy sounds, was ashamed of himself, and went on toward Anna Maria's. The sudden blip of a siren sent him plunging for the safety of a wall. Two, three, five cars sped past him. All carabinieri. A few seconds later, four more, larger cars crowded with plump, choleric officers, almost mashed him against the wall. The fools! They were supposed to protect the people, not assassinate them!

Anna Maria lay in wait on her doorstep. She beckoned him inside and pointed to a bin of fresh onions. Behind the long stalks he could just make out Micio's darting eyes. He purred in recognition, but refused to come out. Anna Maria was feeling noble and chatty. She had rescued the cat from a column of carabinieri jeeps. The noise had disoriented him. Trying to get away from one jeep, he dove under the next, then skittered away into the path of yet another. She simpered nicely at Matteo's praise and even offered to feed Micio, once he stopped spitting and hissing at every noise, if Matteo left her his little packet. He did and hurried on to the newspaper shop and the café. This was not an auspicious beginning to the day.

While drinking his coffee, he marked the columns of *La Nazione* for libelous phrases. He would urge Dr. Testa to take legal action. Lot of good it would do him! That young man was a product of the times. Matteo could argue as much as he liked that the press must be brought to heel, that indiscriminate freedom was poisoning society, and in answer he would receive a nod, a smile, and a change of subject. He bent lower over his paper.

LACEY, SITTING AT A TABLE, had seen Matteo come in and hoped that by holding her paper a bit higher, she might escape his mournful résumé of the day's expectations. He was a good man, a kind one, and invaluable to Peter, but not so early in the morning, most particularly not that morning. She saw him take out his pen and hunch over *La Nazione* and wondered at such concentration. She pulled her copy from the pile in front of her and studied it. No better, no worse than the others. In a picture taken at some official ceremony Peter looked glassy-eyed, more like a man with a head cold than a mysterious past.

"Good morning." Matteo's head popped up above her paper. "Ah. You've seen it! The editors should be held accountable—but Dr. Testa has little taste for such contests. Perhaps you and signora Kendall . . ." Already Lacey was shaking her head to discourage the idea. "Yes, well, you might consider it. That was not the reason for my intrusion. Could you come to the office for a moment? I have some papers for signora Kendall, which I'm sure . . ." Papers? For El? As far as she knew El had nothing pending, but Matteo did not make mistakes. Could there be . . . ? He was very firm. "She wanted them day before yesterday. That was her deadline, signorina. There were complications and unfortunately—I think I betray no confidence, it's the draft of a new will—I know . . ."

How like El to want her affairs completely in order before the robbery. She had not expected a happy end. Still, she had said nothing to the others, had not discouraged them. At times El's mind seemed labyrinthine to Lacey. She hurried to join Matteo.

In the Piazza the clock on the tower pinged three times and then rang seven heavy *tocchi,* and the pigeons took off from the porch in a great storm, pretending to be startled by the sounds they heard four times every hour. Another example, Matteo pointed out, of irresponsibility. San Felice was not Venice. Why did people have to be splattered and feathered by those wretched birds? And exposed to disease? The town council . . . Lacey listened, nodding on cue, but she was really waiting for another sound. She could see down three cobbled streets, each leading to a high portal in the walls and beyond, into the misty countryside. They were deserted still and their gray palaces, blind. In the upper part of town, clocks began their bingbong rounds, and even Matteo smiled. It was, after all, a very satisfactory sound.

They walked up past the loggia where a fishmonger was setting out his trays, and on up the hill to Peter's office. Already on the landing eight red-faced men, restless and uncomfortable in their "good" clothes, waited for Matteo. Seven of them he sent inside. Dr. Testa would be right with them. He looked the eighth man over very sharply and, for some reason Lacey did not understand, seemed unwilling to let him enter the office. The man was solid and square with a pugnacious chin, pink from a new shave, and small eyes like sapphire chips caught by light. Cocked on the back of his head was a low-crowned, almost brimless hat of molded plastic.

He was not intimidated by Matteo and he was also very angry. Why had *they* sent the carabinieri after his son? Matteo was flattered to find himself included among the powerful, but what, exactly, was he talking about? To his knowledge they had not asked the carabinieri to investigate *any* current matter. And who was his son? Tullio Giusti was his name. He had sold a car. Once the title had been cleared, he was to sign the formal papers. And here was the notice that had been sent to him, instructing him to come *at his earliest convenience*. Giusti, Sr., waved it in Matteo's face. Well, he was away, and the delay of a week did not justify a police inquiry or getting his wife worked up and frightened. He would not have it—not for something as simple as a car.

Matteo went back over the story carefully, patiently. Where did Giusti live? Ah, Barone Casale's land; then he must be a cousin of . . . ? Of course they knew each other. Their wives were related. He let Giusti complain about the young. Irresponsible lot. His Tullio . . . always the ladies. Eventually Matteo convinced Giusti that there was no problem about the car. He would note his son's absence on the list. Whenever . . . but he might well give some thought to what *had* brought the carabinieri to his house. It was an apologetic and puzzled father who clumped back down the stairs.

It was an apologetic Matteo who led Lacey through the waiting room too. Inside the telephone was ringing. Lacey heard a shrill voice command Dr. Testa to Captain Nardo's office. Immediately. Matteo was unmoved. Dr. Testa would be informed, as soon as he arrived. That would not do—Matteo hung up. Brigadier Cirillo! *Presuntuoso!* He selected a folder from a stack on his desk, took out some papers . . . and the telephone rang again. Matteo answered and had to jerk the receiver away from his ear. A colonel demanded to know the whereabouts of Dr. Testa. Probably on his way to the office, although he *could* still be in bed. The colonel bellowed that he would not tolerate facetiousness. He also threatened offical steps if Dr. Testa did not present himself at headquarters within fifteen minutes and banged down the telephone.

Matteo managed to fold the papers and seal them in an envelope before the telephone rang again. At the door Lacey met the two young law students who were scrivener-slaves, and so was delayed long enough to hear Matteo say,

"Signora Kendall, *I* would too, but he hasn't . . ."

And so began another busy and disconcerting day in San Felice Val Gufo.

11

THAT MORNING El applied her considerable willpower to being calm and failed. Her worst fears, briefly suppressed, were again rampant. The draft of her will was an evil omen. She tried to read the newspapers. Her attention wandered. Daydreams took ghoulish twists, or if they had not yet, the half-hourly news summaries on the radio steered them to torture and shame. "Arrests in the Tuscan Train Robbery expected at any moment . . . Sources close to the Ministry of the Interior hint . . . Details at noon." Damn it, she wanted them *now*. She called Peter again. She must apologize. His voice—Matteo was austere in his disapproval. He would place another message on the *dottore*'s desk. It might have been the hundredth.

She could not put her finger on it, but something was wrong. What was supposed to have happened had not. What had happened was askew. Lacey might have an idea . . . But when El found her—stretched out on the living-room couch, reading with her book open and her eyes closed—it was obvious Lacey was not haunted by intimations of disaster. She tiptoed away to search for one of those dull jobs that always need doing around a house.

The bathroom cabinets were neat. So was her closet. The winter bedding had been put away. The curtains over the linen shelves were clean. Eventually she had to settle for the chore that from year to year, she slyly avoided: the systematic arrangement of her books. Fiction first. It, at least, could be sorted alphabetically by author.

At some stage in the remodeling, after the cows and pigs had been evicted from the stalls and before the bathroom tiles were in, El had been forced to admit that in everything connected with the house she was impulsive. She had not needed a house. She was not even looking for one, but she liked the way it reared up on the hillside, solid and rectangular and distinctly masked by ranks of windows. Once the louvered shutters, which the weather had long since devoured, were replaced, the front offered such blank, prim dignity that within there could be no surprises. The deception was innocent and so doubly appealing to her, for this was no shoebox house. Time and the addition of stalls and sheds and lofts had distorted the original symmetry of the building into a wobbly, top-heavy **C**. The longer wing had been a storage barn, its stone walls built up only about a meter, the upper part left open on three sides with here and there a stone column to support the roof. Window frames, a fireplace, and a floor of old brick converted it to a living room. A long, wide hall, which had been a cartway through to the barn, was half the trunk of the **C**. The other half, equally long and wide, was a kitchen–dining room. The short branch, just to the right of the front door, was El's study.

At more or less the same time that she had recognized her impetuosity about the house, her attention had focused on the carpenter's astronomical estimate, and she realized, a bit late, how many windows her house had, and therefore how little wall space. What to do with her books, which had roughly the same annual growth rate as the inflation, was no minor problem. With helpfulness that smacked of commercial instinct, the carpenter suggested the hall, then drew up plans for floor-to-ceiling shelves, leaving two panels free where chests and their lamps and pictures might go. It did seem the only logical solution. The hall became "the stacks." Recently tuffets of books had again accumulated on the floor and El knew that sooner or later she would have to delight the carpenter and have him build an identical arrangement on the other side in the dining room.

El settled down in front of the far left-hand-corner shelves with a cloth, a sponge, a pail of water, and a ladder and girded herself for fiction. Alvaro, Austen, Bassani. Fiction, it appeared, had consoled her in some other moment of frustration. Acres of nonfiction awaited. She sat on the ladder trying to plan categories and subcategories. No Dewey Decimal rigmarole. She would divide by language and then roughly by subject—Italy, southern Italy, and "other" would do for a start. Or would it? The least interesting others could be exiled to the high shelves in the corners. Not very scientific. She glanced up. Two bulbous glass lanterns cast pale aberrations of light—rings of light, which were intertwined on the ceiling, blurred with distance to watermark the spines of books and, below, dissolved into speckled shadows. The lanterns needed washing. Not for the first time she wished she had a handyman chained in the garage. The last row of fiction caught her eye. Over an hour later, when Lacey called, warning that the noon news was about to come on, El, still perched on the ladder, was deep in *Peter Abelard*.

"STARTLING DEVELOPMENTS in the Tuscan Train Robbery" was the lead story on the broadcast. Today the announcer was jubilant. "The first banknote from the Tuscan Train Robbery showed up this morning at the main branch of the Bank of Rome. It was one of several 100,000-lire notes included in the deposit of Leonardo Di Giulio, proprietor of a tobacco shop in Via del Corso. Di Giulio, who denies any recollection of the bill's origin, is being held by the police for questioning.

"The center of the investigation has now shifted to Rome, where, it is felt, the next few hours are crucial. The money must be disposed of—either by conventional 'laundering' systems, well known to the police, or by direct export. Special police units guard all airports, stations, and frontier posts. Those who must travel are asked to cooperate with the delays that will inevitably result.

"The appearance of the money in Rome has added a puzzling aspect to the case. How was it brought from San Felice Val Gufo? The roadblocks, so quickly and efficiently organized, preclude transport by car, therefore the police, aided by detailed descriptions of the robbers, are carrying out a station-to-station survey, both north and south of San Felice, in search of anyone who, during the probable time period, saw one man or more, up to four, get on a Rome-bound train with an excessive amount of luggage.

"An early solution to this daring crime is expected. Programs will be interrupted for flash bulletins. . . ." With a good deal less brio the announcer passed on to the nonresults of union meetings and El sat glowering at the radio.

"I like the 'detailed descriptions,'" she finally said. "*Detailed!* One detail is conspicuously absent. I think I'll try Peter again. He'll know what the carabinieri are up to now."

"Pray Caroline didn't hear that broadcast," Lacey called. "Her principles could still get in the way." El threw her hands up over her head and waggled them. Lacey agreed. They were all mad, even El, who would be the last to admit it, just as she would not admit she was in love with Peter. Calling him for information! Why bother with an excuse? She wanted to talk to him. To apologize, be reassured. Why not? Lacey wished Peter would frighten El. Just once, not accept her apology, or not call after a squabble, or ignore her to flirt with her friends. Lacey would be the first to volunteer—and no doubt be vanquished by Hermione. The perfect decoy! El would seethe. But Peter did not play games, not with El. She was capable of such absolute decisions, against herself, that force was dangerous. She would retreat and with El retreat was final.

Lacey understood Peter's point of view. Still . . . and it occurred to her that, if she could sit, worrying over them, the calamity level had taken a spectacular dip. She hadn't had time for idle thoughts of any interest in weeks. It was rather pleasant. Surely Peter had heard El say that she was not going to marry her mistakes: she had done that. Had he heard the rest? That she had not, so far, been really tempted. The men who attracted her, she did not like, and the men she liked, did not attract her. And then, suddenly, Lacey saw it: that was the key. Peter had both attracted her and she liked him: El was frightened. Ah, well then, time was his ally. She did hope they would get on with it. Why eighteen-year-olds in love were merely fatuous and those of a more reasonable age seemed semicomic was a mystery, unless the young were always fatuous and it was only a question of degree. Really, she was not *so* old as . . . She heard quick steps in the hall and knew all was well.

"Matteo put my messages *under* the papers," El reported, as though his treachery were the important discovery of the conversation. "He's so high-handed, but Peter doesn't— Oh, by the way, he's coming for dinner tomorrow night. I mean Peter, and he sent you a message—Arch is back."

Lacey shrugged.

"That's enthusiastic! I thought you liked him."

She did. It would be hard not to like the big, disheveled English doctor with his tales of jungles and bizarre diseases.

"Last summer it almost seemed——"

"What did Peter have to say?" Lacey cut in firmly. "About anything important." To her surprise, El blushed. "Remember? The carabinieri."

"Touchy aren't we? Let's see. He spent the morning with them and—I thought we might have chicken." Growls from Lacey brought her back to the subject.

Peter had been summoned to repeat his story for the colonel assigned to coordinate the investigation. A bluster-and-fawn type. He had staged a lineup of men. No one Peter had ever seen before. The report that a banknote from the robbery had turned up in Rome had triggered a general collapse of men and machinery. The telephone lines went dead. The radio phone blew out and smoked. So did the colonel, who was seized by convulsive paranoia and ranted that they were at the epicenter of a coup, a terrorist attempt to overthrow the government. He would order the area under martial law. That is, later he might. For the moment all arms were to be confiscated.

Captain Nardo could see to the minor matters, such as the robbery and the return of the pension documents and money, which was the first Peter had heard of the night before's excitement. Nardo went into great detail. At four that morning the stationmaster had discovered two garbage bags and a note near the public toilets. Nardo and a demolition crew that had just arrived from Verona went down. No booby traps, no fingerprints. The station police had seen no one suspicious in or near the station.

"Invisible once more," Lacey commented. "This could get discouraging."

Nardo had spoon-fed the information to Peter, as though priming him. What could he say? It was obvious: the robbery was local. How else could the checks and documents be returned so easily—almost twenty-four hours after the robbery? That seemed to be exactly what Nardo wanted. For the colonel's benefit. Apparently he was very difficult. And then Peter left. The colonel was planning massive cross-exchanges of data among all the branches of the police, two or three ministries, and Interpol. By computer, naturally. Nardo almost bit off his tongue. An errand boy in charge of "minor matters" did not remind a colonel that there was no telephone, much less a computer. Not this sort of fixated colonel, who probably thought John XXIII was a Communist sympathizer.

"There was one thing that worried me." El thought for a moment and then went on more cheerfully. "No, men are little boys at heart. It's all right. Peter's going to help Captain Nardo discover where and how porters' jackets are sold. And he said something about samples of typewriters. Here in San Felice. Maybe *we* should help too—sort of Nancy Drew and the Rover Boys?"

"Let's have lunch instead," Lacey suggested. "I like the part about the station police. 'No one suspicious was seen or heard near the station.' You were right—any four women *could* rob the Bank of Italy!"

THAT AFTERNOON nonfiction was reduced to Italy, Southern Italy, and other. No mercy was shown. Lacey at one end of the stacks, El at the other, with the radio between them, they sorted shelf by shelf, talking about the merits and flaws of the treasures they found. Lacey would not allow that El had ever actually read *Ecclesiastic Property in the Economic History of Matera*. Even more improbable was *The Moral Basis of a Backward Society*. "That's what the Italians thought." El laughed and waved it away to the Southern pile.

It was as good an occupation as any and better, certainly, than staring at the telephone, praying it would not ring. It did with maddening regularity: a friend in Rome; an invitation; the stationer in San Felice had the binders El had ordered; and Arch Stanley, back from South America. They were eager about their messages. El was indifferent, though, as she was about to dismiss Arch, she did urge him to join them the next evening.

"Two by two they went into the ark," Lacey simpered. "Honestly, El!" They both went back to work.

Toward the end of the afternoon only the radio seemed to have a voice, one with little variety. It offered rock and roll or what El identified as the newly fashionable "Folklore," the English word kept, but made more exotic by the pronunciation of the final *e*. The Radio Authority was infatuated, it seemed, with all things African, Asian, or Chinese and disenchanted with all things American, the exception being Sylvia Plath, who was mourned as "a poetess unknown and unacclaimed in her own country." At 4:40 an overly plaintive reading of her poetry was interrupted for a news flash. El and Lacey sat motionless on their ladders, staring at the radio.

"A special edition of *Paese Sera* announces that the pension checks stolen in the Tuscan Train Robbery and a letter to the police were found last night at the station of San Felice. Under pressure, a carabinieri press spokesman has admitted the truth of the report. Details on the seven o'clock roundup."

The woman with the whimpering voice went back to Sylvia Plath. In the stacks there was a muted babble of celebration. If Caroline did not call in the next hour, they were home safe.

"Since you're so happy," Lacey said very seriously, "tell

me where in 'other' I'm to put *European Art Around 1400,* a catalogue in German—German!—with illustrations. We need a guide-book and catalogue section."

"The very spirit of 'other,' I'd say." But El's interest was actually on a book she had just found. "Poor Judith Hearne's been shuffling around nonfiction with her lonely passion. How . . . ?"

A deep ragged bark between hawking and honking drowned out her question. Nijinsky had been awakened and was not pleased. "Someone he knows." El went to her study. "It's Henry Maddox," she called and opened the front door. Nijinsky charged in full tilt, was tempted by the familiar smell of El's skirt, but bounded on toward Lacey, who scrambled off her ladder in time to intercept his front feet on their way to her shoulders. "They waltz beautifully," El told Henry, motioning him out of the way. Lacey and Nijinsky whirled round and round and out the front door. In a moment she was back, wiping her face with the backs of her hands.

"I'm an accomplished dog-sitter," she explained to the bewildered Henry. "Also a trainer of dancing bears."

"Impressive on her *curriculum vitae.* Come on." El pushed Henry gently toward a ladder. "No shirking. We'll hand up to you." He looked from one to the other not quite sure whether they were serious or teasing. He still had that trouble with "older people," which to him were all those over twenty-five. Before he could decide, Lacey had shoved a pile of books at him and El stood ready with another. They worked at a frenzied *Modern Times* pace and in less than an hour had the presorted books on their new shelves. The last two tiers would have to wait for another day. El thought they should have tea. Henry said he'd like a beer, please. He had tea.

Delegated to entertain him, Lacey led him off to the living room, where he slumped on the sofa, his legs jackknifed under his chin and his long arms dangling between them, and stared at the rug in speechless misery. She tried Nijinsky. Scissors and snails and . . . No. Cars? Perhaps motorcycles? The light blue eyes flickered up and down again. By the time El came with tea, he was explaining multi-exhaust monsters with enthusiasm that bordered on idolatry.

"The books were dirty, Henry. Go wash your hands," El ordered in a firm, motherly tone that suited neither her age nor condition. "And if you have a comb . . ." The straw bristles were standing out at all angles. He went off obediently, and she whispered to Lacey, "Don't go away. I want to know what you make of it."

For the next half-hour Henry stammered and stumbled and qualified and explained and El listened without helping him. Lacey listened too. The gist of his contorted tale was that he had some money, which he would be willing to change. He knew—that is, he sort of thought—that people were always changing money. Everyone needed to at some point, like when they sold a house, or bought one—or—or—other times too. El led him on with gentle persistence. He seemed earnest, guileless, but Lacey found herself wondering if his offer was as simple as that. And why to El? At this particular moment? Or was he hinting at secret knowledge? A courteous attempt at blackmail. If so, El was giving him no satisfaction. Lacey tried assuming he meant what he said and no more.

In Italy the state is based on the principle that deception, both individual and administrative, is the better part of survival. The private money exchange, one of the results, was a system widely used and never mentioned. A foreign buyer paid the price on his sale contract in lire imported through normal banking channels. The exchange rate was always low. A foreign seller received the price shown on the contract in lire, but the price declared on contracts was seldom more than 50 percent of the money that changed hands, which was a *de facto* accommodation accepted by all involved. With casual pragmatism the state, never one to lose, adjusted the taxes and fees a notch higher. The buyer-seller was often left with a mountain of lire to buy or sell, which did not officially exist and which he, naturally, would like to exchange at the highest rate.

Henry expected to step into the breach. The foreign buyer or seller was greedy. If he bought lire, he preferred 850 for his dollar to 700. If he bought dollars, he preferred paying 1,000 lire for each to 1,200. The illicit buyer shopped around or took the loss. Supply and demand were perpetually out of balance. The customers were in a monetary traffic jam: whichever lane they chose was the one that did not move. Henry's offer, if he had a reasonable amount of money, could help the buyer of a house, for instance. If he was careful, he could keep his money going back and forth and make a nice profit. Lacey thought she saw the real purpose of Henry's visit.

She interrupted whatever they had been saying. "Actually you want to see Dr. Testa, don't you, Henry? He's the one who has to do with all the house contracts and sales of property." Henry's face lit up for the first time. He nodded and kept on nodding, like one of those dolls on the back shelves of cars, whose heads bobble inanely. When he noticed that he was expected to explain, his earnestness compensated for his general incoherence.

"Yes—that's it! Because, you see, I don't know Dr. Testa very well and he might tell my father, who doesn't know anything about this. I—I thought if you talked to him, for me, sort of, then—well, it would be all right." He beamed at El, delighted with his own lucidity. She chose to be stern.

"Henry, *I* can't speak to Peter about this, any more than *you* can. You know that." She waved her hand in a way that canceled all hope. "He knows about it, of course, but *he* can't have anything to do with it. Not in his position. You're not thinking very clearly. Any friends, dependable, discreet friends, who need to change money, I'll send along to you. And I won't forget. Now I think . . ."

Henry was dispatched quickly. El saw him out and came back shaking her head.

"Finesse isn't his forte, but I *did* wonder, last night at the party, if he could be trying . . ." Still shaking her head, she started around the room pulling the curtains, and Lacey took the tray to the kitchen. Suddenly Nijinsky set up a ferocious wailing, howling-growling, and pounded back and forth on the gravel in front of the house. El and Lacey met in the hall and stood together for a moment, listening to his roars of protest. He sounded rabid and definitely carnivorous.

"Someone in uniform. I can tell from his voice." El smiled. "He's a terrible snob. Probably a telegram. We can see from my study." The radio, which no one had thought to turn off, erupted with static and, after an apologetic silence, a dignified voice announced,

"Important news flash. The Minister of Defense has made the following statement in answer to what he has called 'persistent, unfounded, and obviously subversive' rumors. 'At no time in the last forty-eight hours has there been any danger, threat, or even hint of a government takeover by terrorists.' He urges the population to be calm and confident."

" 'Curiouser and curiouser,' " El muttered as they hurried along the hall. Nijinsky sounded as though the kill were near. "*Sic transit . . .*"

". . . one colonel." Lacey finished the thought for her, adding, "Maybe he'll be dramatic and fall on his sword." They leaned against the glass to see out the window. There in the driveway, circled and snarled at by a foaming, toothy Nijinsky, sat the mighty blue-and-white Alfa Romeo of the Second Flying Squad with its red roof light flashing, and inside, white-faced and tending to cringe away from the doors, Brigadier Cirillo and Captain Nardo.

". . . In the Tuscan Train Robbery, arrests are expected at any moment," the radio droned prophetically, echoing El and Lacey's exact thoughts.

12

EL DID NOT GO to carabinieri headquarters until the next morning, and then not as a prisoner, but an interpreter, such being the favor that Captain Nardo had come to ask the night before. It was a delicate situation, he had explained. The person, no better identified, was only marginally involved. He doubted an official record need be kept and would not be, if he could avoid an interpreter from the Ministry. He was himself so tactful that El understood little beyond the obvious. She had been chosen *faute de mieux*, which was never flattering. But she could not refuse him: no sensible person was rude to a carabinieri officer, certainly not El under the circumstances.

By morning dizzying spasms of fear, which she tried to conceal from Lacey, and incidentally herself, alternated with curiosity. In her days of probity she had never been inside carabinieri headquarters, though, like everyone else in town, she had heard a great deal about their feud with the local authorities over a new, more suitable garrison. Indeed, ever since the war, it had been the local *cause célèbre*.

In this semipermanent interim the carabinieri occupied a

sixteenth-century palace on a steep street above the Piazza. It met none of the Ministry's standards. It was neither free-standing nor on high and would not have been impervious to attack, had anyone been inspired to attack it. As each commandant was careful to emphasize, these quarters were temporary, a status that had saved the outside from any indignity worse than a lighted, white plastic sign.

The interior had not fared so well. The cavernous salons were reduced to a rabbit warren of offices, many inevitably without windows. Remnants of an acanthus frieze, once the glory of the ballroom, were still visible in a lavatory and stenciled dadoes peeked out between banks of file cabinets and old-fashioned duplicating machines. Of the frescoes almost nothing remained. A tangle of legs, some soft and feminine, others hoofed and hairy, graced the ceiling of one cubicle, but no torsos emerged on the next. The management of law and order was a serious affair, efficiency and propriety of the essence.

Punctual to the minute, El arrived at nine to find the front door locked and the bell apparently out of order. She pounded on the door, thinking that absurdities begat absurdities. Without warning it flew open and she was launched headfirst into a large hallway. The group of officers nearest her stepped back out of range. Others, huddled together about the room, glanced up and stiffened, fearing, perhaps, a commando raid. Their instincts tended toward survival, not gallantry. Military geegaws, even a monocle or two, flashed in the gloomy light. The duty corporal, who had caught El's arm as she stumbled by, was more helpful and very apologetic.

He would tell the captain she was there. He stepped to the door of his little office and groped around on the table. He seemed to have lost the telephone. El moved closer and peeped around him. The floor was a litter of old, rusty weapons, an armory, flung in any whichway. Here and there the vacant black eyes of shotguns stared out at her.

"The colonel's . . . ?"

The corporal nodded. "And more to come." He had found the telephone under a pile of dueling pistols. After brief words with the captain, he offered further apologies and suggested El might sit on a wicker settee in a corner beyond the front door.

It was very dark, but she unfolded her newspaper anyway and for the benefit of the officers, who fixed her with hooded, speculative eyes, pretended to read. She felt rather than saw them turn back to each other and listened to the murmur of their voices grow as they became engrossed in the supreme tactical problem of every peacetime army: promotions and transfers. These little mozzarella men, neatly packaged in khaki and braid, were or would someday be colonels, the springboard grade for despots. An uneasy thought. Whatever pessimistic conclusions she might have arrived at were interrupted by a voice from the shadows.

"You too!" She lowered the paper and could just make out Peter, standing, grinning above her. "What dastardly crime have you committed? Let your residence permit expire?"

"Funny, I was just wondering about it. Officially I'm an interpreter." She told him of Nardo's visit.

"Wonder who his prisoner is?" He sat down beside her and folded up her paper. "Bound to be someone we know. We'll know the robbers too. I'm convinced we will. Last night I worked out a list of possibilities—for instance, where has the money gone? We've agreed the talent's local, right? They knew exactly how the station functioned. At night. They could guess the confusion *after* the robbery and the roadblocks cutting off escape from the area. Now what would you do? Sit in a house or a barn or a cave, waiting to get caught with the eight hundred million lire you'd stolen, or would you get rid of it? How? El!" He broke off, disappointed and cross. "You're not listening."

"I am. I'm—I'm fascinated." She was, and terrified that his conclusion would be the right one. "How?"

"It's so obvious. They pack it up as fast as they can and take it right back to the station, where things are so upside down no one pays any attention. They ship it somewhere in Italy, so they can avoid customs and the *Finanza*. Then, whenever they want, they quietly pick up their boxes. No prying eyes. And they dispose of the money, however they planned. Another thing . . ." El turned away. He was obsessed by the robbery. Nothing else seemed to interest him. But she was wrong. He put his hand on her shoulder. "You're pale. Are you all right? How about some fresh air?"

"I'm fine," she lied. "Just concentrating." As far as it went, that, at least, was true. She was concentrating on the great internal lurches and shudders that first his theory of the disposal of the money and then his gentleness had churned up inside her. She had an almost irresistible urge to tell him the truth, to cry on his shoulder and be comforted. But—she took a deep breath, and, trying to keep her voice light, asked, "The other thing? What's that?"

"If you think about it, those four or six men all had to have plausible reasons to be free—you know, not expected at work, until at least noon, if not later. Who fits that schedule?"

"Almost nobody," she said very softly, convinced now that he knew and was playing cat and mouse with her.

"You've got an omelet for a brain! There are hundreds— all the night people." The mild slur ruffled El and the long list he reeled off, all men, completed her revival. The time had not come for surrender, much less confessions. ". . . Hospital orderlies, emergency utility crews, firemen, and—*and*, don't forget, the entire foreign colony." Looking very pleased with himself,

Peter stopped. El's heart did one of its acrobatic flip-flops. "Webster, Robert, Eddie Hughes—can't imagine him, but he's unemployed—their sons, that whole crowd at the party. All right, they have things to do, but they don't have to do them at any set time, or report to a timekeeper. They're free—legitimately—if they want to be." He stopped again, waiting for her reaction and maybe her admiration. El knew of only one subject that would distract him and she rejected it. Not now. She might... "Well? What do you think?" She had irritated him even more.

"Have you told the captain your theories?"

"I just figured it out last night. If he's not too busy, I might this—Oh, I almost forgot." He stretched his arm along the back of the settee and leaned closer to her, shielding her from the rest of the room. Had he lost his mind? "*You* were involved too." If she fainted—she never in her life had—this would be the perfect moment. Peter was silent. Finally she could bear it no longer. She looked at him. He was frowning blankly at his own hands, his thoughts far away. Her slight movement had drawn his attention. "Sorry, I was trying again—do you remember two years ago, just after I met you, there was an item in a paper about a man, a Milanese I think, who *did* get money across the border, a lot of it, with some trick? You told me about it. Can you remember how he—?" El started involuntarily and in an effort to hide it, straightened up, which gave her a glimpse of the room over Peter's shoulder.

"There's Cirillo, Peter." El pointed. "Over there, waving." It was the only time she had ever been glad to see him. Peter stood up and in a conversation of gestures arranged to meet Cirillo in the inner hall. Cirillo was holding the door for them.

"Is it revolution or war?" Peter asked, pointing back toward the clusters of would-be commanders in chief.

"Specialists," Cirillo growled, his eyes straight ahead.

"Guerrilla warfare. Sabotage. Infiltration—that is, according to the Ministry." His boots thudded along the hall at an automatic march pace and were answered, it seemed, by a swell of nervous, busy noises, as though the tiles had identified the vibrations of his approach and warned the corporals in their smoky little closets along the corridor of his approach. Chairs scraped. Typewriter keys clopped furiously on paper too quickly inserted to be fastened firmly against the roller. He cocked his head toward the doors. "Everything's screwed up around here. You'll see. And now these foreigners causing trouble. I say send them home where they belong." El cleared her throat loudly. "Present company excluded," he added in a rush. "With you it's different, signora." Peter clucked disapprovingly at him.

"Very '*Italia a Noi!*' The captain would object to such open Fascist sympathies." Cirillo stiffened, but ignored the remark. El hoped Peter would stop goading him. The Brigadier was a natural bully. They turned a second corner.

"Where in the world are we going?" she asked, feeling that each step took them deeper into past regimes.

"Here, at the end," Cirillo muttered. There was a desk in a space slightly wider than the corridor. "The colonel evicted the captain, *he* evicted *me*. This is my new office." He swept up the papers on his desk and locked them in a drawer. He would have treated his own mother no differently: to be suspicious was a moral obligation. "If you'll wait here." And he disappeared into the captain's office.

Seconds later Captain Nardo slipped around the door, closed it, and kept his hand on the knob. A dark man, he was as tall and trim and well pressed as ever, a dandy only slightly disguised in a drab uniform, but his eyes were puffy and his mouth drooped at the corners in uncharacteristic imitation of the bushy moustache he affected to age an otherwise boyish face. His manner echoed the same conscious precision. Ritual courtesies would be observed, impatience and inner frustrations suppressed, along with humor, which was one of his great off-duty charms. He made the conventional amends, none to be taken too literally. He was sorry to inconvenience them. They were both busy. He appreciated their cooperation. Dr. Testa, he need detain only a moment. His statement was ready. El sensed uncertainty and a quick decision. He would just get it. It would be better, perhaps—he opened the door.

"Don't bother." Peter followed him. "I'll sign it in here and be off." Cirillo was too late to do more than bow El in and close the door.

The room, of medium size with a disproportionately high ceiling, was one of the greater and lesser pits created by the haphazard remodeling. A sheen of light reached the upper regions of institutional tan through a high, narrow window, just barely requisitioned from the nobler apartment next door. The glare of horizontal neon bars, placed around the room at human height, revealed the lower regions, where straight chairs and desks, crowded together, looked miserably squat, as though they really belonged in a doll's house. Double occupancy had doubled the documentation and disorder. Stacks of cardboard files, ranged along the walls, on the desktops, and slumped on chairs, where they threatened to slide off, had been excuse enough for the cleaning squad to skip its daily incursion. Ashtrays and wastebaskets were overflowing.

At a table cleared of debris sat a soldier-typist, staring with palpable lust and confusion at Winkie Cromwell, who ignored him. She was smoking, one arm thrown over the back of her chair, her face lifted toward the ceiling in dewy-eyed transport, expressing a deep, as yet unidentified emotion. When Peter and Captain Nardo were well into the room, she swung halfway around in her chair, stared at them, and rose, ever so slowly, tipsily to her feet.

"Peter! How dear of you! How very dear!" she gasped and held out both her hands for him to take. "It's at times like this that one can count one's friends." She gave a strangled sob. This, then, was agony, not ecstasy. Whether caused by a death in the family or a gallstone was still not clear. She heeled very gently toward Peter and sighed. Before she collapsed completely, inextricably into his arms, he shifted the momentum of her body back in the general direction of her chair. El thought he gave her a slight, very slight push. She landed with a thud and gazed up at him, her eyes large and mournful. Peter and Nardo stared back at her, baffled, but fascinated.

What do you suppose they see? El wondered. For instance, that extraordinary costume—a white turtleneck jersey under blue-and-white-striped farmers' overalls, bib, built-in suspenders and all—did they see that? Or the unerring cruelty of the neon? The face was broader, flatter, her skin spongy. Two half-moon smears of brilliant blue eyeshadow, evidently the only make-up she had had time for, were grotesque. They also added the unfinished-clown piquancy so touching to Peter and the captain. El resigned herself: men might be cerebral, but not about women.

With blundering good intentions, the soldier-typist tipped files off a chair and realized, as he lifted it over to El, that he had sent a glacier of papers slithering across the floor. A quick look at his captain, at El, who shook her head, a quick sweep of his boot, and the papers were safely under his desk. He smiled guiltily at El, and they settled down in companionable silence, he to ogle Winkie, she to admire the stags at bay.

"So dear, so very dear," Winkie murmured vaguely at Peter. She seemed almost to shudder. "You will *help* me? Protect me?"

Peter made pompous, raspy noises in his throat, which committed him to nothing in particular. "That is, I assume . . ."

He looked over at Captain Nardo. "It's just a routine statement about—"

"Just a statement—yes." A tight smile confirmed the tacit warning: the subject was closed. Peter refused to understand. The two men glared at each other until finally Nardo drew a long breath, an inverted sigh, to stifle his impatience. "Just a statement—as to the periods in the last weeks, more specifically in the last seventy-two hours, when she can account for the activities of a certain Tullio Giusti." At the name Winkie blinked and two impressively globular tears rolled out and down her cheeks. Nardo would not be sidetracked. "Tullio Giusti is the missing mail-car guard. He was taken into custody this morning at . . ."

"That does not concern her," Peter objected.

"Taken into custody this morning—at her house. Now, Dr. Testa—if you would sign your statement . . ."

"You will help me, won't you, Peter? Please!" Winkie moaned. Too late Peter saw the wisdom of escape. He tried every excuse. He was a witness himself and a public official. El was there to interpret for her. She would also translate the formal statement. "Please, Peter," she moaned again. "It would make all the difference. You'd be on *my* side—not theirs!" She waved generally in the direction of Captain Nardo and the stenographer. Her eyes slipped over El. Not with any animosity. Help, among other things, she expected only from men. "Please. I feel so—so degraded. Yanked out of bed. Not even given time to get my face on—I'm a ghost without it, an absolute ghost! Now the police station! What will people think? For such a silly affair. My Italian friend—"

"At least give the man the dignity of a name," Peter broke in irritably. His appetite for treacle had fallen off. El fished in her mind for neutral thoughts and found the jingle "I never saw a purple cow . . ." It would not go away. Winkie wept noisily.

"Basta!" Captain Nardo shouted and slammed his hand

147

down on a pile of folders. "This is an investigation, not a hanging." He pointed to a chair and ordered Peter to sit on it. He ordered the stenographer to take down his questions and the witness' answers as they were translated. Winkie, he ordered in a slightly more gentle tone to tell the truth. She would have to sign a statement. She would be accountable for its accuracy. Now—her name, place and date of birth, her residence, local address, profession, and passport number.

Winkie, soothed by the banalities of officialese, hitched her chair closer to the desk and leaned an elbow on it, ready for a friendly chat. She blinked at the captain admiringly. He ignored her, looking at El, waiting for her translations. Peter, on his best behavior, never lifted his eyes from the captain's cap and his gloves, neatly folded inside it, on the corner of the desk. The stenographer had trouble with the foreign names. El wrote them out for him and Winkie prattled on in her bilingual patois, until, that is, Captain Nardo led her slowly along to Tullio and the truth seeped through to her: this was *not* a friendly chat. After that she clung to El's words, answered in English, and wrung her large, bony hands. Her evasions and euphemisms did not veil the sordid little story.

Late the summer before she had met Tullio in a local café and had, on her return, "renewed the acquaintance." They found many "areas of mutual interest" and soon a "deeper relationship" (*ahimè!*) developed. Tullio had arranged to take a week of his vacation, which they spent to their "mutual satisfaction" at her house. He then suggested, that is he hinted, that he could arrange for another week of "sick leave." She marveled, really marveled at the laxness of the Italian government. State employees did as they pleased. Disgraceful! However—they had their second week together.

At no time had he been out of her sight. El glossed over the more wanton episodes Winkie offered in proof. They verified little, except possibly a bawdy imagination, and would have driven the stenographer completely gaga. At no time from the fifteenth of May until that morning had they been separated. El kept her voice without inflection and translated word for word, not sure whether Winkie was splitting hairs or simply lying. She had, after all, been at the Bourton-Hamptons'. Tullio had not. Captain Nardo flipped through reports.

"Private, we won't need you for a few minutes. Why don't you step into the hall for a cigarette," he suggested, and picked up two papers he had selected. "Yes, here we are. On the night before the robbery, signora Cromwell, you and . . ."

Winkie admitted that the night before the robbery they had gone out for dinner to a pizzeria, had quarreled over friends of his who had come in: she wanted to join them, he said she wouldn't understand their conversation. Her feelings were hurt, so she left. But she had waited in the car, her car, for him. Maybe half an hour. Oh, was it an hour? She also admitted that she had not gone with him to apply for sick leave and, after prodding from El, that the night after the robbery she had kept a "prior engagement," to her great displeasure. The captain was stern about her elastic approach to accuracy. She whimpered quietly and he relented: with these discrepancies corrected her story agreed with Tullio's, which, as far as the robbery was concerned, cleared him of any suspicion.

The young soldier was called back. Winkie romped through her new improved version and watched him bash away on the typewriter, pouting kittenishly each time he braided the keys together, which was often. She was enjoying herself. Captain Nardo sighed and caught El's eye.

"If you can have it ready, ask her to come day after tomorrow at noon to sign it," he said very quietly and batted his eyes in a mild burlesque of his witness. "Warn her that Tullio may have trouble with the railway authorities. Contrary to her impression there *are* rules and laws that govern state employees." Suddenly he grinned and added *sotto voce,* "They're not enforced, but that's beside the point." A footnote El assumed he did not wish translated.

Winkie was in no hurry. She took out a compact, lipstick, eye liner, and a comb-brush and went about an almost complete toilette. She screwed her face into the particular grimace, every woman has her own, that would allow her to apply eye makeup. She looked like an outsized guppy. Nardo studiously read his reports. Peter gaped at her, his expression bemused, embarrassed, and curious too. He might have stumbled into the wrong bedroom at the wrong moment. Of the three El found Peter the most amusing to watch, which, when he noticed, sent him back to his study of the captain's hat and gloves. In fact he seemed spellbound by them. He frowned at them. He flipped the fingers of the gloves. Finally he propped his chin on his fist and stared at them.

"I've got it," he crowed triumphantly. "Captain, I remember what . . ." Nardo jerked his head up from his papers and narrowed his eyes, slipping them toward Winkie. A shake of the head, an emphatic order to keep still. "But . . ." She had collected her paraphernalia and was shoving it into a large red felt bag. Nardo sprang to his feet.

"Then we'll expect you day after tomorrow," he said so pleasantly he might have referred to a social engagement. "Ask for Brigadier Cirillo." She dithered about. He waited. At last she stood up and swooped over to his desk.

"Captain, you've been *too* kind," she simpered at him. "All rather silly. But now you know Tullio had *nothing* to do with it. There, *do* admit it!" She paused and, remembering that Nardo did not speak English, turned to El. "Be a duck and tell him I hope he'll come to see my house—and me. He's rather cute, don't you think?"

"Sorry, interpreters never make passes at captains." El's smile was guileless, but she felt it twisting to a smirk. "Professional ethics." Winkie glared at her, spun around, and presented her hand to Nardo—to be kissed. Impassive except for a ticklike flutter of his eyebrows, he performed with gentle solemnity. She clung to him, hand and eye, as long as she decently could before swinging quarter-circle, arm outstretched, to offer the same delight to Peter, who, after a moment of doubt, twisted it over and shook it. Without further ado, Winkie swept out, no mean feat in a pair of bibbed overalls.

As the door closed Nardo whispered across the desk to El, "What did you refuse to translate?" She exaggerated a bit.

"She's not Hermione, captain," Peter consoled him. "But she *is* tall and blonde!" Nardo's cheeks crinkled in a grin, even his mustache seemed to droop less dejectedly.

"Which reminds me—there *is* one more question." He considered Peter with a critical frown. "Not official, just curiosity. Tell me—did you really sleep all the way to Rome? With La Hendricks in the compartment?" Peter nodded, proud of his apparently superhuman accomplishment. "Hmm! Really!" Nardo stroked his mustache, musing and unconvinced. "Must be the English blood!"

MOMENTS LATER Matteo opened the door on a scene of unbecoming merriment, the very kind of behavior he deplored in the young.

"Once that—uh—lady left, I thought . . ." he began testily, then stopped and, in something of a huff, tapped his foot, waiting for their attention. "I called, but that brigadier . . ." He tried, gave up, and tried again. "So I came myself. I felt you should know. These . . ." He waved some clippings at them. "Are from today's papers with the text of the letter the thieves left at the station. And here, captain, is the copy you gave Dr. Testa. The variations are obvious." He put the clippings and Nardo's copy of the letter on the desk. "I'll leave you to draw the appropriate conclusions. *I* must get back to the office." He stared pointedly at Peter, bowed to the captain and slightly less deeply to El.

"Thank you for your suggestion about where to find Tullio Giusti," Nardo called after him. "You were right."

"Families can be very trying, but they are useful at times."

"We appreciate your help. It would have taken us much longer to find him." Nardo was doing his formal best. From the door Matteo bestowed a thin-lipped smile on him and left. The captain made a face at Peter. "Must be like spending eight hours a day with your mother-in-law. Well—let's see what he's brought." He looked at the clippings, shook his head, and passed them on, some to Peter, some to El. The copy of the letter he pushed to the front of the desk between them. El knew she must read them with a good show of interest.

Convinti che non deve soffrire la povera gente per le sviste di un governo maldestro, rendiamo gli assegni delle pensioni ed i documenti relativi sottratti per sbaglio durante l'assalto al vagone postale nella stazione di San Felice Val Gufo. Ci teniamo che siano puntualmente pagate—senza i soliti imbroglietti, truffe, longaggini o addirittura lo smarrimento totale. Onde assicurare ciò, mandiamo copie della presente ai giornali, pregando che la pubblichino.

c.c. *Corriere della Sera*
     Il Messaggero
     Paese Sera

[Convinced that the poor must not suffer for the mistakes of an inept government, we are returning the pension checks and relative documents taken by mistake during the robbery of the mail car in the station of San Felice Val Gufo. We are anxious that they should be promptly paid—without the usual imbroglios, frauds, bureaucratic delays, or outright total disappearance. Toward assuring this we are sending copies of this present letter to the newspapers, asking that they should publish it.]

c.c. *Corriere della Sera*
    Il Messaggero
    Paese Sera

Except for an elusive, non-Italian quality, which might be conceptual rather than linguistic, she saw nothing odd about it. She read the top clipping in her lot. Her heart thudded again. Matteo had underlined in red *"copie al,"* followed by the names of the newspapers. She knew without looking back at their letter that it said "c.c." Her mistake? Kate's? It made no difference now. She forced herself to look at the other clippings. She even switched back and forth, comparing them, before she looked up. The captain was coming to the end of his pile of reports. Peter was switching back and forth through the clippings, as she had, his face without expression. She could not decide whether he was intentionally noncommittal for some private reason she did not like to imagine, or whether the abbreviation "c.c." meant nothing to him.

"Well?" Nardo finally asked, tidying his papers. "Matteo's made his point, but I still ..."

"A typographical error?" Peter pondered. "It has to be. There isn't a phrase that fits and ..."

"In Italian, Peter," El specified. Instinct or lightning revelation? Later she was not sure, she simply *knew* on odds it was better to point it out than have them discover it later and wonder at her silence. "In English it's the common abbreviation for 'carbon copy.' I can't think of any other answer."

"So you're saying that whoever wrote that note normally writes in English?" Nardo sounded doubtful. "That gives us someone in this area who writes Italian, but is presumably English or American. The typing is good. Or . . ." Peter waggled his finger at El.

"What did I tell you!" He swiveled around and leaned eagerly across the desk. "Captain, it all fits."

". . . or a clever Italian who knows English well enough to throw us off the track. *You,* for instance, Dr. Testa."

"I'm a two-finger man myself. But listen, I'm serious. If you list the people who had an excuse to be free *all morning*— I did it last night—the foreigners are the largest single group. No one would question their presence anywhere. Maybe Cirillo, but . . ." He brushed aside the idea. "Just think about it—and the letter."

"I'll keep *you* in reserve, but the Americans and English don't strike me as types to rob trains. . . ." Nardo's voice drifted away in speculation. He frowned slightly, stroking the lower fringe of his moustache from the center outward with the thumb and index finger of one hand, feathering it neatly to the line of his upper lip. The habit, the unconscious companion of thought, El found oddly attractive. What sort of private life could he possibly have? Meandering in those byways of feminine logic, she forgot the actual physical person and was startled by his voice, now very positive. "No! Absolutely not! Anyone who robs a train does it for money. You, *dottore,* surely have enough. Our English and Americans have much more than enough . . ."

"Not all of them . . ."

"Dr. Testa! You of all people," Nardo chided. "Every Italian schoolboy knows that *all* foreigners are rich." His grin was wry.

"Many of them work," El objected. "I do."

"Most don't." His voice had assumed the flat resonance of absolute power that El had heard earlier in the hall. "They have *no* reason to steal, *no* way of disposing of the money once they steal it." He glowered first at one, then the other, challenging them to disagree. El was elated, but shrugged, hoping that would be an ambiguous enough answer to please him. Peter was dogged.

"But the mistake on the letter? Their mobility? The foreigners are at least . . ."

"Take the last point. Even the most fluent foreigner, like signora Kendall, can't walk into the local bank and deposit eight hundred million lire cash in her account, or even two hundred million, supposing they divided it evenly, without the cashier asking a lot of nasty questions. Cashiers are dumb, but they'd notice that! How are they to get rid of it? That's the point. Foreigners can't, period."

Peter stood up, shaking his head. "You know your business and I won't have any if I don't get back to my office, but I still think they're among the possibles."

The captain eased himself out from behind the desk and offered his hand. "Proof is all either of us needs," he conceded with a smile. "Did you sign the statement?"

Peter nodded. "*I* almost forgot."

"One thing's on your side—foreigners can't deposit lire, only foreign currency. That's the law. Of course Italy is the country of exceptions." He reached over and flipped the fingers of the captain's gloves, still lying in his cap. "You won't like this either. Your gloves reminded me. The garbage collector, the one I spoke to in the Piazza—*he* was wearing gloves—gray

155

suede gloves." El closed her eyes and hung her head, realizing for the first time that, right or wrong, she did not want to be caught in this mess. And she *was* caught.

She calculated without Captain Nardo. "Gloves! *Gray suede gloves!*" he scoffed, his cheeks flushing angrily. "Gray suede? Why not pea green? You think it's funny—foreigners who rob banks, garbage collectors wearing *gray* suede gloves. Get out of here! My life's already a nightmare without the Anglo-Saxon sense of humor. Now get out!" Again he slammed his fist down on the pile of reports.

For their own separate reasons Peter and El were delighted to obey—immediately and in silence. The officers were still in the hall, discussing peacetime tactics.

13

"WELL, ARCH, where was it this time?" Robert Pound asked, looking beyond Webster, thwarting, for the moment, his further remarks on the villainy of sons. Lacey was grateful. To each his own addiction: hers was not children.

"South America. Seven months of jungle and parasites." Arch Stanley's voice came to them as a hollow rumble from the interior of the fireplace. He was sitting on its wide ledge, coaxing the fire along with professional, rather absentminded precision. "This time I really earned my three months off." Careful not to topple his pyramid, he very gently eased a log. New, more confident flames burst out and he ducked back around to face them, his deep tan slightly reddened by the fire's heat. For a bearish man, he was very graceful. "But what's been going on here—beyond the get-rich-quick schemes of your boys? What about the famous robbery?" Lacey had seen this trick of manner before. He liked to play the boyish innocent, asking quick, artless questions, then widening his light gray eyes, which looked confused, almost naked, as though he habitually wore glasses and had lost them. He had set out, consciously or not, to diagnose the state of the neighborhood. He needed the patient's symptoms.

"What about parasites?" Robert insisted.

"The usual spying on the life-cycles of two or three little pests—and the usual cures—cesspools and water."

"Once in Africa," Robert began, his tone suggesting that his experience had a direct connection to Arch's, "I found a tribe . . ." Beyond him Lacey saw that the gray seamless sky had darkened into twilight. Against it, occasional heavy raindrops were silvery comets, and slightly blurred, across the courtyard in the study, stood El and Peter deep in conference.

"What the hell *are* they up to?" Webster mumbled to himself. Lacey had known he would slough off Africa, but for a moment, just a moment, thought he had eyes in the back of his head. Then she recognized his *idée fixe*.

"Aren't you glad the boys have caught on to the notion they should do *something*?" she asked, getting up. It was time to pull the curtains, even offer them a drink.

" 'Course, as long as it's honest, but the way . . ."

Lacey stopped listening, distracted by a phantom warrior in a crested helmet, who was apparently crawling along very slowly on his hands and knees behind the sofa. At the end table legs blocked his exit. He reversed, even more slowly, with a marked dip and lurch of white plumage.

" 'Jinsky! *Shame* on you!" A long white cockade arched up and flapped wanly. A backward lurch produced the great white body. Seconds later the head reared up, over the back of the sofa and around. The body did its best to follow, rocking the sofa. In his frenzy Nijinsky smeared his jaw and the sodden object it held along Robert's cheek, which earned him a grunt and a swat and sent him scrabbling out of his tunnel, across the room. He braked in a sitting position, collided with Lacey's legs, dumping her back in her chair, and offered his paw.

"Shame on you!" she repeated, trying not to laugh. He looked very apologetic. His gray plug, chewed to gummy perfection, still trailed from his mouth. "Afraid of the rain?" Her voice was too conciliatory. He smiled and dropped his prize on her knee. She shuddered and batted it away. It plopped down near Arch, who grabbed it with the fire tongs.

"Shall I?" he asked, swinging it over the flames. One quick look and she nodded emphatically. There were footsteps in the hall.

"Oh Peter! You left the door open!" El was cross. "Where's that fool Nijinsky gotten to now?"

"In here," Lacey called. The mushy blob already sizzled in the fire. "He's all right." He put his head down on her knee and looked sorrowful. When El came to the door, he got up reluctantly, turned, and slowly rippled from the room.

"Anybody hurt?" Her question brought a chorus of denials, some sympathy for Nijinsky, and Robert's plaintive inquiries about what slimy thing had massaged his face, all of which drowned out the scratching and clawing of Nijinsky's return. He bounded into the room, a gray glove, obviously the unmasticated mate of his first treasure, flapping about his muzzle. Proudly he offered it to Lacey.

"Were you saving it for dessert?" She stuffed it under the cushion of her chair and took his collar. "That was your curtain call." Together they left the room, Nijinsky trying his best to loiter, but resigned, head down. On her way back Lacey stopped in the kitchen for glasses, ice, and a brief consideration of their new logistic problem. Still mulling over the possibilities, she crossed the hall to the living room.

"My God! More noble savages!" Webster bellowed, looking up at her. She almost dropped the tray. "Here, Lacey, let me take that from you." He walked off toward the far end of the room, still talking. "That's a lot of rot and you know it, Robert.

Africans would be better off under colonial rule—and we'd be safer . . ."

"All I said was—*they took care of me,* healed my leg," Robert groaned. Lacey watched Webster lean over to help El get bottles out of a low chest and wished his manners were less correct. She needed a second alone with El to warn her—and she had lost it. She would have to sit like a brooding hen on the glove and wait her chance, she decided, and started casually toward her chair. She lost that too. Without warning Peter, who had been standing near Arch, talking, flung himself into it, wiggled forward, and made a broad gesture with one arm. They were earnestly discussing British politics, a subject neither knew much about, but one that Lacey recognized as sufficiently manly and unsolvable to please.

"And don't start on the evils of colonialism," Webster warned, sauntering back to his place on the sofa. With the men safely lost in world order, Lacey slipped off to the end of the room and whispered to El,

"Did he see the glove?" El shook her head. "Now he's sitting on it."

"If you can, shove it in the woodbox." El looked back over her shoulder. "Listen, Nardo and Peter *are* investigating the 'foreign question.' And watch out for Arch. They've dragged him in too. Given him a 'detailed briefing,' according to Peter. It's to be a very quiet, on-their-own dig into the whereabouts, bank accounts, typewriters—that sort of thing." She poured a jigger of whiskey in a glass, then looked at it doubtfully. "Maybe I shouldn't. Peter has a list of foreign residents. A dozen names were missing—they don't even know . . ."

"El, we haven't time . . ."

"We're to lead Webster and Robert around to the robbery. Should be fun. Of course, we're excluded. You're nonresident,

I'm too noble." With lifted eyebrows and a little on-again, off-again smile she managed to look like an affable idiot. "Oh, and they're looking for an Olivetti portable or Lettera 44, so I made Peter take a sample of *yours*. That seemed a nice touch."

" 'Who knows what evil lurks in the hearts of' women?" Lacey intoned. " 'The shadow *knows*,'—but he'd never tell." She was suddenly aware that strain brought on a deranged cheerfulness.

"She," corrected El and started toward the other end of the room. "Anyone who wants a drink will have to fix his own." Lacey hurried over to stand in front of Peter.

"You stole my chair. The least you can do is get me a drink." She struggled to look him in the eye. The glove, kneaded almost free by Peter's moving about in the chair, now dangled its fingers in full view below the cushion. He crossed his legs and the fingers waggled in a macabre way, as though a woman, suffocating in down, begged for help.

"You just want Arch to yourself." He did not budge.

"Give the lady her chair," Arch said, standing up. "And we'll get the drinks. That's why they keep us around—to bartend."

As soon as she was safely alone, Lacey started burrowing in the wood basket. When she could go no deeper without risking a great clatter and thumping of logs, she palmed the glove, shoved it in and let the wood subside over it. The others were still crowded around the table, with El, Webster, and Robert, standing to one side, looking at the room. Webster studied technicalities of construction. Robert had his glasses off and his nose stuck up against a tall bead-and-pearl altar decoration, one of a pair, each with its own brass urn. Watching them, Lacey was aware of the room as she had not been in a long time.

It was a very large, very Tuscan room with its polished brick floor, its heavy linen draperies, and the towering stone fireplace, but it was also a room of gentle contradictions. El, never one for quaint milking stools or ash settles, had jumbled in the possessions from her various lives—comfortable chairs and sofas, rugs from her American past, with southern Italian altar decorations, fruitwood chests, and medieval etchings—and willed them to get along together. Probably she had seen nothing odd in the disparate parts. They were, after all, the familiar parts of herself, and they had folded into an easy, rather formal whole, not unlike her, except that a room has no unknown dimensions of temperament. This one lulled visitors. They liked themselves, and therefore others, a little better and so were reluctant to leave. Again Lacey felt the contradictions slipping away from her, but she had no doubts of the room's effect, which reminded her of dinner. She was wondering whether it would stretch to Robert and Webster, as it might have to, when Peter and Arch came back with drinks.

"What was that Nijinsky had in his mouth?" Peter asked, handing her a glass. She busily hunted a place to put it down.

"Unidentified sodden object." Arch shrugged. Not satisfied, Peter lifted his eyebrows at Lacey.

"The first. The second looked like one of El's wood-toting gloves," Lacey answered reluctantly. Out of the corner of her eye she could see El, sitting very still on the sofa, listening. To her amazement Peter stooped over and began rooting around in the wood.

" 'Seek and ye shall find,' " El commented to the air.

"*This* is a wood-toting glove?" Peter muttered, straightening up, the glove held up between thumb and forefinger. It was a very clean, soft, expensive gray suede glove.

"My grandmother didn't think so, but her hands were

bigger than mine. Not much else I can do..." El stopped in mock alarm. "Oh dear, Sherlock's still suspicious. Get your magnifying glass and come with me. Upstairs. I have a drawer crammed with her gloves, including a dozen pairs of sixteen-button white kid. She couldn't resist a bargain." Peter had grinned at El's banter, but was obviously still puzzled. She pretended not to notice. "I'm going to be terribly chic. Purple kid for mowing the lawn, taupe, I thought, for silver-polishing, and gray..." He dropped the glove back on the woodpile.

"How did the mutt get them?" he insisted and was roundly jeered. On some earlier junket into the house. Or El had dropped them outside, working. Or... If he must play sleuth, Webster urged him to solve the more challenging mystery he could offer and Peter, bemused by the proliferation of gray suede gloves, fell into the trap. Again they listened to the few facts and many speculations about Alan and Henry's activities, which except for Lacey's adroit flummery, might have turned into a full-fledged seminar on youth: she mentioned the Rolls. Soon they were summoned from cubic displacement and gas consumption by Arch, who had moved along the fireplace ledge for a quiet chat with El.

"I need a witness," he announced. "She's just proposed to me—I think."

"What you need is a fast car," Robert observed and slouched further down in his chair. "How about a Rolls?"

"Bachelors should carry probability insurance." Webster's was a judicial interpretation. "Women are predatory. They're looking for a free ride. A poor, innocent man—"

"Innocent man!" El turned on him. "I resent that."

"But that's what she offered—protection." Arch came to her defense. "A marriage of convenience, so I wouldn't be the victim of my friends. They want to marry me off—preferably to some lonely widow they know." He shook his head, discouraged. "They won't give up and I've no talent for it. None whatever."

"Neither have I," El agreed, doubling her legs up under her. She drifted on, perfectly naturally and without preamble, into a discussion of typewriters. Apparently nothing could have intrigued Webster, Robert, and Arch more. Each had his say. None had the right make, though Robert explained in detail that he had replaced Kate's old Lettera 44 with an electric. He had never been sure: maybe she would have preferred a watch. Webster still used a prewar Remington because its letters were so sharp the *o*'s, *b*'s, *d*'s, and *p*'s cut holes in the paper. He liked the idea that he wrote in filigree. And what were their theories about the robbery? Lacey, who was already feeling a bit like Alice at the Mad Hatter's tea party, decided he also thought in filigree.

"Let's be methodical about it," Arch suggested. "Where were people between say four A.M. and seven A.M. the morning of the robbery? Even some of you were up and out. Peter and Hermione. Kate took an early train, didn't she? Alan and Henry? Where were they? Or anyone else who might be suspect."

"In bed, asleep," El stated without hesitation. The idea seemed to amuse her. "Or if they have good sense, they'll *say* they were." She looked from one to the other for objections. Only Robert tried. Alan and Henry—he wasn't very sure . . . El pounced. "I never said they were *at home* in bed." And caught her mouse. Robert lapsed into abashed silence. Arch was not so easily weaned from the methodical.

"Then take the obvious suspects—railway or post-office employees, even the stationmasters or the police. They'd know about the shipments. Imagine one about to retire on a small pension—"

"That's psychologically wrong." El pounced again. "Remember the kind of Italian who applies for a state job. He wants security. He's not a gambler—too cautious. He'll take a bribe, but he won't risk stealing a billion." Peter was watching El thoughtfully, perplexed by her sudden testiness. Lacey hoped he would credit it to impatience with Arch's prosaic deductions. If she could find a dotty, but just possible suspect . . . "And," El went on triumphantly, "besides, he would need three others, maybe more, as desperate. There aren't that many, that daring, assigned to this little junction. Outsiders he wouldn't trust much. Anyway, it's too geriatric." Arch retreated into the fireplace to fiddle with logs and probably with rebuttals, which Webster made unnecessary.

"No, no, *no*! You people have it all wrong." He leaned back, smiling to himself. "You don't read the papers. These days only two groups get things done efficiently—the Mafia and the feminists! Now what if the Mafia started a women's auxiliary? There's an idea. . . ."

"That's hard to treat as anything but the product of a feverish brain," Robert announced, standing up. "Come on, Webster Algernon, before the firewater gets to your legs. Time to go home, old scout. No fuss—sleep will do wonders." He grabbed Webster's arm, twisted it into a playful hammer lock, and, murmuring nonsense in his ear, propelled him in jumps and jerky side steps toward the front door. "Nice and easy, Webster. Everything'll look better tomorrow. If not, I know a doctor. Nice man. Gentle, understanding . . ."

"Unhand me, you idiot!" Webster struggled good-naturedly.

"Now, now, don't get excited."

"Who's excited? Just think of *Hermione*! Wouldn't she . . . ?"

"Perfect little den mother, our Hermione," said Robert soothingly.

"She'd love it. Always telling men they can't get it . . ."

"Webster! *Not* in front of the ladies. Mind your manners."

At the door they paused long enough to thank El. Webster pushed Robert out, then stuck his head back inside.

"Sometime when this maniac's not around, I'll explain my theory. The trouble is no one *ever* takes me seriously."

GOOD HUMOR PREVAILED through dinner and conversation was hyper-rational, at least by San Felice summer standards. Arch was rather stuffy about Webster's Rolls project. Somehow national pride and honor came into it. El and Peter contributed progress reports. Webster had found what he considered the Roman version of the little old lady who never drove further than the grocery store—a Hungarian countess, whose name, he insisted, was Hammacher Schlemmer. He was sure she was reliable: she lived in Via Giulia. He also confided to El that "she" was known as "Delilah." The Rolls, it was finally established, not the Hungarian countess. In the next month her maiden voyage from Rome to San Felice would be aborted four times and her name modified to "Delilah, the Golden Whore." After a fifth round of costly tinkering, she made it, but no one, with the possible exception of Webster, expected her to see Genoa, much less Albuquerque or Ankara. That evening they underestimated her flair for disruption and passed on to more pressing local affairs, such as the private investigation of the robbery.

Peter proposed that he and Arch divide the foreign colony systematically, which sounded efficient, but in practice went, "I'll take Hermione, you take La Cromwell. Then I get Martha Gelder—no, that's not fair. You take Hermione and La Cromwell, I'll do Martha and Anatolia. Oh God . . ." El suggested an antipathy index, take an average, then . . . Lacey juggled the permutations and soon they were talking about bomb shelters in London, of which both Arch and Peter had dim, little-boy memories, about a suitable bride for Nijinsky, and, by some limpid irrelevance they could never trace, about childhood ambitions.

When they had finished dinner, they stayed at the big round table by the kitchen fire, sipping wine, talking. Arch told them about South America. He was almost apologetic: he should not enjoy what was supposed to be his work. The telephone rang and El went off to answer it, muttering about victims of the Puritan Ethic. She was gone a long time. Peter thought Arch should write a book.

"Ah, the San Felice virus, our own endemic problem!" Arch shook his head. "And what would you call this epic?"

"How does . . . *The Cesspool Connection* strike you?" Lacey asked, giving the title oracular emphasis. "Definitely a Book-of-the-Month. Then a paperback with a red banner 'Soon to Be a Major Motion Picture.' I can just see it. Don't laugh. It's as 'filmatic' as cancer of the prostate and a friend of mine—"

"Which reminds me—how's the script going?" Arch's voice insinuated neutral concern and cheerful sympathy in the exact dosage prescribed for calming disturbed personalities. "Collaborations can be very difficult. Sometimes technical disagreements become per—"

"Before we get to the couch," Peter broke in, leaning toward Lacey. She was busy deploying ranks of bread crumbs about the table and did not look up. "I want to know what it's about, this script. Or is it a secret? You can say yes or no to that, at least." Once the script was mentioned, she had expected the fatal question. She placed the pepper mill in command of one army, the salt mill in command of the other, and sighed.

"It's not a secret, just hard to explain. It's a mystery—

sort of reversed cops and robbers. The bad guys are the good guys, if you see what I mean." She stopped, giving them time to convince themselves they had understood and was delighted by their confused expressions. "You don't. Well, El and I think the 'good guys'—police, authorities, whoever—have some blind spots. The 'bad guys'—criminals, reformers, again whoever— could take advantage of those blind spots. They commit a crime and the chase is the story. *Who* actually gets caught. Now do you see?" If anything Arch and Peter looked more muddled. By the time El came back from the telephone, Lacey had them lost in the complexities of casting. "It's important. The characters' personalities have to fit the actions they are given—or is it vice versa? Otherwise the audience won't believe in them. An El-type, for instance, wouldn't be a plausible streetwalker."

"I would have thought," Peter began tentatively, "that in a mystery it was just the opposite, that El would be the ideal murderer because you'd never suspect her. I grant she couldn't be a house painter, but she could do unexpected horrors in any . . ."

"Funny," El said mostly to herself. "I've painted so many houses!" Lacey knew from her voice that El's tongue was on automatic pilot, her mind elsewhere, chewing over a new woe, and was almost relieved when the telephone rang again. Lacey pressed on, explaining as obliquely as possible that she had meant the general characters before the plot began, while Peter was already busy with the plot. El came to her rescue just in time.

"That was Plum MacIntosh," she announced, as though the name told all.

"His mother was horticulturally confused," Arch suggested helpfully. "Why is it that American names are such a mix of genealogy and Hollywood kitsch?"

"Just French. Plum's an acronym for—" And again the

telephone rang. El left them in midsentence and Lacey, not sure that her silt of complications had effectively buried the script, decided on domestic activity. She would make coffee.

When El reappeared, the kitchen was in reasonable order, the dishes soaking, the Neapolitan coffee pot turned, and Peter, Arch, and Lacey, while they waited for it to drip, were once more settled around the table, pooling their knowledge of Greek beaches. El sat with them so silent and inattentive that Peter reached over for her hand. She shook her head, almost forgetting to smile: nothing wrong. Still Lacey was anxious. She rattled on about beaches, but found herself listening for a distant sound, as El seemed to be.

"Damn!" El said, suddenly standing up. "I thought I'd talked her out of it. Maybe she won't stay." A car engine labored closer and almost stalled. They heard the snarl of gears. The engine raced and again almost stalled. "Not much of a mudder, is she? Oh, sorry—Martha. She's furious about something. Liquor does . . ." She hurried off, leaving that to their imaginations.

At the table conversation progressed in pantomime. Peter's fingers stole silently across the table as into the night, suggesting they escape. Lacey mimed coffee and Arch was for a combination of the two. When the rumble of voices in the hall stopped, they froze, waiting to hear the front door close. Instead the footsteps came toward them. A moment later El, very much the mistress of the house, stood in the doorway.

"Martha's come. Why don't you go in the living room. I'll bring coffee in just a minute." Only an eavesdropper, who could not see the peremptory waves of her hand, would have mistaken it for an invitation. It was an order.

They obeyed and were confronted by what Peter later described as the "arresting sight" of Martha in a red plush caftan. She must have heard them in the hall. She had moved away, glass in hand, from the liquor bottles, thrown back her head, and taken a deep breath, which set in motion a large gold medallion down about where her stomach may have been. It glittered and flashed some secret message of fury, while, in profile, she glared at them from one heavily made-up malevolent eye.

"Oh, I thought you were El." She let out her breath in a gust of disappointment. "Stop milling around. You make my head spin. Peter, do see to the fire. A drink, anyone?" In her role as hostess *pro tem* she turned majestically to each of them, revealing the other eye for their admiration. If the left had been sinister with black elongations and shadings, a Lady Macbeth eye, the right, all silver and blue eyeshadow, was definitely Violetta. Arch was transfixed. Lacey imagined him deciding which Martha he dared ask about typewriters. He collapsed into a chair and stared wistfully at Peter, who, deep in the fireplace, had achieved relative safety. Martha must be distracted from her avowed intent to cause trouble. Lacey grabbed at the first wisp of thought that floated through her mind and chanted,

" 'Fill, oh fill the pirate's glass.' " Not exactly inspired, she thought, snuggling herself as nonchalantly as possible into a nest of cushions on the sofa, but it might bring Martha to herself. O frabjous day!

"Ah, our own little Buttercup!" There was no mistaking Martha's sarcasm. Peter backed out of the fireplace just in time to hear, "*Dear* little Buttercup." He straightened up abruptly and cracked his head on a jutting stone support. Arch stared quizzically at each in turn, his head lowered as though he were looking over Ben Franklin glasses.

"Buttercup, smuttercup," Lacey mumbled, then added, more kindly to Peter. "Nothing to worry about. Just a bit of Gilbert and Sullivan. Some people never get over it." Peter retreated into the fireplace and stayed there, uselessly shifting logs, while she tried to hold her own in a game of Ping-Pong quotations. *The Pirates of Penzance* was a gold mine. " 'It is a glorious thing to be a pirate king,' " she cautioned Martha, who flung back a bit from *The Mikado:* " 'I've got a little list—I've got a little list.' " That broke the nonsense code! Arch would surely know the verse.

> As someday it may happen that a victim must be
>   found
> I've got a little list—I've got a little list
> Of society offenders who might well be underground
> And who never would be missed—who never would
>   be missed.

" 'Let us shut our eyes and talk about the weather,' " Lacey urged. The answer from *Trial by Jury* did not augur well. Defeat, however honorable, was near.

"No! Oh, Martha, no!" Arch groaned in outrage. " 'Dusk.' Not 'dark,' '*dusk*'!"

" 'Dark,' " she snapped, baring her teeth ominously.

"Now, my dear, allow an Englishman his—"

". . . his usual condescension. No, I won't. Especially because you're wrong. *I* know the libretto." Her anger calmed him.

"Just a slight lapse of the memory, I'm sure. The lines go

> You'll soon get used to her looks, said he,
> And a very nice girl, you'll find her.
> She may well pass for forty-three
> In the dusk with the light behind her."

Martha squinted at him through slits in the harlequin makeup, looking evil and coy at the same time. From the doorway El's voice surprised them.

"Didn't your mothers ever tell you it's not nice to talk about your hostess behind her back?" She held a red lacquer tray with small cups and a silver coffee pot. "Besides, you exaggerate." She did a little two-step jig, mouthing "In the dusk with the light behind her," and just reached the table as the cups performed a near-fatal glissade of their own. "That was close!" She looked up straight into Martha's glowering Lady Macbeth eye. "My God! Where'd you get the black eye? Not *Arch*?" For several seconds Martha stood absolutely still. Slowly her eyes widened and, in a movement that was surprisingly agile for so heavy a woman, she bolted from the room. Relief tricked them: they laughed.

Martha stormed back from the hall, shouting, railing at them. They could sneer, condescend to her, make her the butt. They always had. Oh-so-literary ladies! Dabblers! Dilettantes! Plain amateurs! Parasites! As her hysteria mounted the more rococo insults she tried to fling at them tangled on her tongue. She . . . She . . . She spluttered. Two pre-pretentious bitches and their st-st-stooges. Who were they to laugh at *her*? Finally frustrated, still enraged and about to cry, she wheeled around and again left them. Four strides later the door to the bathroom slammed.

"Coffee anyone?" El's voice was so normal, they jumped.

"From Gilbert and Sullivan to Grand Guignol," Lacey fumed. "She's crazy."

"Menopausal," corrected Arch, taking a cup of coffee.

"Jealous, I'd say." Peter reached for his cup, but El had stopped pouring to listen. From the bathroom came the full, deep, and often flat notes of "O don fatale." "Ah, so now it's Verdi. If she'll stick to him, we can have some fun." He cringed as another slithery note came to a bad end.

"Please—not the *Requiem*," Lacey begged. "Couldn't we

172

just ignore the whole thing, pretend it never happened?" Which was not very grown-up, she knew, but she would rather pretend the social parquet had never splintered and warped than feel splintered and warped herself. She noticed El was jangled too. With very wifely distraction she had put a teaspoon of sugar in Peter's coffee and stirred it, before handing it to him. He had the answer! His own operatic voodoo. Imagine Martha in the most ungrateful roles—Norma bedaubed in blue woad or Azucena in rags—then she was funny. How about Amneris?

He broke into a triumphal, tootling whistle and was so intent on conjuring up elephants that he failed to see Martha fling herself into the room, a rose between her teeth, her fingers snapping high over her head. *La*-la-la-la, *la*-la-la-la, she trolled, swooping around Arch, curling back to stroke his cheek and stomping on toward Peter with a flamenco tattoo of heels and lusty bellows. He prepared for the honor about to be bestowed on him by arranging his face into a mask of such greedy, witless enthusiasm that El put her head down on the arm of her chair. Martha's dips and grinds were more gelatinous than sinuous, but, as she snaked back and forth in front of Peter, the red plush did billow and swirl and sway more or less voluptuously to the slowing rhythm and la-las of the *habanera*. Lacey calculated her probable stall speed. She saw El, peeking over her arm like a curious child ready to hide her head at the first hint of disaster. Martha could crash ignominiously into Peter's lap. She purled on, *La*-la-la-la. Peter picked up the red lacquer tray and Martha, glowering suspiciously at him, writhed ever slower until she idled in matronly wiggles.

"Imagine that's John the Baptist's head," he ordered, centering the coffee pot. "Now—on with the dance! Off with the veils!"

"Clot!" she thundered and stamped her foot. "You—you—

ape!" Peter leaned back, looking at her with wide, frank, startled eyes. He was too innocent. Lacey squirmed uncomfortably. She envied Arch his pipe, which at the moment required elaborate attentions from him. "You—you— For your information that was *Carmen*! *Not Salome*! And if you don't know the difference, you should. . . ."

"Should what?" Peter growled unexpectedly. "*You* should learn to recognize a joke. You're *not* the only one who knows *Carmen*. You're *not even* the only amateur who can't sing it— but most of us practice in the shower." He let out, again unexpectedly, the deep gurglings of an aquatic Salome about to dance. Martha threw herself on the sofa and buried her face in the pillows. Peter grabbed a shawl El had thrown over the back of a chair, pulled it around his hips, and began to shimmy. Martha lifted her head, watched for a few seconds, then with a snorting yelp plunged back into the pillows. They heaved with her half-smothered laughter. "Enough! Enough!" Peter quieted the bravos and clapping. "My forte is 'Celeste Aida' of course. I also do an acceptable 'Walkyrie,' but another time. There are more interesting things to talk about. Martha, tell us about the world of journalism," he invited, disentangling himself from the shawl. She resurfaced from the pillows with tears rolling down her cheeks.

"Amateurs! I despise amateurs!" She seemed to grind the words between her teeth. El sat up very straight and Lacey, who had been considering another glass of wine, decided against it. She should have known Martha never lost the thread of her own disgust. Now center stage was hers and Peter was still too innocent, encouraging her. "Bah! Amateurs!" she repeated, straightening the pillows.

She was plagued by amateurs, though for a time it was hard to discover just how. She had been commissioned to write a series of articles about the train robbery. She had come back excited about it, particularly pleased at the idea of solvency. Arch ventured a compliment. His reward was a diatribe on the perfidy of editors, which degenerated into an attack on all employers. White slave trade was redefined. The political solutions . . . Once more Arch tempted her with the joys of solvency. Ah yes, she had come back enthusiastic, optimistic for once, only to find that the train robbers were *amateurs! They* were such inept, simpleminded amateurs that they had given back part of the money. *They* were the amateurs who plagued her. *They* would ruin everything for her. Lowering her head she glared first at El, then at Lacey, who felt a hot wave of resentment churn up in her: did Martha really think . . . ? Martha recognized antagonism and feared it: she veered off on a new tack.

"They have to be local." This was to be an impersonal, analytical evaluation. "Much too simple for such a crime. They'll buy Maseratis or change bills at the local bank or . . ."

"Or get drunk and fight over the loot in public," El added in a deadly still voice.

"Amateurs! The world . . ."

" 'You have delighted us long enough,' " Lacey interrupted, impatient, now that Martha's bluff had been called, with the tyranny of ego. "Let's talk about something else. Or have a drink. Or throw plates at each other." Peter and Arch stood up and declared it time to go home. Martha thought that an excellent idea. She scooped up cups and odd glasses and swept off toward the kitchen, calling over her shoulder that she would just stay a few minutes to discuss unfinished business.

"Oh no she won't," El whispered as the others started for the front door. "It was such a pleasant evening until she came. I'm sorry. Sometimes she . . ." El labored on with her apologies.

Lacey beckoned to Arch, who leaned closer. Had he come with Peter? A nod. Then he did not have a car. She would drive him home. She—wanted to talk to him. From his delight she knew that her unbidden rush of tact had been misunderstood. They need . . . she started to say, turning to Peter and El, and then stopped. From the kitchen came the gentle click of plates and splashing water. El's sigh was a quiet prayer for patience.

"I'll get her out of there," Peter vowed. "If I have to carry her." He marched into the kitchen and moments later came out, leading Martha with his arm around her shoulders.

"Peter, why aren't you married?" she cooed at him. "Wouldn't he be lovely to have around the house, El?" Peter dragged her resolutely toward the door.

"That's a *professional* opinion, I assume." She bridled. He insisted. "Can I quote you? The recommendation of a connoisseur—or is it connoisseuress in feminist English? You should know. . . ." He chattered all the way to the drive, where they said their good-nights. Martha had opened the door of her car when Peter called to her, "Wait! I have a little Gilbert and Sullivan for you."

El turned her face into his shoulder. "I *hate* you!" Her whisper was fierce. "I'll never speak to you again, Peter Testa. *Never!*"

"Well?" Martha was impatient. "And do get it right." Peter looked off into the dark, as though rehearsing it through once to himself, and then recited very clearly,

> "Darwinian man, though well behaved
> At best is only a monkey shaved."

Lacey wasted no time on her errand. She delivered Arch, fully enlightened as to why he was so honored, at his own front door and sped home. Peter's car was still there. In the living room the fire flickered. The softest of whispers suggested that El had changed her mind. *Never* was a dangerous word, Lacey warned herself, as she tiptoed very, very quietly upstairs. She went to bed and to sleep. She had no idea what time Peter left. Nor did she ask.

14

$\mathscr{O}$ ONE EVENING toward the end of the following week Peter went again to play chess with Giordano. Palazzo Maffei was shrouded in darkness and the perfume of lavender in bloom. Behind it, the moon, on the wane so late rising, cast a glow that did not reach the façade. Cypress loomed, and elongated shadows from the battlements seemed to fortify the edges of the lawn.

Peter pulled the bell wire, waited for it to slip back through its hole, and then pulled again and again and again until the bell tolled lugubriously, echoing and reechoing through the empty rooms. Could Giordano have forgotten? Something brushed against his trousers. He jumped away as though he had been stroked by a ghost. A kitten with a raucous purr braided back and forth between his legs. He picked it up and was about to reach for the bell wire again, when, high above his head, rusty iron grated reluctantly on rusty iron, followed by a creak of brittle wood.

"Who's there?" called a deep, gruff voice. "Oh, it's you, Peter. Sorry! I was so busy with my invention I almost forgot. Be right down."

Again the wood of the shutter squeaked and Peter was in the dark, this time with a kitten clawing to get inside his jacket. Giordano's progress down corridors and through salons was announced by lighted windows, one after another, until the grass was a green-and-black checkerboard. At the turn of the key in the lock, the kitten catapulted out of Peter's arms, pranced across the sandy drive, and sat down in front of the door, calm and demure, waiting for it to be opened. Definitely female, Peter decided, as she strutted in, her spiky tail stiff and quivering with anticipation.

"Again?" Giordano grumbled at her more amused than cross. He motioned Peter to come inside. "There's one thing you might as well learn. If a lady has made up her mind, men can do nothing to change it. Look at Caroline. Off to Geneva on a foolish errand—in fact—for a minute I thought *you* might be Caroline. She said tomorrow at the latest. But women have no sense of time." He turned to look at the kitten, who had curled up on an old, three-legged chair that sat propped in a corner, waiting for a cabinetmaker. "All right, *you* can be the first tiger in my animal park." He smiled at her and stooped over to rummage in the bottom drawer of a chest.

"Only this morning I was thinking— Why aren't *we* like the English? 'Stately Homes' and all that. A few lions, a giraffe or two, lots of deer, some tigers. There could be tours of the house, of the 'park.' After a season or two I might even be able to afford a new roof." He stood up, apparently satisfied with an old blanket, which he put over the kitten. "And, of course, a gift shop with all the usual junk," he went on, half to himself, as he closed and relocked the door and reached up above it to pull a small copper lever down from its place between two copper brackets, until it hung vertical and free over the door itself. To Peter it looked like a homemade knife switch to close a circuit. For a moment Giordano stood, admiring it, then shrugged.

"I could wander in looking modest—like the Duke of Bedford. They'd buy out the place," he sighed. "There's always the other side of the coin. Would you help me for a few minutes before we play? I'm almost finished."

That seemed to be the end of the "Stately Homes" of Italy. Giordano did not expect any objection. He wandered off down the hall, confident that Peter would follow him, which he did, too taken with the image of this outsized pixie in his wide-wale corduroys and tweed jacket, maybe even his bedroom slippers, playing the Tuscan Duke of Bedford, to ask questions about where they were going.

Giordano led him up the broad stone stairway and on the first-floor landing turned away from the sitting room where they had played chess. Instead he opened a door into a vast salon, paneled in dull gold damask, with a coffered ceiling and a fireplace at either end. It was cold and empty, possibly a ballroom once, a passage now that did not require comment from Giordano. He took up his ruminations again, the other side of the coin.

He had seen at once that his idea would never work, his Renaissance Castle and his animal park. The locals would come with shotguns cocked, the children would stone the deer, nobody cared to meet a *conte*, and the peasants would disapprove of lions under their olive trees or giraffes in their lettuce patches. And then too, there was the staff. Terrible snobs. They wouldn't stand for it. This, he emphasized, was a major obstacle. At first Peter thought he was joking. The staff, as no one had ever before referred to it, consisted of one deaf, arthritic old man who poddled about in the garden, and two local women, wives of his tenants, who cleaned and laundered and cooked delicious meals, but never quite caught up before they disappeared back to their own families in midafternoon.

"So I gave it up at lunch," he announced. "I'd be bored with it in a week and then Caroline would have to feed the animals. She even forgets to feed *me*!" He opened a door into a long gallery. "So I went back to my old project. Come along. I'll show you."

Past rows of portraits. Giordano pointed out "the family Titian," a corpulent, greedy-eyed ecclesiastic, who, he was careful to note, had been born twenty-five years *after* Titian's death, not that the discrepancy was important, he supposed. Through echoing reception rooms and state bedrooms. Finally, at the far end of a gallery, they climbed a stairway to the library, where Giordano had been working. He scrambled to the top of a ten-foot ladder, jammed nails in his mouth, and began to explain. This was a burglar-alarm system. Miles of wire strung all over the palace. Homemade switches set at each window and door. Open one and a lever would be forced up into its bracket, closing a circuit. Sirens would shrill. It was a simple, brilliant scheme. Peter would see.

Indeed, he might, but at the moment he was having trouble understanding the garbled sounds that did manage to reach him through the hammering. Oblivious, Giordano moved on to his day at the market, which he and his friends judged to be the supreme in spectator sports, because they could watch everything right from their chairs at the café. Good value. Lots of information to be had. They monitored the Mayor's flirtations, discussed other men's wives, the foreigners in San Felice. Too many of them . . . all had CIA connections . . . after Chile . . . strange world . . . his wife was painting their bedroom pink. Peter dusted off a rime of plaster that had sifted down from the ceiling and waited for a clue. Suspicious . . . Robert Pound had sold two of his battered cars, Webster had sold a town . . . bought two farms. The neighborhood was disintegrating into a mad game of Monopoly.

"A whole town?" Peter shouted. Giordano stopped hammering.

"Deafness run in your family?" Giordano peered down at him. "He sold a *church!* Now—move aside. I'm through." Stepping off the ladder, he added, "You can fold it."

WHILE HE LUGGED the ladder down the various stairways and through the galleries to a storeroom off the main hall, Peter reconsidered the question of eccentricity. Nothing bizarre about it really, and very practical. It was not a deviation: you did what you wanted without apology and considered others who did not the true eccentrics. To Giordano, Peter, lurching around with the ladder, was the eccentric. He would have left it in the library for someone else to haul away. Peter saw that the thought processes were reversed, which reminded him he had to find his way back. Giordano had absentmindedly turned out the lights, leaving him to fumble along to the sitting room.

Grapevines twined around the walls and over the ceiling. Birds peeped timidly out from leafy bowers and squirrels cavorted in a perennial game of hide-and-seek through the ribs of the frescoed arbor. The room was a pergola no season could wither. Giordano had lighted the fire and put the chessboard out on a table in front of it with two comfortable chairs drawn up, but obviously was not yet ready to play.

"I'll just connect the batteries and the master switches. They're in the bedroom. Seemed the most practical place." He opened a door perfectly cut in the fresco to be invisible, and disappeared. Moments later the stock of a shotgun floated out through the door and waggled. "Make sure that's loaded.

Shells are in a desk drawer." Interesting place for them, Peter thought, breaking the gun. He looked at the birds, who seemed to watch him, and silently apologized. He found the shells, loaded the gun, and then stood, the Great White Hunter, on the rug in front of the fireplace, waiting for orders. From the next room he heard clinks, metal on metal, and grunts. "Oh no!" Giordano was grief-stricken. "You won't get to hear the sirens," he called. "They're splendid—four made for fireboats. Got them in Livorno. Navy surplus." Peter heard him chortle to himself. "Caroline said I'd *never* use them. Wrong—as usual. Well, if we're lucky, someone will break in tonight. Give me the gun. From now on, I'll sleep with it." Caroline would be enchanted.

GIORDANO TRIED TO CONCENTRATE on the theoretical battle of chess, but other strategies intruded. While he speculated on the thieves he would surely catch, Peter beat him two games in a row. They were setting up the pieces for a third.

"A-Uuu-GA! A-Uuu-GA! A-Uuu-GA!" came a terrible blast in their ears. "A-Uuu-GA! A Uuu-GA!" They both jumped to their feet and looked over their shoulders, as though the fire horns, miraculously come to life, were sneaking up behind them. With each explosion a wave of nausea bounced up under Peter's rib cage. Giordano's eyes bulged, his mouth was wide open. "A-Uuu-GA! A-Uuu-GA!" He stumbled for the bedroom.

"A-Uuu-GA! A-Uuu-GA! BOOM! BOOM!"

Almost before Peter could identify the sound, Giordano was back, still stumbling awkwardly, this time toward the sitting-room window.

"A-Uuu-GA! A-Uuu-GA!" He fumbled with two shells, trying to reload the shotgun, at the same time jabbing at the window catch. Peter grabbed the handle, turned it, and swung the two glass panels wide.

"BOOM! BOOM!"

"A-Uuu-GA! A-Uuu-GA!"

Desperate to make it stop, Peter banged the window closed again and set the circuit switch.

And, of course, "A-Uuu-GA!" blared on, while the two men stood, staring at each other. Remembering the bedroom window at the same moment, they collided in the doorway, but reached the window, shut it, and set the switch.

"A-Uuu-GA! A-Uuu-GA!"

Peter understood why people in burning buildings jumped. He wanted to jump himself, to disappear down a cypress-lined avenue out into the fields away from "A-Uuu-GA!" Instead his mind snapped back on: thought returned. Somewhere a window or a door had been opened and was still open. And it seemed to him that, in the split-second gap between one "A-Uuu-GA!" and the next, he heard a distant sound, not just an echo, a sound wedging itself weakly between the blasts. To get Giordano's attention he had to touch his arm. Watch, he gestured, and closed the index and middle fingers of his right hand into his left fist. He pulled the fingers out. Admittedly he might have been milking a cow. Giordano stared at him, mystified. Peter tried again. His fingers—the plug—from his fist—the socket. Giordano's face lit up. He stooped over and began yanking at the snarl of wires.

Peter raced back to the front window and threw it open again. There, in the beams of a car's headlights, a tall figure in tight pink pants and a filmy white blouse performed a wild Watusi on the lawn. Long hair flailed about, disappearing into the dark to loop forward to the ground and be thrown back, revealing the mask of tragedy, the eyes squeezed shut, the mouth agape. Arms were flung out, imploring, desperate.

"A-Uuu-GA!" It occurred to Peter that it might be better if Giordano did *not* succeed in disconnecting "A-Uuu-GA!"

"A-Uuu-GA! A-Uuu-GA! GA! GA!"

"Assassino! Idiota! You stupid bastard, turn that . . ." For a moment the silence, real, absolute silence, thick as fog, paralyzed them. Naturally Hermione was the first to recover. "Jesus! It's about time."

"Are you all right?" Peter called from the safety of his perch. But there was no answer. He watched as her legs very slowly folded under her, easing her onto the grass, where she sat, rocking back and forth, absorbed in some cabalistic rite. A lumbering figure on all fours detached itself from the shadow of the car and humped along, working its way laboriously toward Hermione. Peter's eyes had adjusted to the darkness and the one brilliant shaft of light. Still, he could not identify the amorphous bear. It collapsed and rolled playfully about on the grass at Hermione's feet.

"Did you catch them?" Giordano. asked, slightly out of breath. When Peter did not answer, but moved away from the window, he stuck his head out and yelled, "This is private property. Trespassers will be . . ."

"Imbecile! That," screamed Hermione, pointing to the body at her feet, *"that* is your WIFE!"

"Oh my God!" Giordano groaned and with uncharacteristic speed sprinted out of the sitting room, through the dark halls, and down the even darker stairs, leaving Peter to follow as best he might.

Out on the lawn Giordano knelt beside Caroline. He frowned at her. Fear had erased the leonine certainty, which gave his features their strength, leaving an unfamiliar petulance that the glare of the headlights intensified. He gibbered at Caroline, ignoring her answers.

"Are you all right? I didn't hit you? Are you sure? Really

185

sure? Are you all right?" She insisted that she was. He went right on, asking over and over again, "Are you all right?"

"Yes, yes! Don't go on so." She looked at Hermione, then at Peter, and winked. "At least now I know I'm not just someone to cook your dinner. Would you . . . ?"

"I didn't hit you?"

"For the last time—no! Don't be silly. Would you have sat by my grave and mourned? No, probably not. To spite me you'd marry an exotic brunette and live happily ever after." He glowered at her, offended.

"Get up! This instant!" he roared, struggling up himself. "Stop this childish behavior. It's inappropriate for a woman in your position." For a moment her eyes glittered. She was tempted, sorely tempted, but decided to let it pass.

"That's my dear Giordano! Back to his old self." She rolled over and stood up, brushing off her stained brown slacks and sweater. He did not help her, preferring to sulk, until she threw her arms around him. "You're sweet, and you would be upset if anything happened to me." He looked pleased and a little shamefaced. He kissed her forehead. Peter stretched out a hand to Hermione, who took it without seeming to notice it, and pulled herself up.

"Oh, he's sweet, all right," she sneered. "But just what the hell was he trying to do?" Peter, to avoid the explanation, suggested they unload the car. If someone would turn on the lights in the hall, the headlights . . . Giordano was already describing the ingenuity of his alarm system to Caroline. With the single-mindedness of the successful inventor he drew her along with him. She could see for herself on the door frame exactly how it worked. Left in the dark with the bags and Hermione, Peter knew he must say something or prepare for her philippic on the stupidity of the male.

"What were *you* doing in Geneva?" was his random choice as he leaned into the trunk of the car.

"I had to be there. *Everybody* knew that, even the police—if it's any business of yours, which I doubt." Suddenly contradicting her huffiness, her voice plunged its entire range to a seductive half-whisper. "Why do we always meet over the bags, darling? This time—at least—there's no rush. Is there?"

Her flowing blouse rustled lightly and Peter felt her body ooze into place like warm wax along his left side. Then she slipped ever so slowly, clingingly, up to nibble his ear, and he found himself enveloped in a cloud of heavy, slightly antiseptic perfume, the kind that has no particular fragrance except expensive.

"They'll never miss us," she mouthed into his ear, tickling, as she undoubtedly intended, the one capricious nerve that would send soft flutters along his spine. If these were the Rites of Spring, was he cast as a satyr? Physically as well as psychologically off balance, he took a half-step backward. A suitcase knifed into his knees. They buckled and he pitched over in tumbling, crashing retreat. Hermione cursed him in every language she knew.

"I thought you ladies believed in free choice," he parried when she stopped for breath. He struggled back to his feet and brushed his trousers with extreme care, which he hoped would double for dignity. He was relieved that seduction had withered to scorn, and still had enough sense not to show it.

"We do, we *do*," she agreed lightly. "It's just that I have such stinking taste. Impulse, Hermione! Beware of it, dear. I must say this one was so slight, I'm sure I'll be able to *eat* my way out of it—very quickly." And sweeping through the *portone*, she too disappeared.

Indeed, for the next hour and a half, while Caroline recounted her misadventures, Hermione put on a remarkable performance. She ate—slowly, constantly, with noisy gusto—almost as though she were determined to work her way, shelf by shelf, through the Maffeis' icebox. She started with whiskey and a hefty wedge of *pecorino,* then moved on to spaghetti with oil and garlic, a wing of cold chicken, a container of yogurt, some leftover, sodden *zuppa inglese*, and to settle it all, a bottle of beer. She was too busy to talk a great deal herself, but did take time out to lead them through two long digressions with all the flights of fancy, erudition, misinformation, and irrationality that made her an intriguing, if outrageous, public speaker. All in all *she* had a very satisfactory evening.

15

CAROLINE WAS POSITIVE that guilt accounted for Giordano's sudden domesticity, but she was touched. He swept the chess set away and stoked the fire. He moved the furniture back, including a small sofa, which belonged in front of the fireplace and on which he insisted she stretch out and rest. He banked her in pillows and covers. By the time Peter had hauled the bags and parcels upstairs, off in the kitchen a kettle was lisping about to boil. Giordano was also a polished butler. He brought whiskey, soda, and glasses on a tray and Caroline's tea on another. She watched him, the corners of her mouth held tight. He was so solemn: she mustn't laugh. Lying back against the pillows, she crossed her legs and laced her fingers together in her lap. She tried to look relaxed, but she was tired. Behind her eyes was a dull ache and she could feel the tightness about her mouth and chin. For her the trip was not over yet. She had to tell Giordano. If the police happened to investigate and she had *not* told him . . . She would have to be very careful in editing her version. She closed her eyes and then almost immediately forced herself to open them. Giordano had cleared his throat. He was waiting. For only a second she hesitated.

"It was the most extraordinary trip," she began, frowning. Although she spoke in Italian, she kept the elongated, very nasal tone that in English lends the phrase such ineffable wonder.

THE MORNING she left San Felice had been misty. As she drove down into the valley the umbrella pines had been large, gray mushrooms and roofs floated alone, silver ribbons of moisture glistening between rows of tiles. Her odd premonition of adventure could not resist the dullness of the *autostrada*. Between Florence and Bologna, she struggled with trucks. As usual the Po Valley was steamy. There were squalls of rain around Milan and then, as she climbed toward Aosta and the Mont Blanc tunnel, the clouds disappeared, the sun came out, and she felt she had discovered summer.

Before she could see the frontier barriers, she came up behind a long line of cars, which at first she thought must be some special convoy. The drivers were out, standing patiently in the road, their papers in hand. Down the way, scowling, a policeman in a crash helmet and boots wielded a stick with a red disk at the end, signaling all trailer trucks and some cars on toward the border. Caroline pulled out to follow them, but when she came level with the policeman—she had been watching the back of the car in front of her, not him—he was in a fury. He waved her to a halt.

"Back to the end of the line," he ordered.

"But why? Those others . . ." She pointed at the cars passing them.

"Are *not* Italian. Now—go back to the end!" He watched her until she swung in behind the last car. She switched off the ignition and sat, telling herself not to lose her temper. Then she got out and went to stand with the others.

Four or five men huddled together, listening to the cackles from a transistor radio. One, a fat young man in an undershirt and dirty trousers, said it was the noon news. Maybe there was a prison break or a bank robbery. A Genovese told her what he had, she gathered, already reported to the others: up ahead four men from the Finance Police were going through car registrations, identity cards, and passports as though looking for typographical errors. The man in the undershirt offered a bottle of wine. No one took any. He tried to discuss the weather with Caroline. Some drifted away, others joined the group. They had packets of *salame* and bits of cheese and loaves of bread. A little boy ran out in front of a car. His mother whacked him on the ears. It struck Caroline that they were shipwrecked on a paved island. She decided to go back to her car, which turned out to be less than a good idea. The young man in the undershirt followed her to lean against the door and regale her with the sexual foibles of foreign women.

Twenty minutes later, only partway through the Swedes-he-had-known, the French still to come, without warning the cars in front of Caroline pulled away. Her admirer dashed off; she moved up and was relieved to see a pair of uniformed men approaching her. They stuck to each other so devotedly that she wondered if, like carabinieri, one read, one wrote. These were thin and unshaven and, unlike carabinieri looked shabby, their collars frayed, their uniforms wrinkled. The one with the thin Rudolph Valentino moustache gave her a limp imitation of a salute and leaned toward her.

"*Favorisca i documenti.*" Caroline handed out her passport and car registration. He consulted his partner. She could not hear them, but all the same they moved away, nodding at each other, turning back to look at her. They studied a sheet of paper, nodded, and again looked at her. Finally the one who talked stepped over to her window.

"Move the car up to the building. Park it at the back and lock it. We'll join you there."

Why did the police arouse panic, even in the innocent? When she twisted the key in the ignition, she forgot to let out the clutch. The car leapt forward in a giant hiccough, grazing Valentino's jacket. Oh no! Now they'd add attempted murder to the charge. Whatever the charge. Caroline realized she did not know. Shaken, she parked the car as instructed, and waited for her captors. A new line was forming.

Neither the architecture nor the atmosphere of frontier posts is inviting, but the traveler seldom has more than a fleeting impression of windows where jaundiced men in uniform study documents, slap them back on the counter, and, without bothering to look up, mutter, "Next." Caroline found herself facing a three-story tower with two long, low tentacles that jutted out from it, all of cream-colored plaster. One narrow door and a long rusty streak from a faulty gutter saved it from total blankness. Penitentiary architecture! No, more likely so many people had to be paid off, there was no money left for windows.

Valentino walked past her, motioning her forward. His partner had already unlocked the door and started upstairs. She followed. Seconds later the footsteps of the second guard fell in behind her. The first landing and one metal door that led into a narrow corridor about eight feet long. At the end two corridors went off, one to the right, one to the left. Along the back wall, the wall without windows, were offices, no more than slots, with glass half-partitions that gave onto the hall and may have relieved the impression of premature burial. Uniformed drones shuffled back and forth. Machines clattered. Caroline had a pervading sense of gray—drab gray uniforms, drab gray paint, rubbed grimy at hip level, even a fusty gray smog of cigarette smoke. She was escorted to one of the two doors opposite the cubicles. Gold letters on black plastic read LT. SPADACCIONE.

Valentino knocked, then took Caroline by the elbow, which she resented, and opened the door. He led her to the exact center of the desk, placed her papers neatly on the blotter where Lieutenant Spadaccione, who was on the telephone, would see them, and ambled back to join his partner on guard duty at the door.

Caroline took a quick look around the room. There was little to see. Two walls, entirely glass, provided a dismal view of six highway lanes. The floor was a cheap grade of white marble chip and bare. Centered in the shorter of the two solid walls were the obligatory plastic crucifix and the President of the Republic's photograph, and below them, off toward the corner, sat a military stenographer, face to the wall, hammering away at a typewriter. It reverberated like a pneumatic drill, forcing Lieutenant Spadaccione to yell into the telephone. His voice was thin, almost shrill, and his head was completely bald. For several minutes Caroline knew no more about him because he had his back to her. As the adieux began—*Non dubiti* ... *Bene* ... *Bene*—he twirled around to his blotter and she was surprised to see a young, cadaverous D'Annunzio, not an aging cherub. It was a messianic face—wide forehead, enormous suffering brown eyes, and long nose. A luxuriant, but carefully trimmed Vandyke extended further than usual along his jaw to join thin sideburns, as though he were determined that the lower half of his face should make up for the follicular failures of his scalp. Fragile, very white fingers worked the passport open—*"Si, si* ... *Dovere* ... *Arrivederla."* He hung up, concentrated on the documents for several minutes, and asked without looking at her,

"May I see your *permesso di soggiorno?*" Caroline recognized the studied discourtesy, never actually rude, as a technique favored by the Italian police academies, but she felt the blood rush to her face.

"I don't have one." Which was a white lie: hers had expired.

"A foreigner living in Italy must have a valid *permesso*." Not satisfied, he offered a chanted footnote. "Article 142 of the integral text of the laws of Public Security." He still had not looked at her.

"Not if you have an Italian passport too."

"May I see it? Why don't you use it?" At a certain point the official must look up either to gloat or avert a flanking maneuver. Spadaccione selected that moment. Caroline saw that his eyes had not one single spark of humor. She fished nervously in her purse, finding everything from dog biscuits to a new spark plug for her motorbike before she felt the plastic folder with her passport. He took it by the corner as though it might be sticky and turned the pages almost without touching them.

Caroline knew she had herself to blame for this complication. She seldom used her British passport, but from the remark of the first policeman, who had forced her back into line, she had the impression a foreign passport would speed the formalities. Now it appeared it might have the opposite effect.

"I'll have to verify these," Spadaccione said, letting his eyes slide past her. "It shouldn't take long."

"Would you tell me what I am supposed to have done? You'll find my papers are in order." To her own ears her voice sounded more pleading than dignified.

THIS WAS MORE than Giordano could accept.

"He suspected *you* of an illegal act! *My* wife! Why that—"

"Oh Giordano, you're *so* Victorian," Hermione said with

her mouth full. She had just attacked her plate of spaghetti with oil and garlic. "Don't be ridiculous. Caroline's as capable as anyone else. Men are all alike! A woman—*your* wife—must be a genteel little saint, except when you turn the key on the chastity belt and *ecco!*—faster than you can say 'Trojan,' she's supposed to be your private whore."

Caroline, who had been watching her husband, snickered at the expression on his face. Fortunately Hermione did not linger on that aspect of her argument.

"Jack the Ripper, yes! Joan the Ripper, no! Why? If there's a warrant out for a hit-and-run driver, it's assumed to be a man. Why? An ax murderer? It's a man—Lizzie Borden to the contrary. I say women are as innately evil and grasping or selfish as men and fully as criminal. They have a *right* to equal suspicion!" She paused, allowing for applause. She waited another beat and when nothing was said, she shrugged. "Hmm, I must have done better the other night in London. They liked it. Women's Right to Equal Suspicion! Even sounds good. Equal Suspicion! They're talking about an amendment to . . . Oh, never mind. There's no point in explaining anything serious tonight. Go on with your story, Caroline."

"But did you object? After all, false arrest—surely you had sense enough—" Giordano would not accept that any of this had happened.

"Of course I did, darling. I told him it was madness, absolute madness." She giggled. "My voice got all squeaky. I don't think I was very impressive. He was very calm and above it all. . . ."

"NOT MADNESS," Spadaccione had insisted pompously. "It's the legal business of the Republic of Italy, which I have the honor—"

"Is there some article in the integral text that says a suspect, if that is what I am, cannot have a chair?" He motioned to the men at the door. A straight chair was placed behind her. He turned away to consult a notebook. After he had scribbled numbers on a pad, he started opening drawers, each of which produced a telephone, three in all. The cautious pronunciations, then the spelling of all the names and places involved in her birth gave her some amusement and plenty of time to study the arrangement. The first call ended with an imperious *"Subito!"* so that telephone was connected to a police switchboard. He dialed the second call and asked for the Consul, so that one was an outside line. He had some difficulty convincing the Consul that he had a right to question a British passport. Again the cautious pronunciations. English made for delightful verbal pratfalls.

"Odd that neither her mother's nor her father's name is given . . ." He looked over at Caroline, frowning. "Oh really? If you say . . . Yes, as soon as possible . . . The consulate in Rome? You can call . . . The lines, I see . . . Most grateful." He hung up and without taking a breath said, "Your husband's name, place of birth, residence, and profession, please." Caroline was not sure "landowner" would be acceptable. "How comfortable," he grunted. "And his title?" Lawyer. Giordano did have a law degree. "By education. By birth?" She objected that titles were illegal. Spadaccione stared at her in his insistent, unblinking way.

"Conte Giordano Bruno Maffei. Are you satisfied?" He drew a stack of files toward him and opened the first folder.

"Smoke, if you like."

"I don't smoke, thank you."

"I do," he said curtly and lighted a cigarette. Not even the perfunctory "Do you mind?" Caroline could not fight her dislike of this man and the others of this new wave. Perhaps the old, sloppier Southerners were less honest, more lecherous, but they were human. Their posturings and their thundering gallantries she preferred, and their imitation of royal court-spiel, even that, she preferred to the pasteurized Spadacciones. His accent had the invented neutrality of a Sardinian television announcer and for what he would call "relax" he undoubtedly read the civil code. To hector him, she asked,

"When the Consul calls back, may I speak to him?" A bored nod. "And I'd like to call my brother-in-law in Geneva. With this delay, he'll be worried." He closed his folder and selected the green telephone, which he had been using when she was brought in the office. The name and number in Geneva? She was intrigued by his efficient, not very good French. "You shouldn't have any trouble reaching him." She smiled pleasantly—she hoped. "He's Director General." He lifted his eyebrows very slightly. Sir Arthur might have been the janitor. Spadaccione handed the receiver to her and again opened his file.

Later Caroline wondered why she had bothered. Arthur was never helpful and this time his only concern was that she arrive in time for dinner. She must not be rude to his guests, who were, *ipso facto*, important. "I might *just* have been able to do something with a French or Swiss official—they're civilized—but nobody can do anything with the Italians." He did not go on and say, as she knew he would like to, that it had not been "quite the thing" for her to marry one either.

For the next half-hour she sat, the Lieutenant concentrated on his folders, and the typist typed, sending letters ricocheting around the walls. Perhaps he was part of the *mise-en-scène,* the Italian adaptation of the Chinese water torture. Eventually both the Central Police Archives and the office of the British Consul confirmed her passports as in order. Spadaccione did not seem surprised. When the Consul called, he gave her the telephone and leaned back in his chair to listen. For the first time it occurred to her that he might understand English. Had she said anything awful to Arthur? Or he to her? With the Englishman's classic distrust of continental telephones he had shouted at her. Oh dear, she couldn't remember.

The Vice-Consul, as he stated himself to be, was so busy justifying his nonintervention that he heard nothing she said. And he addressed her as Countessa, successfully maiming both languages. She corrected him. "Quite, Countessa," he plunged on, and she stopped listening. When she hung up, Spadaccione smiled for the first time. Really it was a malicious leer.

"Now—I presume you're willing to have your car searched." She bobbed her head. "Or, if you prefer, we can impound it. No? All right." He motioned the two men behind her. They moved up to stand on either side of her chair. "First, I must examine the contents of your purse."

The dog biscuits, the spark plug, a collection of other people's calling cards on which she wrote her grocery lists, a screwdriver, a small silver pocketknife, three candies received as change, and a prescription for worm medicine were treated with the same official detachment as all the more conventional female accoutrements—the Gucci billfold and at least a kilo of keys. Once they were laid out neatly on his desk, he listed each item and handed it back to her—everything except the calling cards. He turned them over and over again, trying to decipher the notations, until, though he regretted the inconvenience to her, he felt obliged to keep them. Caroline longed to leave the dog biscuits and the three candies, but decided it might be a blunder.

"Now, about the car. What's in it?"

"One small suitcase of personal clothing and—and . . ." She stuttered, remembering the books. "And a great many cartons of books. My sister's." Then for good measure. "Sir Arthur's wife."

"I see." He shifted his eyes beyond her. "Take her downstairs. I'll call for one of the squads." He swung his chair halfway around and reached for one of the telephones. It was several seconds before Caroline understood that she had been dismissed.

DOWNSTAIRS, STANDING AT THE BACK of her car, were four young men, hardly more than boys, in khaki mechanics' overalls. Under Valentino's direction they removed everything from the car—Caroline's bag, the cartons of books, the maps, rags, tool kit, a spare tire, the jack, and a complete set of automobile bulbs. It was all piled around her, as though she had been evicted. Next came the carpets, the front seats, and the bottom of the back. One of the men tapped around the trunk, pulled down the panel that revealed the springs and canvas of the backseat, and pummeled that. After he had crawled out, he tested the bumper in some mysterious way and decided to remove it. For good measure he unscrewed the license plate and the taillights to look behind them. Enthralled watching him, Caroline had not noticed that the other three were busy removing the door panels. They also looked inside the dome light, under the instrument panel, and into the glove compartment, stripping out the soundproofing material until they reached the metal of the bulkhead that divided the motor from the passenger compartment. They unclamped the metal ring around a plastic hood at the base of the gear shift, lifted the hood, and made sure there was nothing underneath it. When they started prying at the roof lining, Caroline insisted they stop—for just a moment.

"What exactly are they looking for?" she asked Valentino, since he, in some vague way, seemed to be in charge.

"Oh we don't know. We're to do a *thorough* search" was his dogged reply.

"But wouldn't it be easier . . . ?"

One of the young men, the slightest, with dark hair and serious eyes, came over to her. "Don't worry too much. We know how to get it back together. It'll be all right."

Caroline wanted to throw her arms around his neck and sob. He was the first person in all this foolishness to treat her as a rational being. And she had caught his slight Tuscan accent.

"That's enough, Longo." Valentino had remembered that enlisted men were not to sympathize with the victims. Longo ducked back into the car, but was careful not to loosen more of the lining than was absolutely necessary to prove there was nothing hidden there. He started on the sunshades. By then the front headlights were out and the front bumper off. Valentino, though not exactly quivering with expertise, seemed to understand the operation. As a new chasm was about to be opened, he readied himself to peer into it and, finding nothing, stepped on to what he knew would be the next offered for his inspection. When the car had been reduced to a carcass with an engine, and wires trailed, like gaily colored spaghetti, from every orifice, he waved the men to take it away. Alarmed, Caroline rushed over to him.

"Where are they taking it?"

"To the lift. People solder things underneath—drugs, stolen jewelry, ingots—think we're too dumb to find them." The idea had tweaked some nerve of pride in his phlegmatic disposition. "If it's there, we'll find it. *Count* on that!"

"But what?"

"That I don't know. The Lieutenant just said 'full treatment.' Come, if you want, but with all this . . ." He waved at the piles of metallic entrails strewn about on the concrete and, without waiting for an answer, strolled off behind the men who pushed the car.

For the first time Caroline was aware that people were

staring at her from their cars as they waited to pass on to the tunnel. She turned her back to them and sat down on one of the cartons of books. There should be a logical explanation for all this, some clue, maybe in her conversation with Spadaccione. She thought she was considering the situation very practically until she caught herself daydreaming about food—pickles and *bresaola* with parsley, pepper, and oil, *tortellini*—all things that the makeshift café across the way could not supply, even if she could get there. Adversity, like pregnancy, seemed to bring on strange cravings. No, she would put that out of her mind. Her situation . . .

"MY GOD, that's it!" Hermione burst out. *"That's it!* I'm pregnant! That explains—Peter, be a love and get me a footstool. I abort as easily as I conceive, you know. Tipped, they tell me. More like shopworn, I'm afraid. With my feet up I shan't lose it—at least not tonight. Don't anyone worry." Turning to Caroline as though surely she would know the answer, she asked, "Now *who* do you suppose the father is? Wouldn't mind Bengy. Some awfully good genes there—somewhere—can't say they're always obvious. Quite the contrary. Oh God! Not the Swiss banker. Oh, Caroline, I couldn't stand *that*. I refuse even to think about it. I won't! I won't have a child who arrives all smelling of cologne and dry skin without enough juice in it to keep a respectable dandruff virus alive." Frowning, she paused. "Of course, I'll deliver myself. All this modern carrying-on is nonsense. Just brings disease. For centuries women delivered themselves—in the fields. Birth is an entirely normal function that we understand instinctively."

She cocked her knees up and out in an alarmingly realistic way and charged off into a gory pastiche of old wives' tales, do-it-yourself obstetrics (confused), a survey of Aztec birth rites, brief sorties into the questions of heredity vs. environment and the Freudian fallacy, and finally on to the gradual changes to be expected of the mammary glands. Judicious prodding of same evidently did not supply any startling developments, or at least none that she shared with the others.

Obviously Caroline was accustomed to these scampers through ego and id. She allowed this one to seek its own end, but did not allow it to curtail her movements. She listened for a bit, put some wood on the fire, and then brewed herself another pot of tea without disturbing the pace. Hermione did raise her voice to be sure not a word would be lost in the kitchen. Giordano was less experienced. He made several mild attempts at changing the subject, but when Hermione struck her delivery position and seemed launched on specifics, he chose a bird high in the fresco's grape arbor and fixed it with glassy determination.

"And of course the baby will be breast-fed. The correlation between bottle feeding and masturbation—but I'm sorry. Poor darlings! You mustn't let me harangue you this way. Caroline, *do* go on with your story—and if you don't mind I'll just step into the kitchen and get some of that yummy-looking pud." She wasn't sorry at all. She had come to the end of her lecture, if not of her eating. For Caroline the transition was too abrupt. She looked dazed.

"Where was I? Oh, the food—never mind about that. I ate when I arrived at my sister's. Naturally in the middle of Arthur's important dinner party. By then I was filthy. I'm sure he would rather I'd eaten with the servants. Later he did say he thought it very inconsiderate of me. Of *me*! And I'm carting his ruddy books up to him. But Arthur's not the point. Poor man, he seldom is." She stopped and drew little patterns in the air, mapping out her progress with a long forefinger.

"You see," she started again, "I'm being so tiresome about it all because I still think somewhere in what happened there's an explanation of *why* it happened. Be patient! There's not much more."

HALF AN HOUR LATER Valentino had reappeared followed at some distance by the car, which was now pushed by six attendant-mechanics.

"Negative," he reported succinctly. They might have tested for a malignant disease. "Now comes the slow part. At least it's not raining. Here! You two—Longo and what's-your-name, over here." Though she had no idea what the "slow part" might be, other than the reassembly of her car, Caroline was relieved to have Tuscan Longo back. "All right, start on the far pile. While you do that, the signora can sit where she is."

Suddenly Caroline understood what they intended. It was grotesque, absolutely grotesque, but they were going to open every carton and go through the books. Her first instinct was to get mad, throw a tantrum, try the old "You don't know who I am" line. Instead she found herself crying, which infuriated her even more. She'd show them. They could question her, bully her, dismantle her car, bait her, but she would not be defeated by a bunch of pettyfogging little . . . Feeling better, but still ashamed, she went on cursing them to herself until they had emptied the first box, riffled through every book, and gone on to the second. Then she stood up, stalked over to the empty carton, and started cramming the books back in whatever way they would fit. To hell with Arthur! He could sort them as he put them on the shelves in the comfort of his library. She worked furiously to keep up. She did not want to be left in an acre of her own debris. Once Valentino, who had watched without comment, leaned over to pick up a book.

"Don't you *dare* touch anything of mine," she snapped and watched him jump back, putting a box of books and the two young men between them. Probably afraid of dogs too, she thought with some satisfaction.

Valentino did not approach her again, but every so often she heard him mutter in wonder: *"Ma cosa ne fa?"* "But what does she do with them?" Obviously no bibliophile, his suspicions were instantly aroused by a set of Balzac—with uncut pages— that appeared in the next-to-last carton and announcing to the air in general that the Lieutenant must be informed, he vanished through the one lone doorway.

"Do you have a knife?" Caroline whispered to Longo. He nodded. "Does he?" Pointing at the other book handler.

"If he doesn't, we'll borrow one."

When Valentino came back with the Lieutenant, Caroline and her helpers were busily slitting pages. Lieutenant Spadaccione went first to the car, walked around it, and said something to the men. Next he looked into the box at the offending volumes of Balzac.

"The car's almost ready." His tone was so smug Caroline expected to be told she would find it greatly improved. He did not touch the books. Instead he had Valentino open Caroline's suitcase. (Hermione roared he was probably queer for women's bras and panties.) But after a perfunctory blind feel at the contents, he wheeled around and said, "About the Balzac. In my experience those who own Balzac, read him, so I can only agree—those uncut pages *are* suspicious." He looked around for Valentino. "Have them taken upstairs."

"Oh, no. *Basta! Basta proprio!*" Caroline would take no more. The bureaucrat's First Commandment—thou must save face— would not be invoked against her. "How many volumes are there? Twenty? All right, twenty-four. The car's almost ready, the boxes are repacked. If you'll have the men load them and give me a receipt, I'll leave the Balzac with you. And welcome to it! When you're through X-raying them, send them to me—

if you feel like it. If not—burn them. You haven't found a flaming thing in this entire exercise. Now I'm going. Just give me the receipt and that's the end of it. For now. I'll see that . . ." But she never finished the sentence. Spadaccione had turned on his heels and strutted off. Seconds later the door slammed behind him.

While the mechanics fastened on the last pieces of chrome trim and the book-sorters wedged the boxes in the car, Caroline berated herself for a coward. She felt let down and rubbery in the knees. She could not claim victory. Until the battle was over, she had not had the nerve to object—and she admitted to herself that she had only objected. Bravery in the face of the enemy's inevitable surrender is no bravery at all. Why hadn't she had the guts? By God, if she had it to do over again . . . ! Then she remembered. She did have it to do over again. There were almost as many books waiting for her in Aosta!

Out of the corner of her eye she saw a fat little corporal standing in the doorway of the tower. He squinted up at the sky and then waddled over to give her the Balzac receipt. Without a word he scuttled back inside, as though undue exposure to light and air might bring on decomposition. Did she dare go back to Lieutenant Spadaccione? She had to, unless she wanted to face the same mayhem again. She might live through it, but a car was hardly a jigsaw puzzle to be taken apart and put together every few days. She decided she must face him once more and, without giving herself time to find excuses, she walked toward the tower.

As she turned the handle, the door gave way and she and Lieutenant Spadaccione were pitched into each other's arms.

"Still here? You seemed in rather a hurry." He wore aviators' sunglasses, which, with his visored cap, made him seem larger, more imposing.

"They've almost finished, but I thought I'd best warn you."

She hoped her voice sounded composed and aggressive. "Either tomorrow or the next day I have to come back for the rest of my sister's books." Before she dithered into explaining the details of why she must do her sister's errands, she caught herself. Never explain, never! "I trust I shan't be put through *this* again." For a long moment he said nothing. Behind those panes of smoked glass, she knew his eyes were expressionless.

"You needn't worry, Contessa, about further trouble from us. Rather, if I were you, I would think very hard about who hates me. Hates me enough to report me." He paused, but she knew that he had more to say. His beard twitched and he was smiling. "Officially I have only done my duty. However—personally I regret the situation. Could I—would you accept a peace offering? I know a very nice hotel just over the French border where they have delicious pâté and their own wine. You must be hungry. A bit of food—a bit of 'relax' before facing the rest of your trip. Allow me?"

"Forgive me, Lieutenant, but I've had enough adventures for one day."

She walked away from him, got in the car, and drove off, unfortunately with a terrible grinding of gears.

"YOU SEE! You wouldn't take my advice and get a shipper. Oh no! This would be easier. *Easier,* indeed!" snorted Giordano. "All you had to do—"

"Yes, I know. As it turned out, you were right, but two trips to Florence, finding this famous shipper, the papers, the customs, all the rest, sounded worse. So, I made a mistake. You don't think I enjoyed it, do you?" Caroline was almost as cross as her husband.

"But you didn't make the second trip." Peter's was an assumption. Caroline stuck her chin down, way down on her chest, and stared at her hands. Giordano glared at her, and Hermione decided she would just step into the kitchen for a bottle of beer.

"You *didn't,* Caroline . . . ?"

"Oh, don't fuss at me. Please. I'm so tired." And suddenly she really was. "Yes, *of course,* I did it, and that's my fault too. When I arrived so dirty and cross, I told everyone, all those people at Arthur's dinner party, what had happened. So— naturally— Oh, you know Arthur—he refused to let Laura go, said after all *everyone* at the border knew me. I must say he made it sound rather nasty. We had a terrible fight about it, but in the end—of course, I went. That's not the point. Nothing happened the second time. Nothing! The reason I told you all this—and took so long about it too, I know and I'm sorry— is *who* reported me to the Finance Police? *Who* said I was going to smuggle something out? That's the point." She felt herself blush. She had always been a self-conscious liar. They might mistake it for anger.

"Sounds like a scheme that little snipe Webster would think up," Hermione declared, flouncing back from the kitchen with her bottle of beer and a glass.

"Why him?" "Webster's got nothing against Caroline!" "Ridiculous!" They were all talking at once.

"There's more to him than meets the eye," Hermione murmured mysteriously and then made them wait, while she poured her beer, for an explanation. "More to him than meets the eye—though, mind you—nothing that appeals to me. It's just an observation. Have you thought, What does he live on? Where does it come from? What are those 'deals' he's forever scheming to arrange? And the inventions? He has the right kind of mind for smuggling. Report Caroline and then sneak through right behind her, when they're not looking—or for that matter, real-estate swindles, sheep rustling . . ."

"He can use the Rolls," Peter put in, but no one understood.

They talked for a few minutes more, each off following his own theory. Certainly the riddle would not be solved that night. Realizing it was late and Caroline, tired, Peter suggested that everything might be clearer after some sleep, which earned him a sneer from Hermione. With very little enthusiasm he offered to take her home, proof that he was not yet at ease with himself as eccentric.

"You wouldn't mind if I spent the night right here, would you, darlings? Knowing me tubes and such, t'ain't the moment for a good shake-up."

"The sheets are in the closet." Caroline yawned. "I'm going to bed. I can't stay up another minute."

Giordano, the dutiful host, saw Peter to his car. Mention of the alarm system drew no response. He was distant and morose, until they reached the door and he stood, looking into the dark.

"Who could it have been? Who would set the police on her, Peter? As to the police——" His voice had an angry burr. "Just let them come here asking questions! I'll tell them a thing or two. *Who* would want to hurt her? Such a silly, defenseless woman!"

16

IT THE GREAT TUSCAN TRAIN ROBBERY drifted from the front pages of newspapers to the fourth, on back slowly toward sports, and so out of print, forgotten, like the battles of modern wars, by all except those directly involved. The San Feliciani were relieved. Notoriety that threatened their "season" with trippers, reporters, and police had not suited them. It was the antithesis of pastoral charm, on which their prosperity depended. Now they could look forward to summer-as-usual, and for a time it seemed they were right.

THE FIRST MARKET DAY after Caroline's return, gossip eclipsed business. Reports of her encounter with the Finance Police had already reached heights of narrative invention that Boccaccio would not have spurned, when word rippled through the piazzas and cafés that a foreign woman had attacked Cirillo, had beaten him over the head with a package of roast pork. Warm roast pork! In the bank. Sympathies were mixed. *He* had been rushed to the emergency room of the hospital, a curious place for a shampoo. *She* had "associated herself," as the Italians say, with the detention cell, another improbability because it was generally understood there were no women's lock-up facilities.

Matteo actually crossed a café for the pleasure of telling El about it. When she realized that he was threading his way through the crowd toward her, she was surprised. Alone at a table in the backmost corner, waiting for Caroline and Lacey, she had seen him by the counter near the door, bundled in his winter worsteds and sweater vest. Seen him and noticed he looked feverish. Nothing more. They usually limited their courtesies to the civil minimum: if their eyes met, they would nod. Now, suddenly, here he was fired with xenophobic fervor, Brigadier Cirillo's newest champion. A disgraceful incident! Such an insult to sovereign authority must not be tolerated. And most certainly not from a foreigner. The fibers of society . . . They apparently were busy about a sinful life of their own, fraying, raveling, and rotting. Agitation brought specklings of perspiration and unhealthy red blotches to his face. He mopped his forehead with a handkerchief, and El, still mesmerized by the question of fibers, asked if he wasn't hot in such a heavy suit. Perhaps the sweater . . . ? She had been too personal.

"My mother taught us that the human body can do without the protection of wool only between July first and August fifteenth," he told her through lips tight with irritation. "I have never doubted her wisdom. With your permission." He bowed stiffly, turned away and then back again. "I failed to mention that the bill *this person* wished to change was from the robbery. The number is on the Bank of Italy's list. Again—with your permission." And he left her, as bemused as he might have wished, but for reasons he would never have imagined. Her mind raced in search of plausible explanations for the implausible.

None of them—she hesitated over Martha. No, underneath

the bluster she was too frightened—none of them would have snitched from the robbery money. They knew it must not be found in their possession, wanted it well and safely out of the country. A stenographic error in the list? Too convenient, not that the bank was infallible. Saturday was the right day to pass a dubious bill. Greed might overpower the prudence of the shopkeepers, who, since the robbery, had refused to accept 100,000-lire notes. Or, at the worst, there were the banks, jammed with their market-day customers, many of them peasants who had saved their time notes, electric bills, deposits, and withdrawals for this big outing of the week.

It had happened too often to El, to everyone. The clerks, zealous only in their indifference, assembling the batches of required forms with torpid ill will and, finally, folding them into ragged bundles and slipping them into a sort of toast rack beside the one, the only cashier. And he, another artist in slow motion, laying out each set carefully, like an elaborate game of solitaire, inspecting each slip for flaws, turning each check, re-adding each total, and, disgusted, savaging them with purple smears from his battery of rubber stamps. The customers in lines, shifting their weight like bored horses, smoking, sighing, talking disjointedly with their friends about the new taxes, the price of pigs, their wives. A woman, out of breath, elbows her way to the window and asks the cashier, "Could you just change this?" After feeling it, looking at it against the light, he would. Anyone foolish enough to bank on market day expected two or three such obstructions before he could complete his business. Yes, El could see it. But *not* with warm roast pork. Where were Caroline and Lacey? She started another jittery round of speculations.

Caroline arrived first in a flurry of apologies. Several of Giordano's tenants had waylaid her in the Corso, ready for a good grumble, which was also a familiar pattern. Related, like potato planting and garlic harvesting, to the lunar cycle, the monthly ultimatum was a ritual of truculence, and of its kind this was a classic: they demanded the bank be declared off limits to foreigners on market day, and they demanded in all seriousness that Caroline make their cause her own. Sympathy lightly spiced with feudal displeasure had for the moment satisfied them. But what was "The Incident" they complained of so darkly? she asked El and then, refusing to be alarmed, kept the conversation on a peacefully medieval plane, the lower orders at play, until Lacey joined them.

She was hot and out of sorts. A prod in the back with a machine gun—at least where she came from—was *not* normal banking procedure! It was scandalous police terrorism! They should . . . Again El tried to interest them in her misgivings and in reply heard about the oddities of the peasant mind and the abuse of power. 'Twas ever thus. Still, the unknowns nagged at her and she, at them. She did not like surprises.

SO, WHEN CAPTAIN NARDO telephoned right after lunch, she lied. "What a lovely surprise!" she had said, hearing in her own voice a fair imitation of delight. Yes, of course, she could come to headquarters. "Another favor? If I can." She did her best to keep relief from prancing out along the wire.

"Maybe you need a chaperone," Lacey teased her as she got in the car. "I'm not sure about his intentions." Had she seen him she would not have doubted. He was serious, rather courtly, which El found reassuring, and very much to the point.

She had surely heard of the incident at the bank that morning, involving a foreigner, a woman untrained in market-day stoicism. She was very impatient. She wanted to change a 100,000-lire note. Could she . . . ? No one would let her pass.

She too must wait her turn. All might have gone well, if, when she reached the head of the line, the cashier had not asked her to step aside until he could take care of the others and have time to go through the Bank of Italy list. She exploded. She would not move. Behind her people grew restless. The cashier argued, tried to hand money over her shoulder to the next customer, and when she snatched it out of his hand, left the window.

"Brigadier Cirillo's reports tell the rest." Ceremoniously the captain handed El two sheets of paper. A slight cock of his head and a smile suggested a pleasure they were about to share. "As a writer you'll appreciate the language."

When the "undersigned Brigadier Cirillo" entered the bank, people were shouting and pushing. Pursuant to his duty he forced his way to the center of the crowd, where he found the woman, "subject of this report" and as yet unnamed, raving. He attempted to draw her aside, to reason with her. She was not receptive. She would not be deflected or restrained and, determined to escape, she brandished "the only weapon at hand, a parcel, with deplorable results." Such understatement meant there was worse to come. "Momentarily taken aback and unable to act, the undersigned officer," he continued, was obliged to witness, as were all those present, the vilification of *L'Arma Benemerita* (i.e., the Carabinieri), of his own person and that of his father and most especially his mother, as well as other more distant relatives. There followed a list of chilling phrases, which must have galvanized Cirillo to action.

Pursuant always to his duty, he proclaimed her under arrest, for which he received repeated devastating kicks in the shin, later verified at the hospital, where he was treated for multiple abrasions and contusions to his "extremities," judged curable in fourteen days. He closed with the conventional pieties and the announcement that a formal complaint would be found attached.

"Before you go on, two things," Captain Nardo interrupted sternly, waiting to be sure he had her attention. "As you probably know, that 'parcel' he mentions contained roast pork. We convinced Cirillo to overlook that detail. The 100,000-lire note did come from the robbery." He waved his hand. "Now read the rest. The situation will be clearer."

Cirillo's charges—each cited with the relevant paragraphs of the criminal code and the "aggravating circumstances" that required maximum penalties—ran from insult to a public official, to the Republic of Italy, and *L'Arma Benemerita,* through physical assault and resisting arrest. They were filed against one Martha Gelder of no fixed abode, currently of, etc.

El sat, speechless, shaking her head. The captain smiled.

AN UNREPENTANT MARTHA had refused an interpreter, Captain Nardo explained, and, having read the list of her compliments to Cirillo, he was inclined to agree that she did not need one. However—for the protection of all concerned, he had insisted. In times of National Emergency the colonel spurned such niceties and was, even then, grilling her. Nardo made a funny, puckery face, mouth turned down.

"Si salva chi puo." He shrugged. "If your friend keeps quiet— you see my point?" He waited for El to comment. She only nodded. "When in doubt, don't" was a rule she had learned long ago. She prayed Martha had too. What the captain recommended to one witness he did not necessarily admire in another. When he went on, his voice was brusque. The conversation seemed to be at an end before it could become one. "Obviously you *do,* almost too obviously. I had thought you might be willing to help her." He reached over to take the

reports from El and put them in a clean folder, which he marked GELDER, *Martha* in neat printing.

"I would. Of course I would," she said very softly, staring at the top of his head, willing him to look up. At the crown, thick brown hair swirled in a smooth cowlick. Innocent, vulnerable, she thought irrelevantly, and as deceptive as her own eyebrows. His eyes flickered toward her and quickly away. "You will have to tell me how." He put the folder down, a silent compromise: she could not obstruct him, he could not help her—officially.

For twenty minutes he talked. In his choice of subjects he was as eclectic as the Walrus—the Dreyfus Case, Sienese frescoes, the internecine squabbles of the Ministry of the Interior and the Ministry of Foreign Affairs, Kafka, and face—weaving parables and paradoxes that no superior could have objected to, or, for that matter, have understood. El picked her way through them, building whole systems of interpretation, which collapsed with the next flight of fancy. Facts were few, but one was helpful. Martha claimed she had cashed a check at her bank in Rome, the Bank of Naples branch in Piazza di Spagna, for 500,000 lire. In proof she had offered the check stub and three 100,000-lire notes. One she had spent. The fifth she had tried to change that morning. Without warning, Captain Nardo abandoned his short assessment of Late Beethoven and stood up, taking his GELDER, *Martha* folder.

"You'll be my interpreter, won't you? A last favor?" he asked. As she had to the other non sequiturs, she nodded, and he left the room. She would not have long. She must settle on *one* approach. If she had understood, already an adventurous assumption, then this was the situation: Cirillo was offended and insisted on—? Probably an order for obligatory repatriation, which Nardo doubted could be obtained (Ministry vs. Ministry). The Bank of Naples would not confirm Martha's story—or disprove it—until Monday morning. The captain was for gentle arbitration, legality . . . The door opened and Captain Nardo beckoned her to follow him.

Late that afternoon Martha was released in El's custody with the understanding that she was to present herself on Monday at noon. Neither of them would ever discuss what was said on their trip between headquarters and El's house. El was watchful and more caustic than she normally allowed herself to be. Martha was meek, cooperative, and very good company. Their friends were confused.

LESS THAN A WEEK LATER banner headlines in the national papers announced:

SENSATIONAL DEVELOPMENT IN
TUSCAN TRAIN ROBBERY:
CARABINIERI CAPTURE LUIGI LOSCA,
KNOWN AS "THE CARDINAL,"
WITH FOUR HENCHMEN
IN ROME GUNFIGHT

Via Giulia hideout raided.
Brig. of CC spots vital clues.
Immediate summary trial scheduled.

Italian newspaper reports of crimes are socioliterary fantasies, which can bewilder the inexperienced reader. *Il Messaggero*, the unchallenged master of the genre, devoted half the front page and all of the second to the story. The lead article began:

Yesterday afternoon, after an overcast day, dusk came early to Via Giulia. Shopkeepers had put on their lights. Not a few [*sic*] stood in their doorways looking up and down the street apprehensively. These are uneasy times in Rome. Women with net bags, late shoppers, scurried over the cobblestones, eager to reach the safety of their apartments. At the upper end of the street, one of the most fashionable sections of the city, antique stores and art galleries, their windows aglitter with merchandise, were attracting their usual chic trade. Slender, well-groomed women in luxurious fur coats [*in June?*] abandoned their Mercedes anywhere along the street and swept into the shops to idle away a few hours, spend a few million lire, and then move on for "un drink" at one of the numerous meeting spots nearby.

The lower end of the street, less prosperous, not so well lighted, the part that interests us in this particular chronicle, was gloomier. There was something of menace in the air. Outside the door of number 19, Gianmauro Scandamiglio, a native of Grassano (Matera) but a resident of Rome for forty years, thirty-five of them spent as the *portiere* of the aforementioned structure, was leaning against the wall, eating his afternoon snack. He would have preferred *salame* in his bun, but his wife had seen fit to get rid of some leftover spinach omelet. Four doors down, an aged woman (62 years old), a steam presser in a cleaner's establishment, known to the neighborhood as "Zia Nuzza," was busy wielding her iron and analyzing her dreams of the night before to extract the numbers she must play in this week's lottery wheel. She is famous for . . .

Her prophetic powers can be left to delight researchers who may, a hundred years from now, paw through the morgues, hunting picturesque details of this not so picturesque age. Facts were hidden much deeper where only the dogged would discover them.

At 6:20 P.M. the evening before, eight mobile units of the carabinieri (with an arsenal of equipment) had closed off Via Giulia and isolated a building at number 25. Once snipers were in place on nearby roofs, assault troops entered the front door. The rattle of shots was heard and some ten minutes later five prisoners, handcuffed and escorted by armed agents, were brought out and pushed into five separate cars of the Squadra Mobile, which rushed off with sirens blaring to the Questura on the opposite side of the city. (Descriptions of the traffic jam they created would make anyone who ever lived in Rome weep.)

Several hours later a Vice Questore, distinguished for his ability to *speak* the language of written reports, made an official statement to the press. He identified the five prisoners. A wilderness of demographic information followed each name, including a résumé of the individual criminal records, aliases, *and* where exactly and for what they were wanted at the present time. A summary trial would be held within two weeks. The charges were illegal possession of arms—four machine guns, three grenades, ten assorted revolvers, three switchblades, and a hand ax—and conspiracy. This, the Vice Questore explained, was a move to circumvent any attempt by whomsoever to extract them from the justice of the law and did not preclude the filing of other charges as the evidence in connection with the so-called Great Tuscan Train Robbery was correlated.

When questioned about the mechanism of the raid, how these men happened to come to the attention of the police, a question of some malice in view of the number of places they were wanted for a variety of major crimes, the Vice Questore delivered a panegyric on the skill of the carabinieri. Specific information was buried still deeper.

A brigadier of typical intelligence and devotion to duty had followed a slender clue—a 100,000-lire note presented at a San Felice bank by a foreign journalist, a person so distinguished, so obviously extraneous that she need not be identified, who had received it from the Bank of Naples branch in Piazza di Spagna. Working with feverish determination and skill, the Brigadier, assisted by the bank manager, soon established that an *enormous* sum in bills (later revealed to be less than a million lire) from the train robbery was still in the bank's vaults and that, among the many operations transacted on the day of the robbery, Luigi Losca, "The Cardinal," had paid, using his own name, signature, address, and identity card, some 9,600,000 lire in due notes.

Armed with this information the police planned and executed the raid and, if further justification was needed, when Losca was captured, he had on his person, along with other moneys, four 100,000-lire notes from the robbery—obviously what was left of the ten million he had had in his possession. What was obvious to the police was less so to the diligent reader. It could have been his change, given to him by the Bank of Naples, for some ten-million-lire instrument or check used to pay off his time notes. It *was* thoughtful of him to leave his address.

All the papers published pictures of the suspects, who, even allowing for the artistic level of police photography, looked to be middle-echelon thugs, men in their thirties with potato faces, stubble, and veiled eyes. As frequenters of the station café in San Felice, they would have been conspicuously out of place. If the police had not noticed them, the café manager or one of the chaste, frumpy ladies who daily shuttled between home and school classroom would have and would not have classified them as "boys." They could not be the young men who had lurked around the station café before the robbery and thereafter vanished. Several days after the raid one man who had been arrested finally established that he was, indeed, a taxi driver and had simply been helping the other four carry boxes up to Losca's flat. He was released, and one charge had to be dropped for lack of a quorum: conspiracy, according to the law, takes five. Presumably four could claim they were playing bridge.

Among the "color" pieces was a long and laudatory biographical sketch of Achille Cirillo, "the indomitable Brigadier," as he was dubbed, written by none other than Martha Gelder. She had invented a new format for Italy and a new career for herself. In the weeks that followed she spewed out profiles of judges and prosecutors, carabinieri officers, the Scientific Police, of the manufacturers and sellers of arms, of the wholesalers and jobbers of drugs. Collected, her "A Day in the Life of a..." columns would have been a handbook for the Aspiring Criminal or Terrorist with official information supplied by those who had every reason to long for anonymity. Another example of the power of the press. Or the fragility of human ego.

17

THIS LATEST OFFICIAL FROLIC did not sit well with Captain Nardo. The train robbery had spawned and continued to spawn inglorious side effects. And mostly at his expense. He had been relieved of the investigation. His knowledge of the district had been ignored, his opinions, discounted. He had a brigadier, who was a star turn. His men imagined themselves unacclaimed heroes. The energy they might have devoted, even sporadically, to paperwork was now lavished on their peevish complaints and daydreams. Always sluggish, the bureaucratic digestive system had slipped into acute constipation, and the captain was very irascible. When, one evening, he lectured Peter and Arch on the nobility of routine, it was also obvious that the strain had put a severe crimp in his sense of humor.

They were in his office. Peter and Arch had delivered their typewriter samples, expecting mild praise. Arch joked about the hidden dangers of the enterprise. His liver would, he supposed, recover from the noxious liquids he had consumed in the name of courtesy, but on one point he needed professional advice: what technique did Nardo recommend with a lady of licentious bent who insists you come to her bedroom, if you want to see her machine?

"Have her bring it to the living room," Nardo muttered, going right on, glancing through the sheaf of samples, noting the names and makes typed in the corners. After a third run-through he looked up, scowling. "One's missing."

"We didn't seem to get on with that," Arch apologized. "I went up there, but she was—she was . . . ah . . . sunbathing—or something. Close to starkers, she was. Someone else was there and—she did *not* want company, that she made clear. So I gabbled something about a wrong turning and—"

"Brilliant!" the captain snorted in disgust. "On a mountain road without turnings." Arch blushed and took out his pipe.

"We didn't really need her." Peter tried to excuse his partner. "The morning of the robbery she was on the train with me. That night she was in London. She couldn't have . . ."

Their excuses and explanations were brushed aside like cobwebs. Captain Nardo took his text. He was very serious and very much the Commanding Officer instructing the recruits, which at first galled and finally disarmed Peter and Arch. Their resentment melted into grudging sympathy. He was, after all, only working off his frustrations. To encourage him they volunteered for further duty.

Their offer, and particularly their agreement that the robbery was local, seemed to placate him. He did not, however, accept Peter's suggestion that they discuss strategy. To him men were deployed, even ardent volunteer sleuths. He made short work of it. Arch was assigned to the four young men at the station. He should begin with the manager of the café. Tactfully. Always tactfully. He should look into alternative meeting places. Peter, who was more limited in movement and free time, was to trace the tacks and the uniforms. Such inquiries could be managed on the telephone, which was not exactly the high level of detection Peter had imagined for himself. He was also to note any conspicuous contracts, any that surprised him, especially those involving foreigners. The captain took unto himself the delicate business of bank accounts. He had the contacts. Now, best get started. They had lost valuable time. They had their orders.

THE NOBILITY OF ROUTINE still eluded Peter and Arch. Strategy they discussed at length with Lacey and El and were not surprised by their boundless curiosity. The important affairs of men, properly explained, simplified, *could* interest women, they agreed. At times, perhaps, men were too impatient, a flash of intuition, which produced an avalanche of details their listeners did not need.

Arch had interviewed the stationmaster so many times they were almost friends. By scientific method—doctors, he assured them, must piece together their patients' incoherent symptoms—he had built up a description of the four young men who had hung around the station. Now, why had they chosen *that* café? Probably not all of them had cars. If they were still meeting—if, say, three needed to talk to the fourth on his return from a trip, they could have chosen another café convenient to bus lines. And not in town, where they were well known and private conversations were hard to arrange. Did El and Lacey follow him?

El, exasperated by little steps for little people, offered to draw the local bus routes on an ordinance map for him, putting *X*'s where they crossed with the station buses and a star, if there was also a café. She felt ever so slightly guilty about leading him on a wild-goose chase, but she needed to keep him busy and out of mischief. Lacey was to play eager listener to the reports he provided for their delight. She must worry over his beleaguered liver and encourage him if he flagged, freeing El to keep an eye on Peter, who was potentially much more dangerous.

"Where would *you* go for those fancy tacks?" he had asked her one evening.

"My upholsterer," she answered too quickly, without thinking. He had started with hardware stores. In San Felice alone there were more than a dozen, few with telephones and none thus far with nails even distantly related to his sample. Stranger still, no one knew where he might find them. He stared thoughtfully at El and changed the subject. Several evenings later he complained that upholsterers were dilatory craftsmen, hard to find and uncommunicative if trapped. "Talking to men is a waste of their time," she threw over her shoulder. She was cooking dinner. He had come to stand by the sink and talk. After several seconds of silence, she looked around at him. Raised eyebrows were skeptical. "Don't be huffy. To them a man is trouble. He doesn't know what he wants—what material, what color, what it should cost. They discuss those things with the wife."

"I'm not married," he said irrelevantly to an ice tray he had taken out. "All I get is hocus-pocus about staple guns and new glues and gimp. What's gimp? *Never mind!* I don't want to know. Fact remains they don't use nails anymore."

"Ask who their suppliers were," she suggested, dumping string beans in a colander. He flinched at the sudden cloud of steam. "And if they're out of stock, ask who their last large customer was." He still stared at the beans, thinking, then remembered to put the lid on the ice bucket.

"No wonder you confuse me." He blinked at her innocently. "You have a policeman's mind—which, of course, means it's very close to a criminal's. Food for thought—Uhmmm. So, tell me about the uniforms." She stood very still. Did he mean where? or . . . ? No, he needed a new hunting ground. He had started with the classified listings of uniform suppliers—most were in Rome and Florence—and had been regularly snubbed by retired military gentlemen, even by one haughty lady, the owner of the *Boutique della Servitù,* who had informed him with much gurgling of her bogus French *r*'s that she had no call for anything below a footman's jacket. O tempora! O mores!

"Why not try the *comune?* The office of sanitation or maybe the council member for public services would know where they get them." From his expression he considered that uninspired. "Darling, after that crack about the criminal mind, what did you expect? Besides, no matter what it is, I always look first in the market and that sounded too frivolous. I could just imagine . . ." Already she regretted her fling at raillery. His face had lighted up and what she now imagined was nothing she wanted to imagine. He had picked up the ice bucket. When she put her hands on his arms, they seemed to hug it between them. "Peter, dear Peter, give up this silly business." She was so earnest, he must take her seriously. "Please! We could . . ." Shaking his head, he draped an arm around her shoulders.

"We're getting somewhere. You'll see. Come on." And he led her back to the living room, as unaware in his enthusiasm of her rueful thoughts as he had been of her tentative invitation.

THE NEXT SATURDAY, to Matteo's dismay, Peter canceled his appointments and spent the morning at the market, wandering from stall to stall. He stopped wherever men's clothing was displayed. He looked, he fingered, he bargained for trousers he would not own, he actually bought a sweater, and at each he had a quiet chat with the vendor. Discreetly. The real danger was that he might be so discreet he would be merely elliptic, the gentleman crank. He needed a sturdy garment, he explained, one suitable for gardening or the messier jobs to be found around a house in the country. A long smock-coat maybe, the kind garbage collectors wore. Easy to get into—a porter's jacket would do. No, nothing like that. Coveralls, yes. Smocks, no. If he could wait . . . The vendors were courteous and patient, too patient. They had switched to their summer personalities. Peter smiled and went on to the next.

He found nothing and had a very pleasant morning at it, far pleasanter than refereeing the quarrels of his clients, Italian and foreign. He shuddered to think of his own waiting room, where at any hour not less than a dozen people prowled about, hoping to sneak in to see him.

They were there, when he got back, keeping a deceptively close watch on the doors, lingering by them in the not so casual way of children squatting over chairs, then moving regretfully on, in musical chairs. Inflation, anticipation of death, greed, he was not sure which, had driven them to a spree of buying and selling. Captain Nardo could enjoy the land boom. It was not going to ruin his summer, and he began planning an outing— with El. They could go to the market in Arezzo: that would be the excuse, anyway.

THE FOLLOWING WEEK they did. El dreaded going. She dreaded not going. She dreaded what he would find. She prayed she would catch a cold and not have to go. She prayed nothing would keep her from going. She was disgusted with herself and kept right on, nursing her dread. Misery and company—she urged Lacey to join them. Lacey was several steps ahead of her.

"Ohh-h no! No chaperone for Nardo, no chaperone for Peter. Remember Heloise? She . . ."

". . . ended up in a nunnery," El intoned, seeming to relish the gloomy prospect.

"Besides, I have a date with Arch—for a picnic, a swim,

and a bit of subtle country-café-watching. From the *bocce* court!"
She took consolation from El's look of disbelief. "We also serve,
who only learn to bowl. He's teaching me. He says that way
no one will notice us. He *says.*"

"Mad dogs and Englishmen again! Wait—I just thought
of something. Maybe Nijinsky could go with us. It's an—an
idea." Not one she pursued, however, beyond extracting a promise from Peter that he would stop for a load of dog food.

On the appointed morning Peter arrived at El's early and
in high good humor. It was blue and sunny and dry and he had
seen a group of boys straggling listlessly to school, which height-
ened his own sense of truancy. On the way to Arezzo he told
El of his first miserable confused days in an Italian school. The
black smock with the plastic lace collar, the teacher who did
not tolerate questions, the dreary struggle to memorize without
understanding and the *Pensierini,* "little thoughts," that were the
compositions to be written about what one did on Sunday. His
were always of high adventure at Hadrian's Villa or hikes through
the Sabine Hills, while the other boys, reflecting their own more
conventional families, wrote of their new Sunday suits, large
plates of pasta, and gentle strolls through crowded parks. He
was accused of being overly imaginative, the others were praised
for grammatical accuracy. He felt sorry for them, and so did
El, seeing them as Peter saw them and seeing Peter too, a
curious, questioning little boy, always ready for an expedition.
And she realized that he had done it again, beguiled her into
forgetting real life. She let herself drift. It would do no harm,
no more than had already been done. This was not the moment
for self-analysis, which in any event she had tried—and rejected.

The market was a gaudy, sprawling maze. Piazzas and the
narrow streets that normally connected them were choked with
stalls and people. By tradition and police permit like wares clung
to like wares. Vegetables banked one street, cheeses and meats

the next. Cascades of flowers, cunningly arranged in tiers to conceal the tomato-paste tins that held them, graced each corner. Beyond a different commodity was on view: acres of synthetic finery and plastic utensils, yard goods, detergents, figurines, canaries in cages, hand tools and shoes, thousands of pairs, amphitheaters of them. Over each vendor an awning or a giant faded umbrella flapped and, here and there, on sunbaked patches, leftover hippies guarded dirty, tattered blankets strewn with wire jewelry.

For El the first moments at a market were always the same: she was caught up in a pageant. Like a circus, the colors, the hawkers' calls, the sheer quantity of goods and people jumbled together promised excitement, surprises. A dozen stalls later the promise was broken, scuttled by the very elements that had made it. The goods were shoddy. People shoved just to shove. Even the flaming gaiety of the flowers was demeaned by bins of their plastic imitators, and El felt cheated. But not that morning with Peter.

He stormed the market with all the rambunctious aggression Italian men usually save for soccer and seduction. Against the current he plowed through the crowd, shoving and snapping like an habitué. El struggled along behind him as he skipped from counter to counter, tormenting the vendors. He teased them. He mocked them: they were junk dealers. He challenged ceramists, coppersmiths, weavers to produce something worthy of his notice, and when they did, he cajoled them into lowering their price. Not that he intended to buy: just for the fun of it. El was ready to admire, perhaps to choose. Peter was restless. They must move on—unless electric drills were on display. Their infinite variety fascinated him. Did El understand how . . . ? She recognized a man on the brink of investment. She listened to his explanations of speeds and attachments, asked flattering questions and nodded solemnly over his answers, all the while making rather walleyed surveys of the clothing stalls that threatened her existence. The season seemed to be on her side.

Garments fluttered enticingly from the awning supports of every stall—cotton housedresses, the ubiquitous uniform of Italian women, and painted shawls, T-shirts, men's cotton slacks and shirts. No work clothes. Where they should have been, the featured attractions were sleeveless vests looped with cartridge slots, camouflage pants and jackets, and long, flabby waders, which dangled together like dismembered hunters. Summer must be three months of *dolce far niente*. For a few minutes more she was safe.

Peter rushed on, rejecting mechanics' overalls and khaki fatigues from every imaginable army, and flirting with drills. He posed as a gentleman farmer, as a determined gardener, as a handyman, always in need of a jacket or smock heavy enough for protection, loose enough for movement, easy to put on and take off. What did people work in? Garbage men? Porters? That sort of thing. No glimmer of interest. No sudden inspirations. Thank you, and he propelled El away to another counter, another puzzled vendor. She stumbled along obediently, too exhausted by her own dread and too dizzy from her oscillating 180-degree scans in search of "the enemy" to object. Maybe, just maybe he was not there, had not come to the market, the man who had sold them the smocks, the man who would surely recognize her as easily as she would recognize him. Or would she? She would. And then she did—four or five stalls ahead of them, a tall, bulky man, bracketed by rubberized raincoats, stood, picking his teeth and watching the crowd. He was either bored or bilious, probably the latter, given the effect of sun on rubber. It was very hot, El noticed, very hot indeed. Iridescent.

"Peter." By stretching around behind an inert, very fat woman she grabbed the hem of his linen jacket and tugged. "Peter, I—" He looked back impatiently. "It's very hot and there's an errand I want do—over there." She waved vaguely toward the mountains. He tried to ooze around the fat woman, who zipped up her purse and looked suspiciously at both of them.

"I'll come with you." A promise more easily made than kept. The crowd had shifted slightly, leaving Peter pinned with his arms over his head. He switched to Italian. *"Se questa brava signora mai mi farà passare."* She pretended not to hear and set her feet.

"No, no. You wouldn't be interested," El said, desperately edging away. "It's handmade towels and—ah—things like that. Personal things. I'll meet you at the café in Piazza San Francesco in thirty minutes."

"But El, if— Oh! Personal things. Yes, well—" He hesitated, embarrassed. Poor dummy! They haven't made *those* in fifteen years, she thought. "Let's say forty-five minutes. Piazza San . . ." The fat woman had tired of waiting. Peter tilted crazily. "Signora, you could maim someone with that purse." El was sucked away into the crowd. Peter waved, popped free from the fat woman, and bumped and shunted off in the opposite direction.

For the sake of consistency El bought two linen jacquard hand towels with long fringes. The rest of the time she paced more or less slowly around Piazza San Francesco, debating whether or not to meet Peter. Each possibility offered its own complications and no solutions. If he found the smocks and talked to that bulky, brooding man? If the man remembered his odd sale to Lacey and El? Or, if Peter came away empty-handed? And she was not there? How to explain that? A headache, a cramp in her stomach, and a longing for a sunstroke were her rewards. She stopped in the shadow of a building. What rot that women glow! She blotted her face with a handkerchief, which, after a moment's thought, she jammed down the front of her dress and then, deciding to reverse her course, almost knocked Peter down.

"Damn! I was going to surprise you!" He put his hand on her back. "Why so pensive? No luck?" She held up a plastic bag as silent proof. She was staring at a plump package, very approximately wrapped in newspaper, clamped under his arm.

"And you?" Her voice was not up to more. She still stared at the package.

"Yes—and no. You'll see." Her heart sank. He was much too cheerful. "Let's not stop at the café now. If we get Nijinsky's food, we could . . ."

". . . finish it all up in a hurry." Suddenly exhausted, she was aware that she ached all over, every muscle and joint. "You might as well tell me now what's in the package."

"Later—at lunch. I thought we'd go to Gargonza," he went on cheerfully and quickened his steps. "It's cool and the food's good—and—I want to have a long, serious talk with you. So—*Avanti!*"

Standa was an emporium something between a five-and-ten and a department store, one of a chain with singularly Italian anomalies. The merchandise was problematic. Tissue paper and toothpaste were, for instance, "seasonal items"; suntan lotion and paper plates were *not*. The women's department catered to fifteen-year-old bean poles and dropsical matrons, while in the men's department shoes were for Brobdingnagians. Finding exactly what you wanted was fortuitous, except in the grocery section, which stocked the dull standards plus such exotic wares as French pâté, imported liquors, and peanut butter. To make up for its dependability it was in the basement along with hardware, garden furniture, and luggage, and the escalator went down, not up.

Earlier Peter had left his car in the store parking lot, so

they ducked through the jewelry and bathing-suit department, straight onto the absurd escalator, and allowed themselves to be lowered into the housewife's mecca. A wave of cool air met them. Peter gazed wonderingly out across the expanse of aisles and refrigerated bins.

"Maybe I can find a stockman," he commented without conviction. "He might reverse the stairs for a few minutes." But the lure of drills was still too strong. El watched him wander off toward hardware, the tantalizing package clamped firmly under his arm.

She quickly loaded three cases of dog food on one cart, six four-kilo sacks of rice, some scotch, some gin, some tonic water, and a consolation prize, a jar of peanut butter, on another and marched toward the exit with as much dispatch as the herding of two skittish carts through a labyrinth allowed. She maneuvered around a corner, wondering what the cashier would make of her eccentric diet—not that they were interested in anything beyond the perfection of their own makeup—and suddenly found herself released to the hardware department. Ten feet in front of her stood Peter, blindly absorbed by a five-shelf display of nails. Nails! My God! She had forgotten them. Hermione had said—yes, Standa.

A fit of hysterics was the answer. All those cans swept off the shelves. The dozens of eggs, the paper-towel displays. Rice! Or sugar. Either one. The fruit. Instant *macedonia*. The relief. She was no more given to vapors than to hysterics, but she knew she had to sit down. Immediately. A crate of toilet paper, an improvised buffer between the two departments, was only a few steps away. She sank down on it. She saw Peter shake his head and move purposefully away from the nails and screws, back toward the tools. He had not seen her. Maybe he hadn't seen the nails. Maybe . . . Maybe nothing. She was sick unto death of the whole thing. She would confess. Get it over with.

The others . . . ? There she was again. There was no way out until they nibbled her to death. One hand still held on to the handle of a cart. She put her head down on it and tried to think.

"El, what's the matter?" Peter's voice was very soft and just above her. "Are you all right, El!" He sounded so worried.

"No, I'm not all right," she snapped peevishly.

"The heat—there at the market. I shouldn't have—" He stepped around the cart, put his package on top of it, and squatted on his heels in front of her. She could just see his profile and his wrinkled forehead. "Stick your head down, if you feel faint."

"I don't feel faint. That's not *it* and you *know* it." She could not stop herself. A pepper mill seemed to grind in her brain, faster and faster. She looked up at him, meaning to smile, an apology of sorts, and saw instead the package, which was slowly uncurling, shucking its newspaper wrapper. "Stop playing games with me. I can't stand any more of this. Say what you have to say. *All* of it. I deserve it. But *say* it and be done with it. No Gargonza! No explanations! Nothing!"

"But El, this isn't . . ." She had raised her head, determined to "face" in every sense what was coming.

". . . Just say it. Where doesn't make any difference now." His eyes narrowed. They were ice blue, and she knew he was angry. The unnatural strangled quietness of his voice emphasized it, and it occurred to her that this was an outlandish place for the last act of a comedy.

"For once I think I agree with you. *I* can't stand any more of this either. There's no real point in my saying it now. Your answer—well, it's clear." He waved his hand in an upward chop of dismissal. "It was to be an ultimatum—with nice scenery. Either marry me—or don't marry me. I don't like games. Not with my life. Obviously the answer is . . ." His bitterness was gaining momentum. She knew it, knew she must say something, but went on staring over his shoulder.

"What's *that?*" She pointed at the cart. The newspaper had finally wilted away from its contents, exposing a short bolsterlike roll of padded material splattered with the amoeboid shapes of conventional camouflage, except that they were deep red, sky blue, and olive green. Released, it too began to uncurl and stretch out across the bottles and rice sacks.

"A joke. A present, a silly present! A jacket I thought might amuse you." He reached out impatiently and folded the paper back over it. "Get up. We'll check out this stuff and I'll take you home. The subject is closed—for good." He was shifting his weight to stand up, when El put her hands on his shoulders.

"Was that *really* what you were going to say—at Gargonza? Marry you—or—not marry you? Oh Peter, was that *really* it? Really?" A jerky duck of his head was enough. She threw her arms around his neck. "Oh Peter!" And it all happened at once. He lost his balance, falling away from El, who lurched backward and the toilet-paper crate tipped. Peter made a wild grab for her hands, caught them, and provided a staggering, teetering counterbalance that eventually saved them both. If they had not beenlaughing, it would have been easier.

"I *told* you this was the wrong place," he gasped. She hiccoughed. "You deserve that. Let's get out of here. And I warn you—one more chance, just-one-more—at Gargonza."

THERE LUNCH WAS AS PERFECT as the scenery, not that they noticed. In fact the afternoon was one of blissful incoherence until deepening shadows suggested it might end. They coasted back to El's and would coast happily through the sunset with Lacey and Arch, but in the driveway one flaw in their day did finally come to their attention: they had nothing to unload.

Three cases of dog food, six four-kilo sacks of rice, some scotch, some gin, some tonic water, and a jar of peanut butter were still sitting in carts near the toilet paper at Standa. But on the backseat of the car, again rolled into a bolster, lay the red and sky-blue and olive-green camouflage jacket. Neither remembered taking it

18

$\mathcal{L}$ACEY SUSPECTED Matteo was right about the fibers of
society, at least the society of train robbers. A sisterhood they
were not, beyond a tacit, very fragile pact of silence. Each was
privately digesting or otherwise razing her guilt. Caroline had
taken perpetual vows of wifeliness, Italian wifeliness, which
could have been the primary source of Parkinson's Law. On
her mountaintop Hermione communed—with what or whom
was the subject of inspired rumors. Kate dieted and cooked
Robert's favorite dishes in dual atonement. In her free time she
bought cars, Valentino dresses, Ferragamo shoes, and was convinced she was losing her mind. Martha advanced toward the
Pulitzer Prize with unflappable good humor and determination.
El had found her sweet, if not oblivious antidote, and there was
nothing left for Lacey to do but meet Max in Greece. Not that
she minded.

"You wouldn't leave me alone *now?*" El objected. Another
reversal of character! Lacey decided to watch herself closely.
"At least stay for the *festa.*" That was neat. Peter was spending
a few days in Rome with his mother before her annual trip to

England. He would be back in time for the fireworks. "And what about Arch and your bowling?"

"We've decided I'm not Olympic quality. Besides he can't go on forever sitting in cafés." Or if he could . . . ? *That* was up to him. Relieved by her lack of interest, Lacey agreed to stay.

EACH DAY from dawn to dusk she regretted it too.

"*Alone*! El, you're nothing but a con artist," she repeated, taking advantage of an unlikely hush at breakfast the day before the *festa*. "No, 'Jinsky, you've had yours." He was drooling on her knee. Down in the road an engine brayed to life. She stood up, clamping her hands over her ears, a gesture so familiar that Nijinsky lunged to his feet and bounded around in short, hump-backed leaps. He knew they were going for a walk, which in the last few days had sent him into a more joyous frenzy than potato chips. They were all suffering from overexposure to the *festa*.

The disruptions had started very early one morning. A truck, heavily loaded, churned up below the house, stopped to change gears, snorted and belched like an angry dragon, and ground slowly on, up the steep lane, which, fifty-one weeks of the year, was private for the simple reason that it did not really go anywhere. It meandered up and around the fields, never passing another house, to peter out near the top of the hill at a minute chapel and well. The fifty-second week the Madonna del Pozzetto was honored.

Lacey and El sprang from their beds to the windows. In the drive Nijinsky waxed hydrophobic. A few minutes later the truck hurtled back down, its tailgate clanging in ragged syncopation, and shot out onto the main dirt road with a horrendous screech of brakes. They waited for the crash. None came. Instead another truck gunned its motor and grunted its way up the hill. The second load of coarse gravel. Many, many others followed and for each load of coarse, there was a matching load of fine mix.

To save Nijinsky from cardiac arrest, El brought him inside, where by canine logic *she* was to protect him. He rolled his eyes and hyperventilated and slept between fits in the dark safety under El's bed. Still he was a nervous wreck. But then, so were Lacey and El. Each morning they fled from the house and since El did not quite trust Nijinsky alone inside and would not chain him to a tree, where they went, he went too. For him life was pure joy.

After the relay race came the gymkhana event. Tractors, large and small, bulldozers, scrapers, hoists, and one day, for reasons unknown, a cherry picker rendezvoused at the bottom of the drive and spent happy hours nuzzling each other in and out of gulleys and over boulders, engines yelping. Locally this show of diligence was reckoned the Communist party's tribute to the other great power, the Church. According to El it was a purely commercial necessity no administration could ignore. The vendors of ice cream, of beer and soft drinks, of *porchetta* and of trinkets, the cheese merchants and the *salame* merchants and the town band must all take their trucks right to the chapel door, so it followed that ditches must be dug out, ruts leveled, and new gravel spread. Easing the pilgrims' way was incidental.

The diocesan authorities, perhaps remembering that St. George had been declared of dubious origin, therefore to be worshiped *moderately,* took a Jesuitical stand: they shunned the celebration without actually forbidding it. The Madonna of the Well was one of *those,* an embarrassment, and would have vanished, the victim of time and damp, except for the tenacity of a pudgy, red-faced priest, whose extracanonical interests were decayed monuments, pheasants, and young girls. *He* discovered the painting in the chapel of a young mother at a well, surrounded by peasants, and after arduous research, *he* declared her the Madonna of the Well, the only surviving work of a local primitive, Ristonchio da Ristonchi. The miracle was easily found: the well had "never, in the memory of man, gone dry." (Nor had it been used in the memory of man, but that was unimportant.) So she became the patron saint of well drillers and of hunters, a category which at last count involved 98 percent of the male population. With their wives, their children, their picnics, and their shotguns, they invaded the hillside. Beginning at noon and the opening mass, they came in assault waves. By late evening they stumbled around like a routed army with all the urgent, unsolvable needs of one. But they would not leave. They had come for the fireworks and the grand finale when, after three single detonations, muffled thuds really, every man, drunk or sober, fired his shotgun in salute to the Madonna. That was the magic moment. They would wait a year for another such.

Experience had taught El that her house would be treated as a combination beachhead and service area. People parked in the shade of her trees, then asked to fill water jugs or buy wine. They expected to use the bathroom, make telephone calls, leave their babies, visit the house, or simply get out of the sun and rest. Always inclined to relate people to the animals they resembled, she called these the "littering locusts." To defend against them she recruited friends, promising drinks and fireworks in return for guard duty. Other years she had borne the preliminaries alone, wandering the lanes with Nijinsky galumphing happily around her.

"*Alone!* You knew it would be like this!" Lacey complained again late that last afternoon before the *festa*. They were all tired. Up ahead Nijinsky lay in the path, panting. "How could you, El?" Her answer was short and singsong.

"Confucius say, 'Virtue not left to stand alone.'"

"*It* loves company too?" Lacey leaned over to pat Nijinsky. "Next she'll tell me we're the Festal Virgins." He smiled.

IN ROME Peter had a frustrating time too. He often did when he went to see his mother. He would arrive ready to do whatever would please and amuse her, half knowing she would be too busy to see him. She did not need to *see* him, she would insist. To have him home again, safe in his own room, reassured her. And now she was in a terrible rush. Mornings were for errands. Luncheons, canasta parties, tea, and after-dinner coffees absorbed the rest of her day. If he trailed behind her, handing her through traffic and in and out of taxis, the brace of brittle widowers who had permanent claims to such honors would sulk. "I only said I'd go, dear, because I knew you'd like to see your own friends" had always been her gentle apology. "I didn't want you to worry about leaving me."

In late July he had hoped things would be different. His friends were away, as he had been sure hers would be. Instead, talk of recession and summer robberies, inflated by repetition to the modern sack of Rome, had convinced them to economize. They had canceled their summer excursions: after all, Rome without the Romans was very pleasant. With her usual engagements plus her farewell calls and dressmakers' appointments, his mother was busier than ever. Peter, adrift in a hot, semievacuated city, visited museums he had not seen in years. They were, at least, cool.

The day before his mother was to leave he insisted she have lunch with him—alone. He chose a small *trattoria* off Piazza di Spagna where vines covered the courtyard with speckled shade and a naked pipe high in a wall rationed out a trickle of water, which dribbled down through racks of salad greens and finally plopped gently, drop by drop, into a marble sarcophagus. Cool and peaceful, it seemed a place that might calm her flittering long enough for him to talk to her. Seriously.

Peter arrived early, expecting to wait. His mother was as notoriously late for appointments in stationary places as she was early for trains and planes. He should have been warned—she was already sitting at a table, inspecting her neighbors with the birdlike hauteur she used to hide her nearsightedness. She pressed an *aperitivo* on him. It would calm his nerves: he was so cross. He did not want it, but, like most sons, obeyed out of habit and, like most sons, continued to underestimate her perspicacity. Halfway through the pink concoction he abruptly made his announcement, then sat back to enjoy her surprise.

"Thank goodness!" was all she said for a moment. "I was afraid you'd shilly-shally until El found someone else—or was bored with you." Peter stared at her, speechless, letting his silence seem an apology for his lack of initiative, rather than tell her how many times he had been rejected. Her benevolence might not stretch that far. "Never mind, dear," she finally added. "All's well that ends well. I took this out of the safety-deposit box the other day." She patted his hand and pushed a small box over in front of him. Inside was a ring of platinum filigree, studded with small diamonds, and at the center a large, luminous pearl. His father had given it to her on their wedding day, and she had always worn it, until, at his father's death, it had vanished. "I can't bear wearing it now. I want El to have it. He would be so happy too."

With that arranged to her satisfaction she turned to the more normal pleasures of lunch, chattering about dates and dresses and houses, about marriage in general and hers in particular. His father would have been amused, Peter thought. Once again he was surprised to discover that his mother, *his*

241

mother, had ever been "in love." Of course that was a long time ago. Things were different then. Or were they? Mmm . . . ? Mothers have always confounded their children.

His continued to do so. She had already put off her engagements. She planned to spend the day with him. That afternoon they wandered around Rome. That evening they reviewed the family silver and linens she wanted El to have, and early the next afternoon, after the unavoidable station interlude, Peter entrusted her, along with several thousand lire, to the care of the sleeping-car attendant. She fairly pushed Peter out of her compartment and down the corridor. Her last instructions were called out to him from her lowered window.

"You must run, dear. You don't want to miss your train." He had over an hour. "Don't forget to give El my note—and my love—and tell her that with patience I think she can make you into a very satisfactory husband. Though, I'll admit, mothers are not the best judges."

FROM THE VERY BEGINNING the party sideslipped gently toward debacle. By default Lacey took charge of the before-dinner precautions. She tied Nijinsky with a limp, bearded rope to a tree on the back terrace. He quivered with resentment. She sent Peter and El to entertain him, which was an act of faith. They were too engrossed in catching up on the events of the last few days to notice others, or, if they did, briefly, it was with exquisite, glazed courtesy that meant their thoughts were light-years away. Should he choose, Nijinsky could sprint off across country. As long as El was near, he probably would not choose. Probably. Lacey had to take the chance. Arch needed her at the front of the house.

She found him halfway down the drive, waving off a man

in a minibus crammed with screaming children. The frustrated father leaned out the window and shouted that the Communists knew the proper tortures for the likes of Arch! Just wait until they took over! And cursing, he rocketed back down the drive. Arch bowed solemnly and walked up to join Lacey.

"Our sawhorse didn't last sixty seconds," he informed her ruefully. "An energetic type simply got out and threw it over across the ditch. We had words." He chuckled at the thought. The red plastic sacks they had tied to it flopped in the grass by a white oleander bush.

"I brought a bottle of wine—if we can't leave, we can at least..." She shrugged and pointed toward the steps.

"...have our own party." He placed cushions for them on the low wall that bordered the flagstone terrace along the front of the house, and started to work with a corkscrew. "Before someone else comes, I've been trying to tell you about Captain Nardo. He..." He stopped to concentrate. The cork was temperamental. "There! About Captain Nardo. He says we're getting somewhere, that—" A car raced up the drive with its horn blaring. "Now what?" they both groaned and got to their feet. When the dust settled, Alan Pound grinned at them from one of the Bourton-Hamptons' Jaguars. Beside him sat Joan. He jumped out and came over to them, looking, in a beige linen suit and gleaming brown buckle shoes, like the sleek plastic dandy of a clothing ad.

"My mother here?" he demanded rather arrogantly, or so Lacey felt.

"No. Is she supposed to be?"

"She was going to drop by. Maybe that was later," he conceded. Lacey did not help him. He smoothed down his already smooth hair and considered the ground at his feet. "I just don't know," he finally said. He seemed bewildered. "It's sort of complicated. I'm driving Joan to Porto Ercole and Dad expected me—that is, there was this plan—to go to Rome for a few days, just him and me. Now—well, I thought I'd better tell Mother . . ." His voice trailed away. He looked uncertainly at first one, then the other, and then for a moment at the car. "And—I thought she should know about the Captain's visit. Said he was looking for Dad, but he nosed around and talked to me and—well, I thought she . . ."

"Why not leave her a note?" Lacey suggested. "Or better yet, a note for your father." She wished she could ask more about Captain Nardo's visit. He was altogether too busy.

"I did, but if Mother knows things, she sort of . . ."

"Softens the blows," Lacey offered. "I can imagine. He hunched up his shoulders in an effort at savoir faire. She looked over at the car. Joan waved. "Where's Filippo?"

"In the backseat, sleeping it off. He had a bad trip last night." Alan grinned at her. Not to be outdone, Lacey grinned back. That word again with all its new ambiguity! She would not ask. "Well, *ciao,* as they say!" He bounded over to the car, folded himself into the driver's seat, and shot backward down the drive with spectacular grumblings from the twin carburetors. Nijinsky was offended. No respecter of idylls, he let out sharp, baying howls. Lacey looked over her shoulder in time to see Peter and El rush around the corner of the house, confused, but willing to do battle.

"Nice of you to join us," she welcomed them. "If you plan to stay, get some glasses. If not, of course—"

El ignored her sarcasm to stare off toward the road. "Stupid!" Her irritation had no identifiable source. "*Stupid!* Why didn't I see it before? Peter, if you block the bottom of the drive with your car—it's so obvious—no one can drive up. And we could have some peace until the others come." It was her most sensible remark of the evening.

AFTER SUPPER, once chairs, glasses, and bottles for the party had been brought out and the candles flickered gently behind their glass chimneys, they had coffee. To their left the top of the hill was silhouetted against a nimbus of light. Occasional moans might have been appreciation of some wondrous feat or merely a trick of the wind. They were sitting, not talking, just drifting between reality and night dreams and quite content, when a disembodied Winged Victory, wrapped in white gauze, rippled silently toward them. She dipped and banked like a ghostly white bat and disappeared to glide back into sight seconds later from a different part of the garden.

"Come off it, my girl," Arch shouted. "Frightfully bad manners, you know. Scaring people this way."

"Oh shit!" The chiseled enunciation was unmistakably Hermione's. "Englishmen are such bores." Her wings flopped to her sides and she stumped across the flagstones toward them. "In fact *all* men are bores. I've only just escaped from one— by the hardest." She threw herself in a chair. "A madman. Anyone who'd call himself something like Phineas Fogg must be, and he keeps dropping cards on me. *Three* times he's come up. Can you imagine? I hide and—flippo—there's another card in the mailbox. Three times!"

" 'Tis a bit out of the way," Arch mumbled, half to himself. Hermione shushed him and forged on with her tale. Again, just now, she had met this—this Phineas person—on the road, waving and calling at her like a lunatic, trying to stop her. She taught him a lesson! Ran him off into a ditch, she had, and then had gone plummeting on down the mountain at a terrible rate.

"Actually—" She lapsed into private calculations. "Actually that was great fun! Maybe I should go into a rallye! They fascinate me, and now that I have my license, what's to keep me from it?" The dark was merciful. She could not see her listeners wince, and they, survivors of her practice years around San Felice, long years that might have lasted indefinitely had she not found an impressionable inspector, kept their dread imaginings to themselves. "This is perfect country for trial runs. Take . . ." She did, lane by lane, leaving the others to estimate the toll of chickens and children. New arrivals and a general shifting and regrouping saved Siena. Peter went off to move his car and brought Kate back with him. He had found her wandering around in the dark.

"Not wandering," she confided to Lacey. "Just sitting on the wall, thinking. Everything is *so* wrong, and I can't seem to straighten it out. But you talked to Alan. What did he say? Why's he running off? And what about Captain Nardo?" So she knew nothing. Robert was in Perugia seeing a taxidermist. Camels on the lawn, in the living room? Lacey abandoned those seductive visions to listen to Kate. She had to talk. She rambled in circles, closing each with, "Oh Lacey, we're in such a mess!" She thought she was losing her mind. The other night she had thrown a pot at Robert. What was wrong with her? And Alan. He was up to mischief. Robert suspected worse. They kept her in the middle. Maybe that was what wives and mothers were for—if so, she was a flop. "Oh Lacey, we're in such a mess!" She was losing her mind—and they'd never notice. "I must be. There's no other explanation."

Lacey found several, which, if they did not totally convince Kate, did shift her attention to causes. When people strayed into Kate's monologue—Giordano worried about the CIA, Arch in search of ice, Caroline afraid she might miss a secret, others delighted that Peter and El had finally made up their minds— she was silent and forlorn, waiting for them to drift away again and for her cue from Lacey, who never failed her. Lacey did listen too, absently, knowing that Kate had to talk, that words said out loud *to* someone made thoughts real and fears less so.

Kate murmured, and Lacey pondered marriage and children and how the evening would end.

"Friends! Friends!" bellowed a man's voice from somewhere down in the trees. "Don't shoot! I've brought Delilah to meet you." Webster Maddox appeared, blinking in the light. Behind him came a sturdy man dressed in a mélange of clashing checks. He was curiously hairy with wiry curls that bushed around his head and bristling eyebrows that wigwagged for attention. He peered at the shadowy guests, nodding foolishly. "*He's* not Delilah," Webster announced. "Found him walking along the road. Says he's a friend of El's. You here somewhere, El? He's really an editor hunting Hermione. She's gone to ground. Anybody know . . . ?" He stopped and narrowed his eyes, alert to the guilty semi-silence. "There you are. I've caught you. Told him I would."

"*Tant pis,*" Hermione said very clearly, lingering over the phrase as though she liked the sound, almost as though it held a secret, nondictionary meaning for her. And it was the only comment she awarded Plum MacIntosh, alias Phineas Fogg, for his ponderous gallantries and literary anecdotes. His tales of "Poor Scott" were greeted by "*tant pis.*" "Dear Dottie" fared no better. Ignoring the snub, he moved on to "Papa." "Now, 'Papa' . . ." and Kate, suddenly bubbling with good humor, whispered to Lacey, "Have you noticed? His friends all have one thing in common—they're in no condition to deny knowing him." Her merry laugh pealed out over the party.

As they waited for the fireworks, whichever kind, conversation revived. Webster was particularly insistent. They must meet Delilah. No one paid much attention, until El with the energy of desperation prodded them out of their chairs. She was right at the end of the drive, Webster promised them. "Beautiful! Just beautiful! Plum brought her up yesterday. She's his aunt." This genealogical wonder went unchallenged. Even

Hermione, whose face had set in an expression of remote, sphinxlike ennui, straggled obediently down the road with the others. They teased Webster. He shouted at them. They were clots! His beautiful Rolls deserved better. She—his elaborations were cut off by the calls of a young policeman, scrambling up the hill.

"*Signora! Signora! Ah, meno male!*" he sighed with relief on seeing El. "Do you know who that *transatlantico* down there belongs to? It's blocking traffic. See it?" He pointed off toward a golden shimmer. "The brigadier wants the road cleared for fire engines, just in case, and . . ." Webster lowered at the term *transatlantico* and would have argued except that the policeman grabbed him by the arm and hurried him away.

The denouement came to his friends above as *tableaux vivants* revealed, then concealed, and revealed again by the headlights of cars, apparently maneuvering in a game of mechanical jackstraws. Children clung to the goddess of Peace who surmounted the radiator. Webster picked them off, like kittens, by the napes of their necks. He gesticulated to the crowd. In one dark interval he started the motor. It purred in a powerful, genteel way. He put on the headlights, leaving the car an indistinct shapeless hulk. Behind it the policeman went into a wild ballet of gestures. Move aside! To the crowd. Back, back full speed! To Webster. In the dark again, a siren wailed, closer now. The Rolls's engine snarled in answer. Gritty scrapes and whirs, a crunchy ripping, a dull smack, and people screamed. They stumbled and scratched up the hill. The dark blue-and-white Alfa of the Second Flying Squad eased into sight and stopped. Delilah had vanished. In billows of dust. As they settled, her snout emerged, radiator ornament and all, pointed skyward, then her midsection, the frame resting and inclined to teeter on the edge of the road, and finally the rear of her carcass, which clung to a rock ledge, hooked onto it by deep gashes in the pantaloons that so decorously shielded her back wheels. Her rump was invisible in the sandy depths of a drainage ditch, blessedly dry at the moment. While the motor idled with throaty nonchalance, Delilah was sinking, stern-first, like a true transatlantic.

Webster, his face chalky, leered out the side window, waved, and gunned the engine. Dust and rocks skittered out in all directions. She only listed further sternward. He frowned. Again the engine roared, rocks flew through the air, and the stern dredged deeper. Again and again, until suddenly there was a deafening explosion. "Boom-ka-boom!" A low, moaning "Ohhh!" rose from the fields where people stood about, waiting and watching. The fireworks! They searched the sky. Nothing. "Boom-ka-boom" thundered Delilah. Small mushrooms of steam belched from her prow. "Boom-ka-boom," followed this time by "whoosh-whoosh" and the sky was etched with sprays of exploding lights. "Whoosh! Whoosh!" Another barrage went up, flared, and looped gracefully away into the dark.

The bombardment came from all sides. Boom-ka-booms and whooshes alternated, until finally Delilah, for the first time exposing her true autocratic personality, blasted out three decisive, enraged boom-ka-booms. The devout hunters, nearby and above at the chapel, had reached a stage of delirium beyond the subtle distinctions of thuds. They lurched for their guns and shot off their double-barreled salvos. Webster, the unbowed martyr, crawled out of the driver's seat to a hundred-gun salute, then tripped on a rock and slithered feetfirst into the ditch and disappeared. It was, in every way, an original celebration.

So was the epilogue. The priest sued Webster for disturbing the peace and asked damages, insisting that the cost of fireworks, paid for by him, but unused because of Webster, be reimbursed. Webster got into the spirit of the thing and countersued, charging public nuisance. Within the next twenty years there should be a hearing.

Delilah, now definitely the Golden Whore, was salvaged and repaired at great expense, but her colicky eruptions persisted. They were diagnosed as nonterminal addiction to tetraethyl lead. Since withdrawal was impossible and her constitution too frail for her to leave town, her noisy paroxysms became as familiar as the bongings of the town-hall clock, and Webster, her constant companion, resigned himself to being the children's delight, signor Boom-ka-boom.

Early one morning, several days after the *festa,* the first of many trucks thundered by under El's house and again the yard was clogged with machinery. By order of the Mayor the lane was to be paved. In Italy the right things have *always* happened for the wrong reasons.

19

Ⓣ IN SAN FELICE August is a month for caution, even guile. People with swimming pools, a dangerous attraction, talk of serpents. Others hint at cholera or earthquakes. Any expedient will do that keeps acquaintances and acquaintances of acquaintances with their children, their dogs, and their crises—their cars suddenly in need of a mechanic or their teeth in need of a dentist—from settling in to stay. Restaurants, any public place, and large parties, are to be avoided.

Unfortunately that year, for reasons of her own, which had to do with the availability of social and diplomatic potentates, Anatolia Hughes chose mid-August to give a large supper dance in her gardens for Joan Bourton-Hampton and the Prince of Ficuzza e Verdura. They were to be married in September. The neighbors resigned themselves and hunted out the finery they stored at the backs of closets for such unwonted emergencies.

Lacey, tanned and somber after an epic quarrel with Max, came back from Greece just in time for the party. She had little to say about her trip, less about the quarrel, except for a quiet, autistic question she asked herself out loud several times each day: Why can't I remember how it started? El knew the feeling too well to pry. She did ask Arch to join them, which Lacey accepted with a wan smile. Only the script dragged her out of her mental lethargy, and that because she claimed she must get back to New York and wanted to take it with her.

The evening of the party Arch arrived so dashing in dinner clothes, with three exotic medals hanging from rainbow ribbons, that it was difficult to imagine his old threadbare look. El made a fuss over him.

"The medals," he specified, "are for Anatolia. She'll like them." He strutted off and twirled, first to the right, then to the left, in an expert imitation of a mannequin.

"But poor Eddie! He *will* be jealous." El pretended to sympathize. "He's saved all of his—from school, from camp, and of course from the war, even those target-practice ones. I've seen them in a glass case. One says 'Prone' and the other 'Small Bore.' " Scolding her, they got in the car: she must not be unkind; tonight of all nights she must be on her good behavior. "I'm not making it up," she protested. "Just look in his study. They're there. Besides, why tonight?"

"It's a celebration!" Arch sounded excited. "This was my last day of café-watching. We found them! Just in time too. My liver couldn't—" They shouted him down: found who? when? Peter turned onto the main road. Arch stared out the window, smugly concentrating on the view. The light was deceptive. The hills blazed. Below, the fields were cool and dark, secretive in their shadows. Both were very near, yet far away, their true distance mystified by the sun's last deepening before twilight. When Arch was satisfied with their coaxing, he leaned forward excited again and told them about his afternoon.

He had been sure he had found them, but to be safe he had dragged the station café manager with him. There were three young men obviously waiting not too patiently for the fourth. The manager identified all of them, neat as you please. He had even gone to Nardo's with Arch, just in case there were questions. This damned party of Anatolia's! Nardo was so busy protecting the ambassadors she had lured from all over Europe and Africa that he would not get to the suspects until the next morning. Arch had promised to say nothing. No, no—he would not betray . . . As Peter swept around a curve a man lurched up onto the shoulder of the road, running toward the center line, his arms flapping. Peter swerved wildly to the left and braked. The car slued, skittered off the road, then back onto it, and finally came to rest more or less in the right lane.

"Fool!" Peter snorted. "You all right back there?" The answer was muffled. El grabbed for Lacey, who had ended up head-down between the seats. Arch struggled up from his sprawl across the backseat and helped her. By the time she was extricated from the snarls of her long skirt, Peter was out on the road. Slowly the others joined him.

"Look!" El pointed to a field below them. An erratic path, sliced through tall, droop-headed sunflowers, disappeared into trees along a stream. Pounding footsteps behind them brought their attention back to the road. A tall man was running toward them, his head down. Until he called them, El did not recognize Captain Nardo.

"Thank God, you stopped!" He was hatless and red in the face. "We've got to follow that car." Arch was too sensible to be interested in a chase.

"I'm a doctor. Anyone else in your car?"

"My driver. Stunned, I think not hurt. He's working on the radio. Have to get word . . ." Nardo turned to Peter. "Did you see a green car? No. He was ahead of you. We can catch him with this car. Sorry, that's an order. The ladies . . ." Arch had started down the bank toward the field of sunflowers. Lacey followed, holding her skirt up daintily. She shouted that she knew how to run the radio, and disappeared. El, not to be left behind, had jumped in the front seat. Any chase was better than Anatolia's dance. Peter started the engine and let out the clutch, before Nardo could close the back door. He leaned his forearms on the back of the front seats and rested his chin on his hands so that he could see the road. "Straight and as fast as you can. I'll explain later. Faster! Go on!" He was so impatient that El half expected him to propel himself over the front seat. "*Gesù*! No siren!"

El pointed to Lacey's white scarf, which lay wadded on the floor. He handed it to her. She knotted one end into a loop, slipped it over her right hand, and trailed it high and wide of the car. She had to stretch, but she could just reach the horn lever. It let out loud irregular bleats. They drove through a little settlement. Peter scalloped around a cart and a pair of oxen. At the last second El remembered to drag in her arm. The scarf flicked at the oxen.

"Keep it up! He can't go this fast."

Peter skated between two cars and frowned doubtfully. "All he has to do is pull off the road and park," he grumbled, arching slightly toward the backseat. Nardo shook his head.

"He's headed for a special place, one he thinks is safe." They sped by a country wineshop. Men, clustered around a bowls court, pivoted in astonishment, and gaped after them.

"That it?" Peter nodded toward the windshield. Ahead a car lunged into a bend. The front obeyed, but the back wheels with little weight to hold them to the road bounced along, dragging the car out of its turn, almost swinging it about to face them. It rocked uncertainly, then straightened and disappeared.

"Pea-green Fiat 127," Nardo barked. "Watch it! He's turning. Is he green?" Peter shifted roughly down into third and tromped on the brakes. They took the turn on the bias, heeling without overbalancing, and there, three hundred yards in front of them, was the other car: it was green. El released the horn lever and reeled in her streamer. Peter nodded his approval, but kept his eyes on the road.

"A few minutes more and I'll need the lights," he warned.

"So will he," Nardo grumbled. Surprised at his disinterest, El looked over her shoulder. He was hunched down, squinting through the windshield, then back at a piece of paper held cupped in one hand. He jerked his head, convinced at last. "*Dai, dottore! Dai!* We've got him!" The heavier car did not threaten to skip off into the vineyards, as the Fiat did, but it wallowed like a ship on an oily sea.

Suddenly El felt herself flinch from the window and scream. A lightning glimpse of something about to hurtle into them, a man on a scooter! Peter yanked the steering wheel to the left. The car lunged over, scooped back across the road, skidded into a long, sickening glide, and what seemed miles further on, roared back up onto the crown. Peter twirled the steering wheel and stayed off the brakes, as though he were driving on ice. Only when the weight of the car began to slow it did he stroke the brakes, lightly. El and the captain had craned around to see out the back window.

"Man on a Vespa! Keep going!" Nardo ordered. "He's walking. Time later . . ." El slumped in her seat, closed her eyes, and opened them again almost immediately. The pea-green Fiat? In front of them rose a hummock: the dikes, joined by a bridge, of a wide drainage ditch. There was no car in sight. The road was empty and darkening. Peter switched on the lights. On the levee rows of poplars, stiff as pickets, stretched off to the right and left. The car took the approach, the bridge, and the steep swoop-off like a runaway roller coaster. Still the road was deserted. Peter stood on the brakes. Nardo jumped out and ran back toward the bridge. Peter joined him. They searched the murky twilight.

Well above her on the embankment to her left, El could see a car, small, light in color, bumping along, churning up a foam of dust. The beams of its headlights, cut by the close-order ranks of trees, flashed a monotonous semaphore. He would reach town before they could. . . . It was gray. She searched the levee to her right. Small lights twinkled. Fireflies. In August? Small lights twinkled, further away now. And a spark of red. She heard Nardo and Peter running and hurriedly got back in the car.

"Sneaking down around the hill," Nardo panted, slamming the door. Peter threw the car in reverse and lunged back almost onto the bridge, and then swung off to his left. He was lucky. A track wound around through tall grass and up through one row of trees onto the levee. Ahead parking lights changed to headlights and the car picked up speed. In a dip at the end of the makeshift causeway it vanished to pop up seconds later, twisting around a low hill. They shimmied along behind in squalls of dust. Rocks thumped against the underside of the car, ledges ground along it. Peter winced.

"Not a jeep, you know."

"We'll pay," Nardo assured him. The car and its red tail-lights had disappeared again, but the telltale cloud of dust hovered. "He's gone off to our left. Take the—"

"First left," El suggested in a vague voice. Her eyes half closed, she was trying to remap the terrain in her mind.

"No, second!" ordered Nardo. El grabbed for the strap above her door. Second left delivered them into a compost pit the size of a small swimming pool, an unused one, *per fortuna*.

"*First* left," El repeated. Nardo, who had almost fallen into the front seat, was too busy pulling himself back to answer. By the time Peter backed the car out onto the road, there were no lights or dust on their side of the valley. They searched the hillsides. Nothing. "There's a new firebreak up there," El said finally. "They cleared it this spring. Comes out somewhere near the lake, I think."

"This car can't make——"

"All right," Nardo cut him off. "Back to that last wineshop. I'll call from there." Edging the car gently into the dike ruts, Peter asked who or what they were chasing.

"If you need a get-away car this summer," Nardo said, "buy a pea-green 127. It started at the lake . . ."

His explanation was without frills. He had been on his way to see that his men were in place and pay his respects to signora Hughes. He pronounced it Hug-ess. As always when he was in a car, the radio was on. An emergency had interrupted the routine calls. A young man, driving a pea-green Fiat 127, had charged through a roadblock near Castiglione, scattering cara-binieri and injuring one. Two others had scrambled onto their motorcycles and chased him until they were caught by a level crossing. They skirted it and eventually found themselves fol-lowing a pea-green Fiat 127—driven by a woman. The captain was disgusted.

"Anyway I was on a completely different road," he went on. "Not thirty seconds after the call came over, this kid whips around us in—what else? —a pea-green 127 with about the right license, so I tripped the siren. He charged off full-speed. The corporal fought to catch up with him, but he did and was about to force him over, when a car came the other way. The corporal hesitated—can't say I blame him—just too long. We had to dive in behind our boy and we hit something, maybe a road marker and——" He rolled his hands over and over. "Off into the sunflowers we went. You know the rest." Peter had skidded to a stop in front of the wineshop. "I'll only be a minute." Nardo got out and shoved through the crowd of men who had already collected to stare at the car. Peter decided to turn it around, which brought a spate of advice from the bystanders.

"I bet most of those old boys have never driven a car," El whispered, pointing to a row of motorbikes. "Peter, while he's gone—would you take me back to look for that man on the Vespa? It was so close—I—" She did not go on because Peter had jumped out of the car and gone around to look at her side.

"He didn't actually hit us, but the fall—"

"Everything's under control," Nardo announced, getting in the back again. "We'll still catch him, if you hurry." While they cruised along at a relatively lackluster speed, he told them what he had learned. The corporal was all right. Lacey and Arch would be handed over to their hosts. A car and two men had been sent to see about the man on the Vespa, this with a bow to El, who was surprised by his thoughtfulness. They were to help him, apologize, of course, reassure him. In a few minutes, Peter should expect to be overtaken by two motorcycles, his men, who would clear their way through the crowd below the Hug-ess's, *and* he had the registration of the car. That apparently was all he had to tell them. El sidled around in her seat. He had leaned his head back and closed his eyes, but she knew he was not resting. Two motorcycles sped past them, lights flashing. Nardo waved them on and then gave Peter very concise instructions.

"As fast as you can—no slalom race this time—pass under the Hug-ess's, and the old Customs House. After that take the second left. Got it?" Peter bobbed his head. Already they were squeezed in a narrow aisle between parked cars. On ahead cars burrowed tentatively into ditches, others beat a zigzag retreat. El leaned down, almost across Peter, to see up the hill. A carnival of lights played on what, at a distance, looked like an enormous brick of vanilla ice cream decorated with uniform lashings of chocolate. One of the brown-and-white signs Eddie had dotted around the intersections drifted by: TICONDEROGA. He must be a secret admirer of Long Island country clubs, El thought, straightening up.

"How many people has Anatolia asked?" she murmured to Peter, who made a face at her. The road was almost clear, and again Captain Nardo crouched forward searching the hills. There were few enough lights and all of them stationary.

"Easy now," he warned. "It's just beyond that next rise. About fifty meters up there's a dead end to your right." Peter slowed for his turn. "Go beyond it and back into it—as fast as you can. Then cut your lights! Hurry!" Impatience was winning over diplomacy. Peter followed orders, but when he had drawn the car up and started back, he hesitated. On their left was a sheer drop. The road itself was narrow and the slot Nardo had chosen, between a half-ruined barn and a shed, was even more so.

"*Santo Dio!* Back up!" Nardo growled. "There's plenty of room. Or do you want me . . . ?" Peter's answer was a charge backward, cranking on the steering wheel.

"That suit you, Captain?" he asked triumphantly, switching off the ignition and the lights. Nardo pushed at the door handle. The door gave a few inches and smacked against a stone wall. He tried the other side with the same result. Peter had inserted them into a masonry slipcase. "Lots of room, Captain. Lots!" Nardo mumbled noncommittally and rolled down his window. Only the melancholy croaking of frogs broke the silence. El's lighter snapped open with a loud crack—and shut again and the frogs croaked.

"Could he have been ahead of us?" Peter asked *sotto voce*.

"Darling, you don't have to whisper. Even if he came, he couldn't hear us talking, could he, Captain?" Suddenly she stopped.

"Shh, someone's com—" She caught herself and giggled. Lights slipped over the fringe of dry grass at the edge of the road and then stopped moving altogether, focused on the hard dirt track. An asthmatic grinding told the story. The engine, a 500 Fiat from the sound, had stalled. On the third try the starter caught and a little red car chugged sedately up the hill. For several minutes they listened to the frogs. The stone buildings played tricks with the echoes of cars passing below them on the main road. Peter turned questioningly to Nardo.

"No, he was *not* ahead of us. They checked the map for me at headquarters—there are *no* side roads off the firebreak." He unsnapped his holster, took out his pistol, and put it down beside him on the seat. It seemed almost a statement of earnest. "He's had a slow trip to the head of the valley and he'll be careful doubling back, but he'll be along—I promise you, he will." He cocked his head to listen.

On the main road a car slowed as though to turn. Lights eased around the corner. The driver was very cautious. Instinctively Peter and El ducked down, out of sight. The car passed, its engine steady. Again they were in the dark.

"Pea green and going home." Upholstery muted Nardo's voice. His head finally reappeared from between the seats. "Now we wait. We let him get almost there before we start up. Signora, you must know where the Hug-ess's garages are." El explained that the lane they were on passed one gate, which was usually the exit, and, further along a second gate, the entrance to the interior service lane. It looped around by the garages, past Eddie's study, and so out by the exit gate. She suggested they go in by the first gate. Nardo disagreed.

"No. Take the usual entrance. Less conspicuous."

"Yes, the first gate," El mused to herself, pretending not to hear him. "That way anyone who wants to sneak out will run right into us." The captain greeted this second lesson in the decisiveness of Anglo-Saxon women with a chary silence, which Peter aggravated by turning, the obedient driver awaiting instructions.

"She may be right—or not. Boh! Try the first."

"Very wise decision." Peter edged the car out of its slip. "El, tell me when we're getting close. With that high hedge along the back, I won't be able to see where the gate is."

They climbed up, twisting and curving, passing footpaths that branched, but no roads. Finally Ticonderoga came into sight. Anatolia had arranged a fairyland. Trees glistened with minute lights and a glow from the gardens flushed the upper stories of the house. The service buildings had not had such elaborate attention. They were dark shapes. Then the tall hedge cut off their view.

"See the lights? There, through the bushes?" El strained forward. "That's Eddie's studio. Slowly— Now, Peter! Turn!" There was no opening in sight, but Peter turned, swinging blindly into the hedge. A stone wall, in front of them, spun off to their left. Eddie's studio, lights blazing. Peter cut across one corner of the flagged terrace. "Sharp right," El ordered, and he swept into an opening, skinned by a parked Jaguar, and brought the car around in a tight U that put the headlights straight on a row of six garage doors. Two were open. One stall was empty. In the other was a pea-green Fiat 127. The license number was right.

"Stay in the car. Don't move until I tell you." Nardo very quietly opened the back door and was swallowed up by the dark. The garages were shadow and glare. He materialized as trouser creases at the edge of the dark near the row of garages. From the left, presumably from one of the other stalls where Peter and El had not been able to see him, a tall, thin man in a khaki shirt and trousers walked casually toward the pea-green car. Nardo stepped into the light. He had the pistol in his hand.

"Stand still with your hands over your head." His other instructions were too quiet for them to hear. The gun waggled and the young man put his hands on the roof of the car, his head hanging, hidden, between his arms. At another waggle he spread his legs. When the captain was satisfied, he called, "*Dottore,* I'll need your help."

El watched as Peter felt for a light switch and found one. The jagged shadows melted into the orderly clutter of a well-kept garage. The young man's face was still covered, but the stiff, straw-colored hair was all too familiar. Henry Maddox! Why Henry? To hell with Captain Nardo. She wasn't a carabiniere. She slipped off her sandals, eased quietly out of the car, pushing the door just to, so that the dome light was off, and padded across the gravel.

"What's going on, captain?" Henry's question would have sounded natural, if his voice had not quavered. "Just came out to get my clothes from the car—not to steal anything. I-I left them—this afternoon. Signora Hughes let me use her car— ah—for a while." He lifted his head, blinked into the light, and saw Peter. "Oh, you here too, Dr. Testa. I . . ." His hands started to slide down from the roof of the car.

"Get the hands back." Nardo waggled the gun again. "*Dottore,* feel up and down his legs and arms, pockets—you know. You've seen it in films. And *you,* signorino, stand—*still.*" Peter started tentatively on Henry's shoulders and back. Down his left side, down his right—and stopped at the right-hand trousers pocket.

"Henry Maddox, you're a fool," he muttered in English and winkled out a .22 pistol, just as El walked into the garage. She stuck out her hand.

"Give it to me, I'll . . ." and she nodded at Captain Nardo, who, not in the least taken aback by her arrival, strolled around the far side of the car and felt the radiator.

"You can take your hands down, signorino. It's unfortunate, but I'll have to ask your friends to be witnesses." Over Peter's shoulder El could only see the top of Henry's head and one cheek. Trickles of sweat ran from his sideburns down his chin. Probably had no handkerchief. Sleeves were more his style. She was called to order by an invitation to feel the radiator, to note the crackling of the muffler, a second indication that the car had recently been on a hot trip. With that established Captain Nardo put his foot on the front bumper and considered Henry in silence. He was in no hurry. When he did speak his voice was flat, officially courteous. Had Signor Maddox run a road-block that evening at Castiglione? Had he shortly thereafter ignored a police siren and failed to pull over? Had he then broken every speed law, trying to reach the levee and the firebreak? He had known he was being followed, but—was he aware that *they* had followed him?

Henry stood, shaking his head, dazed, but, El noticed, his eyes darted around, wildly searching for something. He'll bolt, the dummy. She moved around behind him. Peter, too, had noticed. He pushed himself away from the fender he had been leaning against and stepped directly in front of Henry.

"Signor Maddox, where have you been the last few days?" the captain asked blandly. "Your friends were anxious. They were waiting for you in the usual place." He paused, smiling. If he had hoped for an answer, he was disappointed. "We have a lot to talk about. I'll need to see your passport and your driver's license. Why don't we find a more comfortable place? Perhaps Mr. Hug-ess's study. Signora, would you see if we'd be disturbing anyone there, while we help signor Maddox collect his luggage?" Henry stumbled back several steps, turning to run, and crashed into El, who put an arm around his waist, almost flirtatiously.

"Come on, Henry. If we hurry, we won't miss much of

263

the dancing." The plaintive, reedy notes of "Arrivederci Roma" floated up from the gardens. "I'll help you get the bag." She opened the car door, but before she could release the seat lock, Henry had pushed her aside and was groping around in the backseat. He shifted sweaters and old pairs of sneakers and some books. It seemed to take him a long time. Eventually he snaked out a small brown plastic suitcase, the right size for a weekend trip.

"Is that all?" Nardo asked, taking his foot off the bumper. He came along the length of the car on the side away from them in a leisurely, aimless way. "Or would you like to claim the one by Dr. Testa's feet?" Peter moved two or three quick steps to his right, incidentally blocking the door into the next stall, and there, partially hidden by an oil drum, was a small canvas duffel. Henry stared at it and seemed to go limp. Captain Nardo waved El away to the safe side of the car before he said very quietly, "And we'd better have that brown paper bag you shoved under the sweaters too!" Henry put his head down and lunged for the door, straight into Captain Nardo's bear hug. A second later Peter had Henry's arms twisted behind him.

"I'm an American citizen," Henry roared. "No Italian policeman can touch me! This is police brutality!" He slipped up an octave closer to hysteria. "Illegal search! I know my rights." He struggled without conviction. Arrogance was dissolving into the fear it had always been. Peter's leverage on his arms did the rest. Henry slumped back against him.

"That's better." The captain made it sound like high praise. He straightened his jacket. "I'm sure we can trust you to cooperate. You *are* subject to the law of the country you're in, but Italy's very civilized. There's no death penalty. Now—we'll collect the luggage, if you, signora, will . . ." El had already started across the drive.

THERE WAS NO ANSWER to her knock. The door was open, lights blazed. Two steps across the entry brought her into a small living room where a fleecy white rug and deep bulging upholstery in floral chintz achieved the look of synthetic comfort preferred by American hotel decorators. Alabaster chess figures, as tall as schoolboys, had been converted to lamps and stood about on low tables looking majestic and slightly foolish with their dark green shades over their brows. From her podium just inside the door the queen stared at El with such baleful disapproval that El almost apologized for her intrusion. But she was not intruding: the room was empty.

She looked into the room that opened off to her left, Eddie's study. It had the same general air of deep pile and chintz, terracotta this time, and was also empty, which left the bedroom on the other side to be inspected. Halfway across the living room she became aware of the hisses and snorts of an accomplished snorer. Through the bedroom door she saw the toes of black shoes pointing toward the ceiling. Eddie lay spread-eagled on his back. Above him hung a black banner, roughly the size of the bed, with an orange seal and giant letters, also in orange, "Go Tigers!" In his immaculate dinner clothes he might have been waiting for the undertaker. On the chest beside the bed was a full glass of whiskey. El thought it unlikely that they could disturb him, or he, them. To be doubly sure, she closed the door. When she looked up, Henry, with his two bags, stood in the entry door. Behind him were Peter and the captain, who carried the brown paper bag.

Henry was instructed to sit on a sofa, which was well away from the door and relatively comfortable. He was allowed to keep his bags, but was requested to empty his pockets. His passport and license, please. And with them the first complication: he had no license. He had sent it home to be renewed.

"And you want us to think that was why you ran the roadblock," Nardo concluded. "No, don't bother to deny it. Two carabinieri will be here, any time now, to identify you. Tell me, do you always carry a pistol when you go to get your luggage out of a car?" Nardo was sitting in a barrel-backed chair opposite him with a coffee table between them. Without taking his eyes off Henry, he reached under his chair, fished around for the paper bag, and placed it on the table between them. Henry grabbed for it. The captain snatched it away, out of range.

"You have no right to touch my things. You can't search me!" His voice cracked, out of control. "It's illegal. It must be! Dr. Testa, do something!" Peter only shook his head.

"I'll see the *verbale* states that Mr. Maddox objected and protested against my intrusion into his private affairs," Nardo promised, watching Henry very closely. "He did not voluntarily allow me to see the contents of what will be by then 'the aforementioned parcels.' " And without warning, he turned the brown paper bag upside down over the table and shook it. A wide, boyish smile spread over his face: he had performed a miracle. Bills cascaded over the table, flopping off onto the floor as the rubber bands that had held them snapped. He shook the bag again. Four checks, clipped together, slithered out and, with a thump, a small notebook. The captain looked at them and put them aside to fluff up the loose bills with his fingers. One bundle, still intact, he riffled and riffled again rather unpleasantly under Henry's nose.

"You have a lot to explain, signor Maddox—especially *this*." Again Nardo rippled the bills at him. Henry shook his head. "Why did you hang around the station before the robbery? Where, indeed, did this money come from?" Still Henry shook his head and said nothing. "Remember, whether you tell me or not, I can hold you—the roadblock; my man injured; driving without a license; illegal possession of firearms—so you do yourself no favor." Henry's reaction was to stare at his sneakers. "Or better yet." Nardo actually smiled, enjoying his inspiration. "Yes, much better, even if it does ruin the party. I'll have your partners—signor Hug-ess, the younger; signor Pound, the younger; *and* the guest of honor, *Il Principe*—brought here. Together . . ."

"El, for God's sake do something," Henry begged quietly, desperately in English. "Help me, can't you?" His head was turned toward her, away from Peter, and his voice deliberately slurred, so that El doubted Peter could catch more than occasional words of the plea. "I can explain everything—really, the whole thing—but he'd never believe me! Never!"

"At this point, you haven't much choice, Henry. You *must* convince him," El whispered, knowing she offered no comfort. "He'll never charge you with the robbery. I won't let him." For once what sounded like reassurance offered to a child was the truth. In that instant and without elaborate analysis El had decided. No one would be falsely accused of the robbery. There was only one alternative: either Henry convinced Nardo, or . . .

HALF AN HOUR LATER carabinieri were busy counting money and comparing treasury numbers, Peter was out searching for Webster, the captain was dictating his preliminary report to a stenographer, and El, who to everyone's surprise and irritation, had refused to be Henry's interpreter, asked Nardo if she might be driven home. A disgruntled Brigadier Cirillo obliged and gave her her first and only glimpse of the party that would be variously remembered and distorted by the guests and those San Feliciani who only heard about it. Memory is selective and importance a quirky judgment, but, if no two versions matched, it was universally agreed that of stellar performers there had been an embarrassing supply.

Sometime after dinner Alan Pound eloped with La Bounton-

Hampton—and a Bourton-Hampton Jaguar. In the search that followed, the ubiquitous Plum MacIntosh, bloody and decidedly daunted, had to be extracted with pruning shears from a jungle of blackberry brambles. He declined to explain. Hermione, herself slightly tattered, announced she had been "ravaged" in the garden. When pressed for details, her reply was a cryptic, "I have me standards." Martha Gelder in an overexuberant tango display dipped right into the swimming pool, almost drowning her partner. And if that was not confusion enough, Webster, it was said, had come to blows with Captain Nardo. The next day, busy as he was, Webster took time to deny there was any truth in the rumor: he had challenged the captain to a duel.

The national press concentrated on the solution to the train robbery, on Henry's arrest, and the search for Alan Pound, now a double fugitive. Since few facts were known and the carabinieri issued no statements, the dance, featured in all its real and imagined opulence, slowly transmogrified into an orgy at the court of Franz Josef.

On the local scene repercussions continued for the next forty-eight hours. Anatolia Hughes put their house up for sale and dragged a confused Eddie off to Scotland. It was understood she wished to buy a castle. The Prince of Ficuzza e Verdura, who apparently felt slighted, filed suits against everyone in the neighborhood and then retired to a nursing home. His lawyer stated that he had had a nervous breakdown.

One final, much sadder decision received no publicity: El told Peter that she could never marry him. This was irrevocable: he must forget her. With gloomy dignity he retired to England for a vacation.

20

THREE WEEKS LATER, one morning when it happened to be Lacey's turn to meet the postman at the end of the drive, a letter from Peter arrived. A very thick letter. She gave it to El, who looked at it and put it on the corner of her desk.

"Did you do the camera angles for exterior forty-three?" she asked, shuffling through a pile of papers.

"There, in front of your typewriter. Aren't you going to read your letter?"

El studied the directions. "Wouldn't a high camera be better?"

"The last exterior was high, not that it makes much difference. The director will do it his way. Aren't you—?"

"In the meantime *I* have to imagine what I'm seeing." No one could fault her on that. El had become a monster of concentrated imagination. Maybe she hadn't noticed the return address.

"Aren't you—?"

"No, Lacey, I'm *not*. When we break for lunch—satisfied? Now, if what's-her-name says . . . ?"

"Want a cup of coffee?" El shook her head. Lacey, not entirely sure El had not rejected the dialogue, rather than the coffee, went off to the kitchen. It was her round to be tactful and jaunty, and she knew it, but it was wearing. So far, useless too. While she waited for the water to boil, she found herself staring out the window at some morning glories furled in on themselves, fighting the sunlight. El was like that. Squinched up, all color and shape willfully disguised. The letter might pry out a reaction. Any reaction would be better than none. Lacey had her coffee in the kitchen, giving El time, hoping—but when she went back to the study, the letter was still on the corner of the desk, unopened.

"What about a drizzle in this scene? Summer and sun can get monotonous."

"That a personal opinion?" If so, it would be the first in days.

"No, purely visual. Change, interesting colors. Now if . . ." Their rearrangements of the climate consumed the rest of the morning.

After a late lunch El took the letter and slumped down on the sofa, drawing her knees up and letting her head slip forward and down until her chin rested on her breastbone. Back to the womb, Lacey thought, as she did each time El folded herself into her modified fetal position. Out loud she thought she would take Nijinsky for a walk.

"Don't be long. Palermo awaits us!" El cautioned without looking up. Lacey stifled a rude remark. What was the use with someone who called *this* a "compromise schedule"? No, she wouldn't forget . . . How could she? Her days were laid out with regimental precision—by El. Eight hours were grudgingly allowed for sleep, or at least lying in bed: she had an impression El did not sleep much. Four hours were inevitably "wasted" on bathing, shopping, cooking, eating—that is, staying alive. Which left exactly six hours for the script and six hours for unraveling Henry and Co.'s business venture. That was El's idea of a compromise and closely related, Lacey believed, to her estimate of the human attention span. It was all part of their bargain, the only way to finish the script *and* keep El from confessing. Every step of Henry's operation, every lira they traced to its origin, would move him further from the train robbery. Even Captain Nardo could be convinced, and they, of course, had one advantage: they knew Henry had told the truth.

HENRY AND HIS PARTNERS, Alan Pound, Nick Hughes, and Prince Filippo, had set themselves up as exchange agents. The original capital had been limited. By promising to return to college, Alan had "conned" (Henry's word) his father out of $10,000. Henry, who had enough sense not to try the same ploy on Webster, had saved only $2,000. He offered the entire sum. For Nick Hughes with control of his trust fund this was a minor investment. He matched the sum Alan and Henry had put in with $12,000 of his own. Filippo was penniless, but vital to the operation: he was their source of well-to-do Sicilians begging to have dollars in exchange for lire.

They had been surprisingly businesslike. They wrote out a formal agreement, which stated their working capital at $24,000 and the division of their profits to be 30 percent to Alan, 18 percent to Henry, who was to do most of the legwork, 37 percent to Nick with the proviso that he had *no* duties, and 15 percent to Filippo for his Sicilian contacts. "Reasonable expenses" were to come from profits. Not trusting Filippo, Henry, Alan, and Nick specified that, when the group was dissolved, before profits were divided, each partner would be paid his ante. The Prince could not claim 15 percent of the whole.

Dollars they sold at 1,000 lire or even 1,100 lire when the

customer was too desperate to bargain. They bought dollars at 800 lire, which gave their American clients a 10 percent profit. Henry's endurance was phenomenal. When Filippo went to Sicily, Henry accompanied him, carrying the money. Filippo met his customers in cafés. Henry waited in the street. When Filippo brought the lire to him, he handed over the dollars or dollar checks. Ultimately the system had a weakness: Henry was actually introduced to only one of Filippo's customers.

When the Sicilian round was accomplished, Henry had to rush back and find fresh Americans. After his not too subtle approach to Peter through El, he became more cautious. He found that he could acquire the same information, more safely, by listening to the endless "house" conversations, which at summer cocktail parties were as common as peanuts. To his father's consternation he also developed a passionate interest in music festivals. Spoleto—and a hundred orchestra musicians with dollars and in need of lire—drew him like a magnet. To reassure his father he talked of a girl. Perhaps too graphically. Webster was eager to meet her.

All this had gone smoothly until Alan decided unexpectedly to take his money out. He would be leaving soon, he explained. Since he was in a hurry, the partners agreed to pay him in dollars and, if necessary, fend for themselves in changing their shares. When, a few days before the dance, four of Henry's prospects let him know they were ready to change their money, there was a train strike. In a wild rush he borrowed Anatolia's car and wove his way through the hordes on vacation. A night drive to Naples, out along the Amalfi coast to his client. Back and on to Circeo. Another client and a breakdown with the car. Finally at noon the day of the dance, through Rome in terrible traffic and on north with stops at Orvieto and Todi. He pushed hard to get back, hoping not to be noticeably late and at least in time with Alan's money.

If only he had had a driver's license to show, he would not have been caught bucketing around the countryside with thirty-one million lire and checks for $20,000 in a brown paper bag! Twenty-four thousand dollars had turned into $58,600!

Captain Nardo was very sympathetic. False-ingenuous, El claimed, but she was prejudiced. He had no trouble believing Henry. Indeed, they had been exchanging money. Money from the robbery! Could Henry give any other explanation for how he came by forty-seven million lire? He was not impressive. He stammered that money just did that, if you kept it working, making a profit on each exchange. They had more than doubled their stake. One more full cycle and they would have tripled it. Money just did that. And exactly who were these people who had so obligingly made Henry and Co. rich men? The Italians, who had supplied the lire, naturally, because the lire were in question. Names slipped Henry's mind, some he had never known, and Captain Nardo reverted to the week before the robbery.

The notebook with its clutter of calculations was the key. Or so El and Lacey had to believe. The captain was amused by their interest in it, but did not object to giving them a copy. While he carried on the serious business of connecting Henry and his partners to the robbery, El and Lacey could dabble about, trying to prove that the young men had merely tripped into the shadier side of private enterprise. He even called every few days to ask jokingly how their investigation was going. More and more of their "wasted" time was given over to angst.

Webster was their sole collaborator. As they reconstructed Henry's travels, they asked his father for names of anyone he knew in that area. Literally anyone. He had a copy of Henry's statement, which was some help, and he was periodically allowed to see him. Through him they sent questions, intended to jog Henry's memory, which, it evolved, was wishful thinking. Besides not having lived long enough to have any use for a memory, Henry had spent too many sleepless nights in second-class train compartments. A bewildered echo was his peak performance. After a week of supposition and telephone calls, El and Lacey established that July fourth he had been in Spoleto, staying with a friend of his mother's. How much and for whom, they had Webster ask, had he changed money? "Oh sure, I remember that. They had a picnic and I ate ten hot dogs" was the residue from that trip. The business details had evaporated. El and Lacey tracked down the orchestra manager, the first violin, and the choirmaster, who gave them names. Henry had spent the week-end—"That's right, I had to borrow some pajamas!"—and was much in demand. They documented between $5,000 and $6,000 changed: Lacey's projections from his notebook would have been closer to $7,500. His young customers, now in America, safely out of Italian jurisdiction, were willing to describe their trans-actions in writing. Several remembered friends who had changed money. Letters duly arrived. El and Lacey felt they were making progress, but it was slow. Slow and expensive: the telephone company, alerted to El's excesses by a nosy computer, demanded a deposit against future long-distance calls.

The resident Americans were easier to find and harder to convince. One sculptor, who was vociferously modest about his million-dollar commissions, feared the Finance Police when it came to $5,000 of illegal exchange. Another very nervous gentle-man, who should have known better, had found true love—but his wife must *never* know. The others on principle were reluctant to be mixed up in the affair. They already were, as El pointed out to them, but she was satisfied. Captain Nardo could explore the dangers of reticence before the law with them. If worse came to worse, El had tapes of her conversations.

The Sicilians remained. Who were they? Alan had disap-peared, Nick really knew nothing, and Filippo, who could have identified the Italian beneficiaries of the scheme, was incommunicado with his nervous breakdown. Questioning, his lawyer informed the carabinieri, could aggravate his condition: medical certificates were offered in proof. So, once more, they were dependent on Henry's wayward memory. They badgered him with questions. They threatened to give up the cause. They insulted him. Nothing. Finally Webster showed real ingenuity and took him a history of Sicily. Two days later Henry dredged out of his mind the name and surname of the one man he had met. A week passed and again nothing. Suddenly, one morning, from where he did not know, came a second name. At the time it had sounded romantic to him, medieval. Yes, he was sure the name was right. Did it help?

Yes and no. It was a common Sicilian surname, of which the Palermo telephone book listed forty-seven. Lacey, who had once lived there for three months, working on a film, thought she could weed out the undesirables. First she eliminated a hairdresser, a baker, a garage, a dental technician, a Monsignor, and a fishmonger as unlikely dabblers in international finance. Then with the help of a large-scale map, she tried sociosnobbery and crossed off those whose addresses were substandard or apt to be offices. El suggested a Ouija board. Toward the end she was following hunches: certain names seemed to vibrate invitingly. Nineteen made the final cut.

Their plan was simple and highly fallible. Any number of the men could be related to each other, might know each other's business arrangements, and certainly would be inclined to question El about what exactly her proposition was, which must be avoided. They decided she should call between eleven and twelve, or between six and seven, both hours when a husband was not apt to be at home, and ask to speak to him. Really. Could she perhaps then speak to the signora? She explained with exaggerated hesitancy that she was a friend of Filippo's, the young

Prince of Ficuzza e Verdura. She believed that the lady's husband was also a friend . . . If Filippo was repudiated, El offered abject apologies, she must have been given the wrong number, and went on to the next innocent signora of the same name.

If Filippo was recognized, she rushed into a prolix, ladylike pitch. Filippo had told her, weeks ago, before his "troubles"—yes, sad, isn't it?—that she might call signor X should the Americans (carefully male, not to make the poor wife suspicious of her husband's other possible secret ventures), should the Americans he liked be available. El, of course, didn't know if he . . . Naturally he might not . . . She had to be away for a few days. If he was interested, could he—would it be asking too much?—could he call her secretary? Did she have a pen at hand? El left the legitimate Roman number of Josey Bruno, a legitimate secretary-typist, who at times did work for her. She had been told that if a Sicilian gentleman called, asking for El, she was to insist he give his first name and telephone number before she told him El would be in touch with him by the middle of the next week.

They had thirteen outright rejections, fourteen counting the hysterical wife who accused El of delivering her husband's death warrant from the Mafia, and five nibbles. That afternoon they were to call the secretary-typist to hear which, if any, of the Sicilian gentlemen had been hooked.

On their return from their walk Lacey and Nijinsky met El about to drive off in her car. Nijinsky whimpered and danced as though he had not seen her in a week. She opened the car door.

"Come on," she ordered. "Get in!" He crouched and edged back behind Lacey's legs. Slowly he sank to the ground. "I've decided, when the male animal insists, he should be taken up! And they'd act like *that*!" Nijinsky's tail gave one tentative flop. "I'm just going in town to pick up a book. Be right back." Her voice was clipped, efficient, her face, neutral, but at the cost, it seemed, of some effort. The letter? Lacey wondered, then had a sudden thought.

"But, El, he doesn't open for an hour and a half."

"I woke him up from his nap. I *need* the book." The car rolled gently downhill. El stuck her head out the window. "Read Peter's letter——he specifically wants you to. It's on the coffee table." She let out the clutch and was gone.

AT FIRST Lacey thought she would wait to read the letter until El came back. She spread her chart of Henry's doings out on her desk and pored over it, comparing it occasionally with her balance sheet of proven exchanges. There were still gaps. That there always would be, considering the young men had in toto shuffled $200,000 and 140 million lire, was marginal consolation. One more look and she might discover ... The system worked when she hunted for things she had misplaced, but not that afternoon. Too much of her mind toyed with the letter. Curiosity was no sin and she had been asked to read it. Enough excuses. She went to the living room, stretched out comfortably on the sofa, and reached for the letter. Several photocopies fell out of the envelope, and the letter itself, neatly typed, except for the frequent juxtaposition of *m*'s and commas, which was one of the maddening tricks played by a slightly different keyboard.

> My dear, dear El:
>
> If you read this, rather than throw it, unopened, in the wastebasket, all is not lost. Don't sling it away yet. There will be *no* special pleadings, *no* wailing, and *no* apologies.
>
> First, the *convenevoli*. England is chill and damp. What else would one expect? In spite of it we do a great deal

277

of garden sitting. On shipboard the English used to wrap themselves in blankets and brave the gales on deck. Why don't they do the same in their gardens? Anyway, I do and imagine myself to look like that famous picture of Lytton Strachey in a sling chair with blanket and fedora. Mother is thriving on it and has already acquired another desiccated widower, who spent his army years in India and is therefore more English than the English. He has followed us to Cambridge. Next week we go to Salisbury. Mother has not yet told me why. I am only the driver. So much for the conventional news.

As you can imagine, I have had a great deal of free time in which to think—primarily about you, I'll admit, and for a change of pace, about the robbery. It took me a while to realize the two subjects would not be separated. I bought a notebook (yes, my usual pedestrian habit!) and listed the puzzles, mostly minor, that bothered me. (See items 1–5 of the sheets in longhand.)

Lacey sorted through the bundle until she found two pages covered in Peter's fine, very English writing.

1. When did garbage collectors start wearing gray suede gloves? When did El?
2. The small man who walked confidently into the ladies' loo did *not* come out. (Why haven't I thought of that before?) Which means he was perfectly comfortable? No explanation, unless *he* was a she!
3. After the B–Hs' party El and Lacey went out for cigarettes. Time coincides with return of checks and documents. Query: Do women change their clothes at that hour to go out and buy cigarettes?
4. Where was money stored? Certainly not Rome.

5. The clipping El saw in the *Corriere* years ago? Lugano, it was.

Lacey turned back to the letter, feeling numb.

We were still in London, the city that provides anything you need. A boyhood friend of mine is now an editor of *The Observer*. He told me where to look and arranged proper credentials. I enclose a xerox of what I found.

Lacey only glanced at the newspaper clipping. She knew what it said. She had a copy herself. A Milanese businessman had been arrested at the Italian-Swiss border, carrying a large sum of money, which had only one obvious destination, a Swiss bank. The first episode of the story had taken place some months before—there followed an exact description of the *modus operandi* they had used, denunciation to the police, total dismantling of the car, the need for other trips through the border mentioned, etc. The businessman took millions through on his various trips and would never have been caught, if, several months later, he had not greedily tried the same trick just one more time. He was caught. Lacey shook her head and returned to Peter's letter.

Which, logically, brought me to Caroline and also, I thought, explained my fourth question. It's all in my notes. We heard a lot about her trip to Geneva, didn't we? And for good reason.

Hermione's banker interested me too. How convenient that she should be in Geneva at the same time. How you must have laughed at Arch and me! Crates of books were the perfect place to store stolen money, particularly if they were consigned to the very station from which the money was stolen. Switzerland is the land of vanishing money and an aroused banker, even Swiss, would undoubtedly break rules to please Hermione.

You can see from my list that I've spent some time with Gilbert and Sullivan too. Martha would not expect me to have such a good memory, but I understand the messages, the threats she was hurling at you, actually at Lacey. I wondered why you bothered to rescue her from Cirillo, but I see now—you had to!

About our trip to the market and Standa. I had sensed a bubbling hysteria, but after Gargonza, it never went through my mind again. Until these last days. When that newspaper bundle blossomed into a jacket, rather than what you expected (and feared), you relaxed. From then on it was easy to piece together.

All this and my notes to convince you that I really do *know*. I'm not fishing. Of course, I can't give you the names on the Swiss records, or the numbers of the accounts, or explain why in God's name you returned the checks and documents. Maybe one day you'll tell me.

For all your meticulous planning and execution, there was one thing you forgot. Have you noticed? If not, you will soon. Once you had the money, took it safely out of Italy, and invested it, what did you mean to do? Give it back, no doubt. But how? *That* is and has been your real problem. By now you may have another: did your associates agree?

If I were there, I would bring it myself. I can't ask Matteo to do it. He's too inquisitive, so I'll just have to suggest you buy a copy of the Penal Code and study closely section 62, headed Common Extenuating Circumstances. Especially paragraphs 1 and 6. I believe that is your best chance. I've enclosed a list of Ministers, under-Ministers, and their families for your consideration.

I've explained the unsettled status of our engagement to Mother. Her reaction, which she hardly expected me to retail to you, I thought funny. You remind her of Maxine Elliott (I think she was an actress of Mother's vintage). When her engagement was reported, she's supposed to have said she wouldn't marry God! I'm not God, but however this ends, remember that in Italy husbands are not required to testify against their wives. I love you.

Peter

P.S. I have forgotten to tell you that the day of Anatolia's party a cousin of Matteo's came to see me. At times I think he's related to everyone in town. The cousin was upset and afraid. He was the post-office employee who stopped to help Hermione the morning of the robbery. He was under terrible pressure from his partner and the other postal clerks and railway men who knew about it, to go to the police. He felt it would be betrayal. Hermione, in her secret way, had done him a tremendous favor. I talked to the director of the post office and we both went to Nardo. No problem there and no interest. You probably couldn't think of it this way, but it would be assumed that the nails that punctured the post van's tires also punctured Hermione's. There was no other obvious conclusion, and you're right, men cling to the obvious. Not women, I find.

Please let Lacey read this. Though she'll hate me for saying so, she has great common sense. If anyone can get around your stubbornness, she can.

When Lacey heard quiet footsteps in the hall, she was almost through a second reading. Reluctantly she rolled off the sofa and went along to the study, where she found El clawing the wrapping paper off the book.

"Time to call Josey." El was too intent on thumbing through the book to answer. "El—it's *time* . . ."

"In a minute. Wrong paragraph." She frowned, went back to the front, and started through again. This time she found it. Watching her crouched over section sixty-two, Lacey knew she would have to wait. Finally El let out a long breath. "It just might—listen to this! Paragraph one—'to have acted from motives of particular moral or social value,' and paragraph six—'to have, before judgment is passed, completely repaid the damages . . . and when possible by the restitution of same, or before judgment . . . to have voluntarily and effectively acted to cancel or attenuate the damaging or dangerous consequences of the crime.' Lacey, we could—all right, all right! I'll call Josey. We have some studying to do, you and I."

As soon as El started dialing, Lacey pulled the book out from under her elbow. El clutched for it, missed, and Josey answered her telephone all at the same moment. Through the fog of her own speculations Lacey heard El repeat two numbers, two names: Marco and Luca. Lacey almost made a crack about the apostles, but the expression on El's face changed her mind.

"The Questura? Rome, not Palermo. Are you *sure*?" El said in shocked disbelief. "Josey, if you think you're being funny, this isn't . . . Really? What did you tell him? Um, uh-huh. Always better. Yes, you were exactly right, but you didn't mention Marco and Luca did . . . ? Good! Perfect! Josey, thank you so much. . . ." While El tactfully reassured Josey, Lacey's mind reeled through the possibilities. For the moment the penal code was forgotten.

El put the receiver down with exaggerated care, then slumped over the desk, her head propped in her hands. "That blew it! One of our ladies who nibbled was suspicious. She also happens to have a brother high up in the Questura of Rome, so—you guessed the rest. He paid Josey a little visit. In fact he just left. Threatened her with all sorts of things, the nicest, I gather, was banishment to Calabria for two years. She gave him my name and telephone number, explained that I was writing about Sicily, maybe about the Mafia, she wasn't sure, and had asked her to take any messages. She often did that. She did not know who I had called and in this case there had been no replies. You don't suppose they tapped her telephone?" El's head jerked up at the thought. They stared at each other.

"Call Nardo and ask for an appointment. Right now. We've got enough to insist—"

"I have to type the names and addresses. He'd never be able to read my jumble of notes. As soon as—"

"*Now,* El, so we've offered, before he can demand." Lacey was already folding her financial charts and balance sheets together. She stopped abruptly to listen. A barrage of gravel clattered against the wall, as Nijinsky charged off, snarling, and tires crunched on the drive. "Prepare for the auto-da-fé!"

From Captain Nardo's point of view, burning at the stake would have been too merciful for them, but after an hour of bluster and recriminations, he deigned to accept their dossier on Henry's travels and clients. Both sides extracted a price: *they* must stay out of the investigation, *he* must follow up their line.

El saw him out, smiling graciously. "How nice, captain," she murmured sweetly. "We can all return, now, to our proper professions." Only by closing the door very quickly did she avoid bloodshed.

"SCHMERZ!" EL SHOUTED one evening, as their six hours of strategy and study, which had taken over Henry's time allotment, were about at an end. "I never appreciated German enough! *Schmerz! SCHMERZ!* So satisfactory. Sounds like pain, doesn't it. Whoopee!" She picked up the penal code and flung it out the door. It bumped and skipped across the bricks of the hall floor. " 'Good-bye to All That.' " Lacey stood up, stretched, and let herself crumple onto the rug. She did several experimental leg lifts and groaned. El watched, not really seeing her, thinking that this was the moment, perhaps the only chance she would have, to thank her. The script was finished. Tomorrow would settle—lots of things. She did not know exactly how to start.

"Why so serious?" Lacey had opened her eyes and was smiling rather blearily at the ceiling.

"Do you think it'll work?" El was whispering.

"It will. It will. It's flawless, and God knows it ought to be, all the times we've been through it. After tomorrow, the rest is easy. Beh—relatively easy."

"After tomorrow! It'll be a long day. Remind me, I have to be at the café at eight—in the morning." Lacey rolled over and looked at her, puzzled. "Martha's calling from the station before she takes the train up. As of yesterday she only uses public telephones. Hers is tapped, mine is tapped, everybody's—"

"She's paranoid," Lacey snorted, twisting to her feet. "And Kate's no better. Cirillo follows her everywhere she goes—I ask you. They're all cuckoo." El nodded, remembering Hermione's defiant question: Why *should* they give the money back, when obviously no one could catch them? "Caroline says it's dangerous to be seen together," Lacey went on, building her own case. "Much more peculiar if we are *not* seen together, I'd say." She leaned on the front of El's desk. "And you, to keep peace, agree that instead of a cup of coffee right here in comfort,

284

we'll meet on top of a treeless hill. Does that make any sense? Oh sure, we can't be surprised, overheard, or taped, but it's crazy."

"And if they don't want to give it back?" El hated the forlorn tone she heard in her own voice.

"Cheer up! If they take the money, they don't dare stay in Italy. Too dangerous. Be logical—Caroline's not going to leave, neither is Kate. Martha would starve if she did—so stick to the old democratic majority rule." She went to her own desk and began dumping papers into the wastebasket. "Martha would say we need a shredder. To hell with them! I need a drink and some dinner. How about you?"

"In stages," El agreed. As they crossed the hall to the kitchen, she stopped and stood dead still, thinking. "Can you imagine IBM's board meeting on a bald hill?"

"No, but then I can't imagine six grown women stealing a million dollars from a mail train. Can you?"

IN MID-AFTERNOON of the next day, which was cold and dark, six women collected on top of a bare hill and sat in a circle, like Druids, waving their arms. A large, black cloud churned directly over them, but they were too busy with their ritual to notice. Foreigners were like that, or so a peasant, a forestry guard, a plumber for the aqueduct, and a telephone lineman thought, as they watched from their separate vantage points, relishing what must, surely, happen. The women wrangled and waved their arms and when all had been said, sat in contemplative silence. Then five hands were raised and with supreme timing the cloud burst, pelting them with hailstones, the size of which would, in time, become legendary. The women stumbled around, gathering their things, tying scarves over their heads. One umbrella was blown inside out. They slipped and rolled down the hillside with icy grapeshot battering at them. The peasant, the forestry guard, the plumber, and the lineman each enjoyed the scene in his own way and each instantly forgot it. One more example of what he already knew, that foreigners were strange, very strange indeed.

EPILOGUE

ON A CLEAR SUNNY DAY in January Peter and El were married at the *comune* of San Felice Val Gufo. Webster drove them—Peter, El, Arch, and Lacey, who had returned from the real world of Movieola cubicles for the event—to the Piazza in Delilah. Polished and elaborately festooned with roses, she was in fine fettle and, as they soon found out, in fine voice. Their arrival in front of the long staircase was a stirring performance, only surpassed by the dramatic extravaganza of their departure after the ceremony. Delilah gave her all, trumpeting, coughing, emitting plumes of steam, ominous puffs of black exhaust, and occasional straightforward explosions, until it was decided the men should push her and Lacey should steer. El, alone in the backseat, bowed gently and waved to the crowd. It was a regal progress through the countryside, slightly marred by unseemly mirth.

At the wedding breakfast the guests were almost too much themselves. Hermione's further visits to Switzerland had permanently squelched any lingering interest in bankers. Instead she presented her newest trophy, a young doctor, a gynecologist, who, beyond his staggering good looks, offered obvious domestic advantages. Quite unintentionally he disrupted the party. Martha was overwhelmed. She batted her eyes and clung to his arm, whispering she would like to interview him. On a kind impulse Caroline rescued him and roused Giordano's jealousy. He forbade her to speak to this—this charlatan again, and she obeyed. The last weeks she had been very docile: relief can have that effect. Wine and Webster's prattle about a fantastic gold mine, spiced by Hermione's raunchy commentary on what they could expect from A Day in the Life of a Gynecologist, created a noisy semblance of jubilation. Matteo watched beyond speech. Peter's mother tried to win him with tales of other times, other places, but was already herself distrait: her train, she must not miss her train.

And all the while Arch honed another theory of the robbery for Lacey, who excused her lack of appreciation by saying champagne always gave her the giggles.

MUCH HAD HAPPENED that fall. Once the two Sicilians were faced with the police, they were thoughtful enough to exchange favors with their friends, that is, they allowed the friends, who had put them in touch with Prince Filippo, to share their punishment. They will be tried sometime and released by benefit of amnesty or other political machination. Their money grows undisturbed. The Prince trotted across the Swiss border one dark night and was next seen, in the magazines preferred by hairdressers, with a biscuit heiress, whose family had a sumptuous house at Porto Ercole. When exactly he might see and enjoy it, legally, remained moot.

Henry Maddox and Nick Hughes were escorted to the Italian border and invited not to return. Henry went off to finish college, and Nick, who would never give up leisure as an art form, retired to Scotland. There may be a way to corrupt salmon. Somewhere near Leeds Alan Pound was serving his apprenticeship in two mutually incompatible fields—management and marriage. Kate's optimism billowed: she predicted a brilliant career.

Then early in January, before Italy had recovered from the Christmas moratorium, a new scandal hit. A letter addressed to the *Corte dei Conti,* a court which acts as General Auditor or Comptroller, was published by the *Corriere della Sera, Il Messaggero,* and *Paese Sera.* Had it been left to the discretion of the court, its fate might have been very different, but carbon copies to newspapers of such divergent persuasions had again ensured wide publicity.

> Enclosed are cashier's checks to the amount of 959,406,250 lire, which sum, including legally earned interest and increased exchange rates over a six-month investment period, represents the current value of 802,037,000 lire "borrowed" from the State funds at the station of San Felice Val Gufo on May 24, 197__ by person or persons unknown. The careful investment of said funds, aided by the Treasury's willful mismanagement of the lire, has produced a growth of 19.2% (or an annual rate of 38 + %).

> As it will be easy to ascertain, the bulk of these moneys has been on deposit with a highly respected Swiss bank. To avoid unpleasantness with the Swiss authorities, let it be specified that numbered accounts were assigned to Currer Bell, Mary Ann Evans, Aurore Lucie Dupin, and Mary Godwin, all persons of sound literary reputation, whose present status places them above suspicion. Diligent investigation will re-

veal that the initials of either their real names or pseudonyms coincide with those of members of the current Italian government, their wives, or close relatives. It is presumed that diligent investigation is the *proper* business of the Court and that the Court will wish to arrive at the truth as well as truncate the disgraceful flight of Italian capital, so easily arranged and so devastating to national economy. The time for fiscal responsibility and morality in public office has come. Reform is long overdue.

That this matter should not go unnoticed, copies of this communication will be mailed to the newspapers listed below.

The court, absorbed by the procedures necessary to show a profit in the accounts, had neither the time nor the inclination for careful investigation. The press, however, did. In less than a week one Minister, one under-Minister, one wife, and one daughter of Ministers had been identified as the probable holders of the numbered accounts. They were certainly in no danger of prosecution. Another scandal would have pushed them, unharmed, offstage into prosperous private life, but among Italian politicians there is vast brotherly compassion—or fear. With unprecedented zeal the judiciary declared the investigation of The Great Tuscan Train Robbery closed. A criminal act did not exist. No loss could be proven. Whatever, at first glance, might have appeared criminal was, in fact, an act of moral reclamation without criminal intent. The archives were sealed. They could be reopened, but it seems unlikely.

There was, as well, one positive result: the day after Peter and El's marriage, amidst accusations and wails of innocence, the government was forced to resign. In Italy the right things have always happened for the wrong reasons.

As to the script that caused all the trouble, it was judged by producers to be too farfetched, too implausible for a film, which may be for the best and suggests that in the United States the wrong things happen for what seem the right reasons.

The world was a muddle, but El was not discouraged. She had remembered an intriguing article about the Vatican Bank. Nuns are the truly invisible women: priests never notice them, much less the police. Now if . . .

PORTSMOUTH, NEW HAMPSHIRE 03801